ABOUT TH

Siobhian R. Hodges is a Leicestershire-based writer, administrator, and author of the new novel **Killing a Dead Man**. She has wanted to be a writer for as long as she can remember, completing her first novel when she was just thirteen.

Siobhian has a BA (Hons) in Creative Writing and Film Studies from De Montfort University and an MA in Creative Writing from Loughborough University. During her studies, she was both scriptwriter and script editor for *Gatling Gun Productions* – a non-for-profit film company set up by her dad and sister. With her experience in and passion for film, Siobhian's novels and short stories can often be described as cinematic.

Although her debut novel, *Killing a Dead Man*, took ten years to complete, Siobhian has simultaneously been planning and writing six other YA thrillers that we can soon expect to see.

In her free time, Siobhian enjoys reading, long walks with her partner, and raiding the biscuit cupboard! Her favourite authors are Patrick Ness and Kevin Brooks – if you haven't read their work, you definitely should!

Want to know more about Siobhian R. Hodges or
Killing a Dead Man?

Visit her website at
www.siobhianrhodgesauthor.com
and follow her blog.

You can also find Siobhian on:
Facebook: SiobhianR.HodgesAuthor
Twitter: @SiobhianAuthor
YouTube: Siobhian R. Hodges Author

To Jessica,

Thank you for your support
— enjoy!

All the best,

S.R.

KILLING

A

DEAD

MAN

SIOBHIAN R. HODGES

Cover Design and Book Layout by
Michael Webster.

First Edition

hello@siobhianrhodgesauthor.com
www.siobhianrhodgesauthor.com

Siobhian R. Hodges
Author

For my sister, Aisleen,
and my brother, Ciaran.

PROLOGUE
FIVE YEARS EARLIER

When I got back to the hotel room, Mum and Dad were furious and Danny was still missing.

The tears had already started and my legs shook so much I could barely stand. Ten-year-olds shouldn't feel this kind of panic. It felt just like one of those nightmares that makes you sweaty and breathless.

Dad stepped forward, gripping my arms to keep me steady. I'd never seen him look so serious. It made my stomach churn. "Where's your brother?" he asked.

"I don't know!"

They were just as worried as I was. Dad ordered me and Mum to stay put and call the police while he searched the streets. He had a picture of Danny on his phone that he was going to show to anyone he crossed paths with. He'd question the whole of Devon if that's what it took.

The hotel door hadn't even closed behind him

when Mum picked up the phone and started dialling. The call didn't last long as long as I thought it would. We waited together but I guess the seriousness of what was happening didn't hit me until the police turned up. Their uniforms terrified me. Back home, Dad was a constable himself, so I was used to being around police – just not like this. They weren't here for a casual chat with Dad; they were here for Danny. That made everything different.

One was called PC Halls, but I forgot the second woman's name as soon as she'd said it. She had red hair, though, like my Uncle Ryan.

Mum pulled me towards her as the two policewomen scribbled stuff down in their tatty black notebooks. They asked me a ton of questions and I answered as best I could, telling them about the kids we'd been with and the game we'd been playing – I knew their names, but I didn't know where they lived. I told them we left the beach even though we promised Mum and Dad that we wouldn't. And then I told them about the forest: the gap in the fence, the brook, the clearing, the barn, the dead tree...

I told them that Danny hadn't even wanted to be there in the first place, that I'd left him, that this was all my fault.

Mum held my hand the entire time. She said nothing as the policewomen explained the next steps they were going to take. She didn't even seem mad that we'd broken our promise.

When PC Halls and PC Red-hair finally left, it

was almost three a.m. I'd never stayed up that late before. Mum closed the door behind them and then turned to me.

"Go to bed, Jordan," was all she said. No more questions. No more hand-holding.

I don't know if she expected me to sleep. How could I, with Danny still out there? Instead, I closed the bedroom door behind me and shut myself off. *I left him*, was all I could think, *Why did I leave him …?*

I sat on the floor with my knees propped up, leaning against the wall next to the door at the end of my bed. The light from the living room lit the threshold. Mum was silent and I ended up in a sort of trance, staring at Danny's empty bed through blurry eyes.

I wasn't sure what time it was when Dad came back, but the sun had just started to bleed into my room. Mum burst into a fit of tears, an explosion of agony. I knew exactly what that meant: still no Danny.

I clutched my aching stomach and pressed my face into my knees, suppressing a sob of my own. A stab wound would've hurt less than this.

Days dragged and nights lingered. Time passed but nothing changed. My head was filled with worry and empty of everything all at the same time. The hotel manager said we could stay another week without charge while the police looked for Danny, but we didn't need that long. It was only five torturous days later, on a sweltering Saturday afternoon, when we got the call: "We think we've found your son," Police Detective Cooper said. He'd taken over the case three days ago. He was the one who told us Danny was lying by a creek in the forest we'd been playing in. Dad went to identify the body.

My brother had been murdered.

* * *

The funeral was back at home in a plain town called Woodlock. There were no clouds in the mid-August sky, just the strong rays from a sun too bright for mourners.

Mum cried into a handful of wet tissues. Her eyes seemed bloodshot all the time now, and her thin face was always red and puffy. She'd stopped wearing make-up, hardly ever washed her hair and seemed to live in the same baggy jumper and jeans. She'd made an effort today, though: black dress, flat shoes, veiled hat. She still wasn't wearing make-up, but at least her hair was clean.

Dad stood between us, his body locked in place, standing tall but looking twice his age. He stared into the distance as he held my mum, keeping her from collapsing to the ground.

I stood on my own, away from everyone, feeling the full weight of loneliness pressing hard on my chest. I'd stopped listening to the priest. I didn't believe in all that Heaven and Hell stuff, and I didn't need to hear about all the hearts Danny had touched or whatever. I *knew* it was a tragedy. I *knew* he'd be missed. I was living it every damn day. Nobody could put our loss into words. Danny had been taken from us and I wanted whoever did it to suffer in a way no one had ever suffered before.

So far, the police had no leads and hardly any evidence to go on. Whoever did this had covered their tracks well. The case was still open, but it didn't look like the monster would be caught any time soon.

I stared down at the small coffin as it was lowered into the ground. *How the hell did this happen?*

The air was still and – other than Mum crying and the priest priesting – the cemetery was silent. I took a breath. This wasn't right. It should've been *me* in that coffin, forever buried beneath cold dirt. Not Danny.

I balled up my fists, digging my fingernails into the palms of my hands as I imagined pressing something sharp into the killer's empty heart.

That's when I felt it.

A cold hand gripped my left shoulder. The only person close enough to reach me, though, was my dad. I looked up at him, but both his hands were still holding Mum.

My forehead started tingling. I looked away, confused ... And there he was.

It was him. I *know* it was. I couldn't see him but ... I could feel his presence. I know that sounds weird, but I don't know how else to describe it. It was just a *feeling*, like if you close your eyes in a room full of people you can still sense them there.

The air was cold and heavy where he stood, even when he lifted his hand from my shoulder. I smiled at him and then I felt him smiling back.

"What are you looking at?" Dad asked, finally noticing me.

"Nothing," I said. I didn't tell him I'd sensed my brother until a week after the funeral. Danny had followed us home and he barely left my side after that. Mum got really upset whenever I brought it up but I could hardly keep quiet about it. They needed to know that Danny was still with us. I'm not sure why they couldn't sense their own son, same as I wasn't sure why they sent me to see a psychiatrist less than a year later. I wasn't crazy or anything. But at least I still had Danny to help me through it all.

CHAPTER ONE
TUESDAY - PRESENT DAY

"Fight! Fight! Fight! Fight!"

The class gathered round for a piece of the action, encircling me and Matt. Mr Anderson had only left to fetch extra copies of *Othello* but that's all the time Matt would need to plant a few swift punches in my sorry face. I looked from the grinning crowd to Matt's hard stare.

"What's the matter?" he snarled. "Afraid I'll smash your face in?"

My mouth was as dry as the dust under the supply cupboards. I watched him outstretch his arms and flex his fingers. The gesture was saying *come and get me,* but I wasn't taking the bait. He was far bigger than me, the result of his deep-fried diet.

"Where's your imaginary friend now?" he sneered.

"I don't have an imaginary friend—"

"*Liar.* Kevin said he saw you talking to yourself

again in registration this morning. That's why you don't have any *real* friends!"

He cracked his knuckles, and as I scanned the kids around us, searching for a gap in the crowd, Matt took a step towards me.

He shoved me in the chest and the crowd made a noise.

"Come on, wuss," Matt said, looking me up and down. "Fight back or I'll kick your teeth in."

My palms grew moist. *You'll kick my teeth in no matter what I do,* I thought.

He outstretched his arms again, this time as if offering me an easy shot. I didn't move. Surely, he wasn't serious.

Matt shrugged. "Suit yourself."

His beefy knuckles slammed across my face and the crowd cheered again. Fucking... Ow! I stumbled but managed to avoid the humiliation of falling over. The gloves were off.

I saw Matt ready himself for another punch but when it came, I somehow dodged it. That's when the air turned cooler, thicker, beside me. My forehead tingled and my body buzzed with a new energy. Although I couldn't see him, there was no mistaking Danny's presence.

And there was nothing I could do to stop him intervening. He felt colder than usual — a sign I'd come to recognise as him gearing up for something.

Please, I thought, directing it to Danny. *Don't do anything dangerous ...*

He'd already left my side, though.

"You just gonna stand there or what?" Matt said. He took a step towards me and then seemed to trip on nothing, landing by my feet. The response was instant. Everyone burst out laughing.

"You're in for it now," one of Matt's friends said to me, as though I was the one who'd pushed him over.

I ignored him, stifling a laugh of my own. To everyone else, it looked like he'd lost his balance or tripped on his shoelace. I knew better. He was lucky that was all Danny did to him.

Matt's acne-riddled face was redder than usual with a combination of rage and embarrassment. "Think that's funny, do yuh?" he spat.

He got to his feet and squared up to me. Just thirty seconds ago I would've felt threatened, but with Danny next to me I knew I was safe. I just prayed he wouldn't take it too far this time. My brother was so mad. Goosebumps had formed along my pale arms and I even noticed a couple of bystanders glance up at the closed windows, checking for the source of the sudden draught. It wasn't the weather. Danny was about to unleash an attack Matt would never be able to match.

Matt rolled up his sleeves and I tensed, bracing myself for whatever he had planned. I was trying to think of all the humiliating ways Danny might choose to get back at him when I heard Mr Anderson's muffled voice outside our classroom. It was over, and Matt knew it.

The temperature in the room returned to normal. Satisfied that Matt was no longer a threat, Danny was gone again.

"It's a good job your brother's dead," Matt muttered. "Otherwise there'd be two ugly wimps I'd have to beat the shit outta."

He shoulder-barged me on his way back to his desk but the pit of my stomach had already dropped to my feet. He only wanted to get a reaction out of me. I knew that.

My hands started shaking. I couldn't control it. I ground my teeth together as though trying to crush his hideous words – and then something inside me snapped.

I went for him.

"YOU'RE SCUM!" I yelled, spittle flying from my lips.

The circle of kids was broken, their cries a mixture of surprise and excitement as we rolled on the floor with each other, punching and kicking.

I scored a few good hits and the adrenaline masked the pain from Matt's blows. I was vaguely aware of Mr Anderson telling us to break it up but my instincts had taken over. Matt was going to get what was coming to him.

We crashed into one of the desks, knocking off somebody's work and pencil case. My elbow skidded on a sheet of paper and Matt took his chance, ending the fight with three heavy punches before

Mr Anderson managed to drag him off me.

"I said break it up!" Mr Anderson shouted.

Someone restrained me from behind. I looked up and, to my embarrassment, found Mr Johnston – the head of the English department – holding me back. "That's *enough,* the pair of you!" he bellowed, right by my ear.

I flinched. I'd never heard a teacher shout so loud before. I'm guessing it was a first for Matt, too, because it wiped the perpetual snarl from his face. "Right, pack your things," Mr Johnston said.

"But *he* started it!" Matt dared to protest, pointing an accusing finger at me.

Mr Johnston held up his hand. "I don't want to hear it." He looked at us both in turn, nostrils flaring, his thick eyebrows so furrowed they almost joined in the middle. "This is *unacceptable* behaviour. I'm taking you both to Mrs Patel."

I swallowed. I'd never been sent to her office before. I'd heard from others that she could be ruthless – not that I was expecting anything less.

As Matt and I gathered our things, Mr Johnston added, "If you boys give me *any* form of trouble, I'll be sure to suggest a punishment far more severe than a couple of weeks' suspension. Do I make myself clear?"

"Yes sir," I muttered.

Matt nodded, and then the two of us were marched out of the classroom.

The adrenaline had worn off by this point. In

its place was a horrible taste in my mouth. I didn't know how Matt could walk so tall. I kept my head down, shoulders slumped, not wanting to be seen by anyone.

A sickly feeling formed in the pit of my stomach as I imagined the number of different punishments I could face. And don't even get me started on Mum and Dad's reaction to all this.

CHAPTER TWO

I scuffed my shoes on the thin carpet outside reception and wondered how many other pairs of feet had done the same while waiting to see the head teacher.

Mr Anderson had come down a few minutes before to hand over a small pile of papers to Mrs Patel. I'm not sure what they were but he passed me without a glance, and that bothered me. Everyone knew Matt was a troublemaker but why blank me like I was no better? I decided I didn't like Anderson anymore.

Surprisingly, Matt didn't say a word the entire time we sat there. I reckon it was because "parental back-up" was on the way. Mrs Patel refused to see us until our parents showed, and since Matt literally lived around the corner, his mum got there first. She looked like she smoked at least forty a day. And even though her clothes hung off her stick-thin body, I could see traces of Matt in the over-confident walk, the set glare, the jutted chin …

The receptionist ushered her and Matt through to Mrs Patel's office, leaving me by myself. The waiting area was quiet once again – until the receptionist sat back down at her desk, and then shouting erupted from Mrs Patel's office. I only heard one voice, though, as if Matt's mother was having an argument with herself. I tried to make out what she was saying but other than *"It ain' 'is fault!"* and *"Yoo don' know nothink!"*, I couldn't decipher much.

She was still going on when my own mum turned up.

The receptionist welcomed her and, since Mum's stomach was the size of a beach ball, offered to bring the signing-in book over to her in the waiting room. Mum refused, though, signing herself in at the front desk like everyone else. She was past eight months now. I'd soon be a brother to someone again, and here I was causing unnecessary stress. I felt even shittier now.

I looked down at my feet. It was a good call because I could feel her gaze before she'd even squiggled her curly signature, her scowl clear enough to picture without looking.

"Aren't you going to tell me what happened before we go in?" she asked. Her voice was flat, but it was better than yelling. That would come later.

She lowered herself into the plastic chair next to me.

I said nothing.

"Jordan, this is serious. I thought things were getting better."

"They *are* getting better."

"Then why am I here?"

I sighed. Matt's crow of a mother didn't lay into *him* as soon as she got in.

"I just don't want this bullying stuff to start up again," Mum said.

"I'm not getting bullied!" That was a lie. Whenever anyone found out about Danny – about how I still talked to him – they just couldn't help but tease me. It'd died down a little since Christmas but the snide remarks and shoves in the corridors were still there. It was just easier not to tell anyone. I knew Mum and Dad wanted to help but having them demand teachers to confront people like Matt only made it A) humiliating, and B) worse. They *wanted* a reaction. Reporting petty crap only escalated everything.

"Really? Well from what I can see –"

"For God's sake, Mum. Can you just –"

I was about to say something I might regret when Mrs Patel's door finally opened. We both turned to watch her lead Matt and his crow-mother to reception. The pair of them looked fed up, like this was a complete waste of their time. Personally, I think they were just craving another smoke. And then I heard Mrs Patel say firmly to Matt, "Don't forget to come and see me on Monday."

Matt had been suspended. I bit the inside of my cheek. Did that mean *I* would be suspended?

The bell above my head rang for lunch. Man, how I wished I was anywhere else right then.

Mum looked at me – God knows what she was thinking – and then Mrs Patel called us in. I could still hear Matt's mother bitching in reception as the door closed behind us, trapping us in a room that smelt of lemon. Whether Mrs Patel had eaten one at break or it was a type of air freshener, I wasn't sure. It reminded me of my local dentist, though. I hated it.

Mrs Patel shook Mum's hand before gesturing for us to take a seat in front of her desk. The chairs looked much comfier than the plastic ones in the waiting room.

We sat down (I was right – they were much comfier) and for a brief moment I thought about how out of place Matt's mother must have looked. Mrs Patel's office was super-organised. All her documents were in plastic wallets piled in two silver filing racks on her desk, and at least a dozen labelled ring binders were stacked on shelves and in cupboards. It wouldn't surprise me if she'd colour-coded everything too.

"Thank you for coming at such short notice, Mrs Richardson," Mrs Patel began. "But we have a very strict 'no fighting' policy here at Doorston High school that Jordan broke today. Isn't that right?" She turned to me, cupping her hands and placing them lightly on her desk. That's when I noticed the thin stack of papers Mr Anderson had handed over earlier. They looked like statements. He must have made the class write them when Matt and I left. "Would you mind telling us what happened in your English class today?"

"A fight broke out," I said dumbly.

Mum's face said it all.

"Yes, I'm quite aware of that," Mrs Patel continued. "What I want to know is, who did what and why."

I couldn't look at either of them. Instead, I focused on a groove on the side of Mrs Patel's desk and began to talk.

I told them how Matt had always been the bully class clown, and how he just had something in for me ever since we started Doorston High. I didn't tell them *why* he had something in for me. I didn't want Mum to know and it was irrelevant anyway.

"So Matt threw the first punch?" Mrs Patel confirmed, after I'd finished my story. She checked this against a few of the statements.

"Yes, Miss," I said, noticing how stiff Mum looked beside me.

"But apparently you lunged at him. Is that right?"

"Does it matter?" Mum said, her voice a notch away from sounding exasperated. "I'd lunge at him too if he hit me. It's self-defence!"

"Mrs Richardson, I believe you're missing the point." She indicated a particular statement in her hand. "The fight had already ended. Matt was walking away. It says so in all the statements." She turned to me. "Or are they all making it up?"

"No..." I began, but Mum interjected again.

"There's only so much a person can take before they —"

"Before they lash out, yes," Mrs Patel finished. Her voice was calm but her eyes were as sharp as blades. "What Jordan *should* have done was approach a member of staff right away."

"There should have been a teacher there anyway! Who was supervising at the time?"

There was a brief pause. I wasn't sure where this was going but I couldn't see either woman backing down. I quickly jumped in with the answer I'd been meaning to give before Mum had interrupted.

"I only went for him because he mentioned my brother." I didn't know who had reported what or how much they had told, but Mrs Patel looked taken aback by this. "He said he was glad my brother was dead, before threatening us both."

I thought Mum was rigid before. Now she looked as though all her joints had been set with cement. She wrinkled up her nose, as though a bad smell had entered the room.

"I wasn't aware of that," Mrs Patel confessed. For the first time throughout this entire conversation, she looked uneasy. "Nevertheless —"

"What do you mean, 'nevertheless'? My son is on medication because of his brother's death — it's in your school's medical files. Look it up!" Mum leaned forward, gripping the polished wooden armrests hard enough to make her knuckles milky white. "If Jordan is going to be ... *tormented* about it, then I'm glad he 'lashed out'. He was defending himself and I'll back him up every step of the way."

For some reason, I felt like crying. Not because I was sad. Too much was going on, I guess, and seeing Mum so pent-up from what had happened ... I thought she would've blamed me. Instead, she was defending me. I took a breath and kept it together. I was sure I'd get a rollicking once we were alone but for now, she was on my side.

Mrs Patel cleared her throat. "I understand that Jordan's circumstances are different, but that does not justify what he did in class. *Nevertheless ...*" She emphasised where she left off, pausing briefly, for whatever reason. Mum raised her eyebrows, waiting to hear how Mrs Patel was going to spin this. "... Besides the odd hiccup from when he's been bullied, I see that Jordan has a clean record." Mrs Patel turned back to me. "I'll be letting you off with a warning, Jordan."

I relaxed a little. She was still going on about how, if I got into any more trouble I should tell someone immediately, and that she would ask my teachers to keep an eye out for me. All the usual stuff they're supposed to tell you, basically. It wasn't enough for Mum, though.

When it became clear that Mrs Patel was wrapping

up the conversation, Mum asked, "What about the other boy? What's going to happen to him?"

"I've suspended him for the remainder of the week. When he returns, he'll be on a one-month contract where he will have to report back to me every lunch time so I can monitor his class behaviour."

I could see Mum mulling this over. I still doubted it was enough for her, but she didn't say anything.

I was waiting for Mrs Patel to dismiss us when she surprised me by asking if I needed to take the rest of the day off.

"I think that would probably be best," Mum said, and although I didn't say anything, I agreed. The thought of facing everyone in class after lunch was overwhelming.

"Very well." Mrs Patel shook Mum's hand again and walked us through to reception. Two girls from the year above me were now in the same plastic waiting-room chairs Mum and I had sat in. They didn't look like troublemakers. Then again, neither did I.

"Make sure you catch up on the lesson you'll be missing," Mrs Patel said to me after I'd signed out. "And don't forget to revise for your exams."

I nodded – as if I was actually going to do that. I was biting the inside of my cheek again. This time it was to contain a smile that was pressing forward with the thought of freedom. Surely, if you were involved in a fight you weren't supposed to be rewarded? Leaving school almost two hours early was a godsend!

Or so I thought.

It wasn't until I saw the look on Mum's face that I realised this was far from a reward. Matt may have been suspended and put on contract, but I seemed to have a much harsher punishment: driving home alone with Mum.

CHAPTER THREE

It was raining when we left school and neither of us had a coat. By the time we reached the car, our hair was damp and sticking to our faces. Mum unlocked the doors with a tired sigh before yanking the handle. She was annoyed, no question. I got in the passenger seat even though I was more than tempted to sit in the back. I just wanted to be as far away from her as possible.

Matt was probably playing on his Xbox right now. As if he or his crow-mother gave a damn about what happened.

I waited out the silence while Mum turned on the ignition, switched on the wipers and put the car in gear. Her bump was about an inch away from the wheel. Give it another week and I doubt she'd be able to drive.

I looked outside, at the rain that had already changed to a misty drizzle. The roads were practically empty. I was used to weekend traffic and rush-hour that lasted from three until seven. It wasn't until we passed the zebra crossing further down Forest Road that Mum finally spoke.

"What was it about?" she asked.

I looked up at her blankly.

"The fight," she said. "What was it about? Why did he start on you?"

"He just doesn't like me."

"Why?"

"I dunno. He thinks I'm weird." I folded my arms and leaned back in my seat. "Oh, and I'm fine by the way. Thank you *very* much for asking. I'm sure the swelling on my lip will go down eventually."

Mum slammed on the left indicator before turning onto Vaughan Street. "Don't use that tone with me, Jordan. I'm just trying to get to the bottom of this."

"It's sorted! You heard Mrs Patel – Matt's suspended. It won't happen again."

"That Mrs Patel doesn't know a thing," she muttered under her breath; but I was sitting right next to her so it was hard to miss. Picking up on my previous comment, though, she asked, "Why does he think you're weird?"

She knew the answer; she just wanted me to say it. But those conversations never went well. We usually both ended up shouting and one of us almost always ended up crying.

I groaned, already trying to organise my defence.

If she wanted to go down this route, then so be it. I was just thankful she was in the driver's seat. It meant she couldn't look at me for longer than a few short seconds at a time. "Because he can't see Danny."

Mum's hands clenched around the wheel. Only slightly, but I still noticed it. "You can't see him either, Jordan."

"Well, no …" I admitted. "But I can sense him. He shows me signs –"

"No, he doesn't!"

The sudden increase in volume made me flinch. Talking about Danny pained her, and I knew it always would. I also knew that, for some reason, she would persist in talking about him.

The green light up ahead changed to red. Mum cursed, as though it was this short delay that had pissed her off and not me. I glanced at her again, but one look told me it would be stupid to say anything. Even a compliment would be dangerous at this point.

While we sat idling at the final set of traffic lights before our house, I watched the dice swing on the elastic string tied around the rear-view mirror. They used to smell of vanilla, but Grandad had smoked in the car so many times that they now stank of something I can't quite describe.

"Where is he then?"

Mum's voice startled me. "What d'you mean?"

"Where's Danny?" she asked again, humouring

me. "Is he in this car? Is he behind me right now?"

"No."

"Where then?"

"I don't know! He isn't *always* with me. He disappears sometimes." I had no idea where he disappeared to; I didn't know where spirits visited when they weren't around. Maybe there was a Heaven. Maybe they spent time with other relatives. Or perhaps all they did was drift around, watching other people live their lives. All I knew was that sometimes he was close by and other times he wasn't.

The lights changed. Mum took off the handbrake and we were off again, for the remaining minute of the journey.

"Well isn't *that* convenient," she snapped. I recognised the tone immediately. We'd waded too far into the topic. She spat the next few words, unable to contain herself any longer. "He's dead, Jordan. Just leave it."

I never said he wasn't dead, I thought.

Surprisingly, Mum didn't say another word until we had reversed onto the drive. She switched off the engine, took out the keys and turned to me. "Have you been taking your medication?"

She was talking about my antipsychotic drugs for my so-called schizophrenia. I breathed heavily through my nose. I'd already decided I couldn't tell her the truth.

"Yes."

Mum looked at me closely, as though she knew

the correct answer and was watching me fail her cruel test of honesty. "If I find out you're lying, you're going to be in so much trouble."

"I'm not lying!" I broke eye contact first. Pulling the handle, I got out the car and walked up the drive.

During spring and summer, our front garden was usually the brightest on Kendal Drive. Right now, though, there was only sodden grass and waterlogged soil. It was nearly the end of March, but I figured Dad wouldn't have time for planting amaryllises or whatever they're called this year. He'd be too busy with the baby.

I unlocked the front door and headed straight to the kitchen for a snack. I thought Mum would follow me through to continue arguing but fortunately, after placing the car keys in the trinket dish on the hallway windowsill, she went upstairs. I took a breath. Thank God for that ...

I reached for a packet of crisps from the top cupboard, and as I did, I felt Danny approach me from behind. It was a rush of energy that made my spine tingle. "Mum thinks I'm crazy," I told him, shutting the cupboard door. "Can you show her a sign? Let her know you're here?"

He knocked the crisps out my hand. Danny hadn't aged a bit. He would always stay his mischievous ten-year-old self.

"I'm being serious!" I picked them up, opened the packet and ate a handful.

He *used* to show himself to Mum and Dad.

Four years ago, he'd open cupboards, move chairs and leave messages … At first they thought I was playing games, then they thought I was attention-seeking, until eventually deciding I must have been delusional. Trying to convince them it was really their dead son only made things worse. I think Danny realised he was the reason I was having so many arguments with them. So he stopped trying to get through to them.

It's easy enough to talk with Danny but that's only because I've been doing it for years. To start with, I found that he only ever appeared when I was thinking of him — which was pretty much all the time back then. It wasn't until I got older and researched into it a bit more that I figured out how it all worked. Basically, people and spirits are on a different frequency. Like a radio, I guess — you have to tune it to get the right waves. Spirits have to lower their frequency and we have to raise ours so both of us sort of meet in the middle. Meditation often works. All I do is clear my mind and direct my thoughts at Danny. He'll then put ideas or pictures in my head. It can still get confusing differentiating between my own random thoughts and Danny's, but I'm getting better at it.

Danny tried snatching the blue crisp packet out of my hands again. This time I kept a firm grip. "Nice try," I laughed, and at that moment I heard the floorboards creak above me. Mum was in my room.

"Seriously?" I left the packet on the side as I ran out of the kitchen and up the stairs. She was searching for my tablets.

"Mum!" I stood in the doorway, watching her rifle through all my drawers. My desk looked like it had already been raided and my wardrobe doors were wide open. "What are you doing? Get out my room!"

She straightened up, pressing her hands into the small of her back to relieve some of the pressure that had built up there. "Where are they?" she said.

"Where are *what?*" I asked, trying and failing to sound somewhat innocent.

Her expression hardened. "Your medication. I want to see it. *Now.*"

I sighed. There was no avoiding it.

I could feel Mum watching me the entire time as I dragged the chair by my desk over to my wardrobe. I knew I was about to get grounded for life. This was so unfair …

At the very top, lying in all the dust and cobwebs, crammed next to a stack of old board games, were the five unopened boxes of clozapine tablets. I took the top one, hoping she didn't see the others, before climbing back down with it. Mum's hand was already outstretched, waiting. I passed them over and realised I was holding my breath.

She broke the seal. Every single capsule was there and accounted for. I was so dead.

At first I wondered how loud she was going to

yell and whether it would top Mr Johnston. Instead, she spoke in a deadpan tone. "What do you have to say for yourself?"

I looked at the floor – at the carpet, which needed hoovering. What was I supposed to say? That I was sorry for not taking tablets I knew I shouldn't be taking? No way! I wasn't having a relapse, and my outburst about Danny was not another "episode". I couldn't hear imaginary voices – Danny was real. Instead, I looked back at her and said, quite simply, "I don't want to take them."

"You *have* to take them."

"Why? Because you and Dad don't believe me? I'm not crazy. I don't need that stuff. You can't *force* me to take them."

Mum put her hand to her forehead. "I can't be doing with this right now. I'm calling your dad. I'll let him deal with you." She turned to leave, still carrying my medication.

"I don't need 'dealing with'. What I *need* is to be left alone!"

She didn't reply. I was glad, because I already felt like punching a brick wall. I balled up my fists and listened to the sound of her footsteps as she headed downstairs. She was done for now, but the conversation was far from over.

What did it matter what Dad said anyway? I'm not taking those tablets. The reason they don't sense Danny is because they don't let him in; they don't keep an open mind. That's *their* problem – not mine.

I lay back on my bed, staring up at the plain ceiling and half wanting it to cave in on me.

CHAPTER FOUR

Technically, I wasn't grounded yet. So I made the most of my PS4 privileges and continued to work my way through the *Assassin's Creed* game I was replaying. I was trying to get all the trophies so I could finally complete it. I kept the volume low to listen out for Mum, but she didn't come upstairs. She must have been busy preparing dinner.

Sure enough, by the time Dad got home, the familiar smell of Mum's famous chicken casserole had drifted up to my room. I knew I should have at least offered to help, but ... *come on*. After the argument we'd just had, on what planet would that have been a good idea? So I stayed in my room, sitting cross-legged on my bed while being chased by virtual guards – until Dad called me down for dinner.

I said nothing as I joined them at the kitchen table. I wasn't sure if she'd told Dad about school and my meds yet. I mean, I'm sure she *had,* but Dad wasn't acting like he knew. Maybe he was too knackered to lay into me yet. That suited me.

Food had already been dished up so I dug in, picking out bits of onion as I went and leaving them on the side of my plate. Then, just as I was getting used to the silence beneath the chewing and clinking cutlery, Dad asked the question I'd been dreading: "How was school?"

It didn't sound like he was trying to catch me out, but I could hardly lie with Mum sitting with us. "Not one've my best days," I admitted.

"I can tell." He gestured to the side of my face, at one of the many marks Matt must have left behind. The stinging had turned into a dull ache that only purple bruises made. "What happened? Are you all right –?"

"I'm fine."

"You should at least think about putting some ice on it." Unlike Mum, he left it at that, tucking back into his casserole. He complimented her cooking, asked how she and the baby were doing, and then went on about the new receptionist down at the police station. From how he described her, a blindfolded chimp could do a better job. Then he told us how my Uncle Ryan almost got hit by a school bus this morning and that someone down the road was having their driveway tarmacked …

For a while, everything felt so normal that I almost forgot about the fight with Matt and the argument with Mum — until the last few forkfuls, when Dad turned to me.

"Jordan," he said. "Before you rush off upstairs again, I want a quick word with you."

I bit my tongue, trying hard not to sigh. It was no mystery what he wanted to talk about, especially since Mum had gone unusually quiet. "Sure," I said.

There was no point pretending I might finish the rest of my dinner. I stood up to empty my leftovers in the bin, rinsed my plate and loaded it in the dishwasher. Mum and Dad were talking about another trip to Mothercare before the due date, so I left them to it, heading into the front room instead.

Nan always complained about how cluttered our house was, but the front room was by far the busiest. The TV was flanked by shelves rammed with DVDs and Blu-rays, a mishmash of cheap ornaments lined the mantelpiece, and framed photographs covered the walls. Dad even had stacks of his old CDs by the electric fireplace, though he'd been using Spotify for years now. It was the sort of mess that usually made me feel at home. Right now, though, I wanted to be as far away from it all as possible.

I sat in the one-seater chair, switched on the TV and rested my feet on the coffee table in front of me. Dad was obviously going to take Mum's side. I just wished he'd hurry the hell up.

Once I'd flicked through every movie channel we had (and *still* not finding anything worth watching), Dad finally walked in, carrying a fresh cup of tea and half a pack of custard creams.

"So …" he began, letting the word hang there while he placed his drink and biscuits on the coffee table between us. He sat in his usual spot, where the back of the settee sagged and the seat drooped like a deflated tyre. After rearranging the cushions to make himself comfortable, he continued. "Your mum told me that you haven't been taking your tablets." When I gave no reply, he shrugged and asked me why not.

"I don't need them," I said, repeating what I'd told Mum.

Dad sighed. "Jordan, mate –"

"I know what you're going to say," I cut him off, "but I've made up my mind. I'm not taking them."

"Dr Ashton seems to think you need them," he said.

I cringed at the name. Dr Ashton, my therapist, was a boring little man whose words Mum and Dad clung to as though they were sacred. For the past three years, every time I've seen him for these stupid counselling sessions (and I mean *every* time), he's dressed in a tailored suit with polished shoes and designer glasses, all trying to hide the fact that he's a tedious old git with piggy eyes and stout piggy legs. It was his attitude that really got my back up, though. I could never tell if he was being patronising or just over-sympathetic – and of the two, I couldn't decide which I hated more.

What I had was a "psychotic illness", he claimed – which *supposedly* means I can't always distinguish between what's real and what's imaginary. Dumb, right? And whenever I disagreed (because everything he said was bull) he put it down to "denial". To call the whole thing infuriating would be an understatement.

Usually, I had to put up with him for a single two-hour session once a month, which meant another three weeks before I had to visit his stuffy office again. I almost choked on my own saliva, though, when I heard I'd have to see him sooner.

"I rang the hospital and booked an appointment for you to see Dr Ashton this Friday," Dad said casually, as though his words hadn't just shattered any plans I might've had to enjoy the rest of this evening. Matt had got off lightly, the dick.

"I can't miss school this Friday," I said, trying to think up a believable excuse. "I have a mock exam in maths."

"You'll have to take the paper home with you then. Or sit it at a lunch time." Dad wasn't budging an inch. I sulked as he continued, "We've told him about the fight you had with that Matthew kid, and about you not taking your medication. He seems quite concerned about you. He wanted to see you as soon as possible."

"I wish you wouldn't tell him everything …"

"So, Friday. 10:30. Got it?"

"Whatever …" I flicked through the channels until I found a football match to watch. *Stupid Dr Ashton.* An early appointment with Piggy-eyed Man was the cherry on top. At least there was some solace in knowing things could only get better from here.

Dad ate one of his custard creams and then picked up a biro and yesterday's paper from the coffee table. His unfinished crossword was waiting for him.

On TV, two commentators speculated on a lucky save made by Kasper Schmeichel. I was just starting to get into the game when a sharp chill raced up my spine.

"You all right?" Dad asked, noticing me shiver.

I nodded, pretending to be interested in Leicester losing to Arsenal 3-0. Danny had just entered the room. He never usually made me feel this cold, not even when I was in Mr Anderson's classroom. "Is the heating on?" I asked, trying to disguise the odd behaviour.

"I don't think so," he said. "Why? You cold?"

If there was a prize for the world's dumbest question, Dad would've won it. Even if the heating *was* on, though, I knew it wouldn't have made a difference. The only way the room would heat up was if my brother left it.

The air around me suddenly became thick, like I was sitting in a swamp. Danny was standing in front of me.

I toyed with the remote, pretending I hadn't noticed. He was probably bored, and I wasn't in the mood for playing games right now.

The temperature dipped lower: he was determined

to get my attention. I turned my head, looking past where Danny must've been, and focused on Dad. "Are you cold?"

"No, I'm all right," he said, writing in a something-across answer.

"I must be coming down with something ..."

"You're not trying to get out of Friday, are you?"

"No! I was just saying." I shook my head and turned back to the game. "Never mind." Why did everything have to come down to stupid Dr Ashton?

By this point, I was surprised I couldn't see my own breath – and even more surprised that Dad couldn't feel the drop in temperature. Still, I refused to acknowledge Danny. Sometimes he got stubborn. I just had to wait it out.

The decreasing temperature was just about bearable but not the sudden sharp sting I felt on the back of my hand.

I suppressed a yelp, so it ended up sounding like a short whimper instead.

"You okay?" Dad said.

"Huh?" I watched the colour return on a small patch of skin on the back of my hand. The little swine had pinched me!

"You made a noise."

"Did I?" I wasn't sure why I said that.

"*Yes.*"

"Oh ..."

There was a brief pause before Dad spoke up again. "So you're okay then?"

I shrugged. "Yeah, I'm fine."

He sighed his *Teenagers ... what are they like?* sigh before returning to his crossword.

I started drumming my fingers on the arm of the chair, staring at the screen but not really watching, as the room grew colder and colder. Something wasn't right. Danny had never acted like this. For the briefest of moments, I actually felt afraid.

"I'm going to finish my homework," I said, getting up out of my chair. I headed upstairs, not giving Dad a chance to reply. What was Danny playing at?

Outside my room, the temperature was back to normal, but I could still feel the sting of Danny's pinch on my hand. I took a breath, reaching for the door-handle. Whatever had upset my brother, I knew I wasn't going to like it.

As I entered my room, I was instantly greeted by the same icy chill from downstairs. Danny was already here.

CHAPTER FIVE

I shut the door behind me and then spoke in a loud, concerned whisper. "What's the matter with you?"

All my PS4 games were knocked off the shelf above my bed.

"What was that for?" I asked, keeping my volume in check. If Mum or Dad overheard me, they'd be straight on the phone to Dr Ashton, telling him that it was happening again, that I was "hearing voices".

I made my way over to the bed and started putting my games back on the shelf. Their plastic cases were warm from the energy Danny had passed through them. Before I could finish, the computer chair in front of my desk made its way to the centre of the room and started spinning.

I left the games in a heap on my shelf and made my way over to it. The momentum was making a draught and with every spin there was an ominous clicking sound. There must've been a loose screw somewhere under the seat.

I knew Danny was sitting there, spinning himself dizzy (if ghosts could get dizzy). He was going to break it if he wasn't careful. That's how he broke the last two, and I always have to dip into my savings to buy another one.

"Can you stop that," I said, more as an order than a question.

He kept spinning.

"Danny, you're going to break it."

He spun even faster.

"For God's sake, Danny. It's a chair, not a frickin' toy. Now stop it."

I reached out and managed to pull the chair to a halt. It too was warm. Now that the clicking had stopped, the room was eerily silent. I wondered whether I should've just let him continue. He clearly needed to vent. If it wasn't the chair, what else would it be?

"OW!"

I covered my mouth to stop Mum or Dad hearing me as the computer chair Danny had just rammed into me wheeled to the other side of the room. I sat on my bed to inspect the damage. I don't know if he meant to run over my toe, but he did, and it bloody well *hurt.*

When I took off my sock, I was instantly drawn to the red swelling on my little toe. I bit my tongue but, *God,* how I wanted to scream at him. A sigh was all I could manage, though, when the games I'd just put away landed on top of me. Honestly, I don't know why I hadn't expected this.

"What's *wrong* with you?" I hissed, trying to work out my brother's exact position. This wasn't boredom; this was something else. And I would've sounded sympathetic if my toe wasn't still throbbing. "Look, I can't help you if you're throwing stuff around and ramming chairs into me, so just ..."

Oh no.

I watched the lamp by my laptop creep to the edge of my desk. And then it fell.

I dived towards it, catching it in my clammy palms. It was a save like one of Schmeichel's if I ever saw one. Taking a breath, I placed the lamp back on the desk and let my heart recover from taking on the form of a jackhammer.

"Danny ..." I sighed. "Please, just stop this and tell me what's wr —"

The bin beside me tipped over, spilling everything that was inside. He was acting faster than I could react.

I stooped down, picked up the bin and started collecting the crumpled bits of rubbish, when a quiet sound from across the room stole my full attention. I turned and managed to dodge just in time—

The computer chair slammed into the wall behind me, knocking the bin over again. I got that he was annoyed, but this was ridiculous.

"All right, that's *enough*. No more, you hear me?

No more." I got to my feet and glared around the room. And just like that, the icy chill of his temper was replaced by the minor drop in temperature that usually came with his presence. Maybe Danny had calmed down –

CRASH!

Or not.

The board games from the top of my wardrobe – all neatly stacked and ready to be flogged on eBay – fell to the floor. I cringed, unable to draw my eyes away from all the scattered pieces of Battleship, Connect Four, Guess Who, Mouse Trap, Jenga, Monopoly, Scrabble ...

Mum and Dad had to have heard that.

"Crap."

Multicoloured Monopoly money was fanned out everywhere; Jenga blocks and tiny battleships had rolled under the bed. I made my way towards the mess, not quite sure where to begin tidying. I had a feeling I'd be finding various counters on my floor for the next month.

"Okay, this time you've gone *too far,* Danny. You better help me clear this up or I'll –" Danny began to line up the Scrabble pieces. "No, I mean put the pieces in the goddamn boxes. I'm not playing games. These toys were from when we were like *seven.* You might not be, but I'm too old for this kind of stuff – not to mention being extremely pissed off with you for trashing our room!"

As I spoke, Danny continued lining up the

letters.

"Are you even listening to me?"

Still he carried on.

I crouched down, grabbed a handful of the letters he was arranging and poured them into the little green letter sack. I was just about to grab another handful when Danny pulled a tuft of my hair.

"*OW!* Pack it in!" I said, rubbing my scalp.

He didn't, though, and I'd be an idiot to think he'd ever listen to me. I stared straight ahead, watching the letters line up exactly as before, only now more were added and I could see that they were beginning to form actual words:

I_1 N_1 W_2 O_2

K_3 L_2 D_1 E_1

Letters were still darting about on the floor as Danny tried to find the right tiles. Then I heard the front-room door open. My body stiffened.

I could tell it was Mum by the slow footsteps climbing the stairs. Seconds later, there was a knock on my door. "Jordan?" she said, her voice muffled from the other side. "Are you okay?"

"Yeah," I called back, unable to look away from the letters Danny was arranging. I was ready to dart over and block the door if she tried to come in.

"We heard a bang," Mum continued.

"I'm just ... sorting some stuff out."

"What on Earth does that mean?"

"Uh ..." I edged closer to the door. "Tidying!"

I heard Mum sigh. "Okay," she said, and I bet she rolled her eyes. She must've been sick of me today because she walked away without another word.

The letters were still now. Danny's message stared up at me as plain as the game of Scrabble itself, yet the words they formed meant so much more. No wonder Danny was acting so strange.

Even as I listened to the sound of Mum's footsteps fade downstairs, I couldn't relax. I re-read the message, over and over again:

$$I \quad N\ O \quad W\ H\ O$$

$$K\ I\ L\ L\ E\ D \quad M\ E$$

FiVE YEARS EARLiER

It took forever to drive down to Devon. There were too many roadworks, too much traffic, and halfway there the sat-nav stopped working. I gave up asking when we'd get there because it was always the same answer and I didn't know when "soon" was. Basically, a lot longer than I thought.

I was about to die of boredom when Dad pulled into some huge car park. At first I thought it was another toilet break but then it hit me – we were finally there!

Dad parked the car and before he'd even switched off the engine, Danny and I climbed out. It felt good to stretch my legs, and the air was much cooler than inside the car.

Across from us was a large brown building with lots of different coloured flags on its roof. It looked like a giant sandcastle. Above the entrance, gold block letters spelled out "The Brookston Manor

Hotel", just like in the leaflet Dad had showed us.

I breathed in the salty smell of the sea. In the corner of the car park where the stone wall ended, concrete steps covered in sand led down to the beach. I walked towards them until I could see the foamy waves lapping onto shore.

"Jordan!"

I turned at the sound of Mum's voice. She and Dad were busy unloading two big suitcases from the boot. "Don't wander off," she said, as if I was about to make a run for it.

Me and Danny looked at each other. They'd want to unpack every last bag before we went anywhere. Realistically, I wasn't sure how much patience they expected us to have.

"When can we go on the beach?" Danny asked.

"Later," Mum said, lifting the coolbox from the back seat. "Can't you see we're busy? We still need to check into the hotel. The faster you help us unpack, the faster we can go somewhere."

Called it.

Me and Danny interrupted her with a ten-year-old's "I-can't-believe-our-luck" groan.

"Hey ... There's no rush, boys," Dad said, slamming the boot shut. All our stuff was bunched together in a small pile next to the car. He lifted the biggest suitcase, then quickly grabbed a plastic carrier bag that had been leaning against it to stop it falling. "You don't want to do everything all in one day, do you? You'll be bored by the end of the week."

"No we won't," I said. How could anyone get bored on holiday? He was only saying that because *they* were tired. Why didn't grown-ups ever get excited?

"Me and Jordan could go by ourselves," Danny suggested, but Mum wasn't having any of it.

"Don't be ridiculous," she said.

"I'm not! The beach is right outside the hotel. You'd probably see us from our room."

"Daniel —"

Dad interrupted before she could say another word."Actually, Debbie, that might not be such a bad idea," he said, and I'm not sure who was more surprised: Mum, or me and Danny. "You know they won't unpack things the way you want them to. They'll just be under your feet so we might as well let them play for a bit."

"Jason ..." Mum started.

"As long as they promise not to leave the beach, we know where they are."

Danny and I held our breaths. We could tell Mum didn't like the idea of letting us go by ourselves. Her eyes narrowed as she tried finding a reason to persuade Dad otherwise. I guess she couldn't think of one, though. "Make sure you're back by four," she said to us, as stern as ever.

Danny and I nodded before she could change her mind.

"And don't forget to ask reception for our room

number," she added. "You won't know where we're staying, otherwise."

"We will," me and Danny said at the same time. We smiled at her, but I could tell she still wasn't convinced.

Danny grabbed the plastic carrier-bag with our buckets and spades and began rifling through some other bags. "I've got an idea," he told me. "Let's build a sand-mansion for our dinosaurs!"

He was talking about the pack of mini plastic dinosaurs Mum had bought us at the start of the summer holidays. They were so cool and pretty realistic-looking … we just *had* to bring them with us.

"Great idea!" I said. I knew exactly where they were. I fished them out of the side compartment of our suitcase before Dad could wheel it away with the rest of our stuff and put them in the carrier bag with our buckets and spades. Then, after a final warning from Mum, we made our way across the car park to the concrete steps.

It looked very busy. There were deckchairs and windbreakers everywhere, and some guys surfing on the grey waves. I wish I knew how to surf. Then again, I didn't really like the sea. It was too cold, and I remember Dad telling us a few years ago that the current could drag a full-grown man away from shore. The beach was much safer.

We took off our shoes and socks and made our way down, sand filling the gaps between our toes. It didn't take long to find an empty spot. On our left, two women were lying on towels sunbathing, and on the other side of us was a group of kids playing football.

Danny dropped the plastic carrier bag in the sand and pulled out a spade to start digging. I picked up my spade too and began filling a bucket with sand. The plan, I knew without asking, was to build the dinosaurs' sand-mansion as high as we could.

I'm not sure how much time passed but eventually the two women next to us left with their towels and a young couple with a sleepy dog took their place. We'd have to head back to the hotel soon.

"Shall I dig a moat?" I suggested, when we were almost finished. Danny was just adding in the finer details with the end of his spade – windows, a door, brick lines … He was good at that kind of stuff.

"Yeah! Then we can fill it up with sea water."

My moat had only gone halfway around the mansion, though, when a football came crashing through the middle of it. All our hard work had been for nothing. There was no way we could rebuild it in the time we had left.

"Idiots …" Danny muttered. We should've picked a different spot.

I looked up from the wreckage and saw one of the boys from the group next to us heading over. He looked a bit like somebody in our class back at home, only thinner and with fewer freckles. The boy grinned and apologised. I couldn't tell if the whole thing was an accident or not.

His scruffy blonde hair stuck to his face and beads of sweat dripped from his forehead. When he reached us, he asked for his ball back. He was polite enough but that wasn't the point.

Danny stood, picked up the ball and tossed it to him with some force. The boy caught it with a heavy *whack* to his chest. I couldn't tell if that was an accident either.

"Nice throw," the boy said, stopping just in front of us. "What's your names?"

"Danny," my brother said.

"Jordan," I said, getting to my feet.

He nodded. "I'm Lewis." Another grin spread across his face as he asked, "Are you twins?"

"Yeah," I said, when it became clear Danny wasn't going to answer.

"Cool." Lewis looked down at the ruined sand-mansion behind us. "Hey, when you've finished building your castle, do you wanna come play football with us?" He nodded over to the two girls and four boys messing around in the space they were using as a football pitch. The corners and goalposts were marked out by their hoodies.

"Okay," I said, and at the same time Danny said, "Maybe ..." in a voice that really meant "no".

I looked at him, but he turned away.

"Chill, it was only an idea," Lewis laughed. "If you change your minds, we're just over there." And then he started making his way back to his mates.

I waited until I thought he was out of earshot before asking Danny, "How come you don't wanna play football?"

"They just wrecked our sand-mansion!"

"It was an accident —"

"As if!"

"Come on, Danny. We haven't played a proper match in weeks!" Two months, to be precise. Half our team back in Woodlock had quit, so our coach had no choice but to cancel any upcoming matches until we had enough players again. "Besides, they don't seem that bad. It could be fun."

"I thought we were having fun building *this*?" He gestured to the pile of sand between us.

"We were! But we have all week to redo it. Chances are we might never see these guys again."

"So?"

I stared back at our destroyed sand-mansion and said nothing. *"So" I wanted to play football ...*

Danny sighed. It was the sound of defeat. I didn't look up, though, until he said he would play.

We put on our shoes, packed up our toys and left them in the carrier bag on the sideline of their imaginary football pitch. Lewis beamed at us from what might have been the halfway line before jogging over. "Glad you guys decided to join us," he said, then started introducing us to everyone: "This is Shane, Sophie, Leanne, Mike, Dave and Ben." Even though he pointed to them all in turn, it would take a while before the names stuck to the right faces.

When it came to me and Danny, Lewis mixed up our names. We didn't bother correcting him. They'd never be able to tell us apart anyway.

"How old are you guys?" one of the girls – Leanne, I think – asked.

"Ten."

"We're all twelve ..." She stopped short, glancing up at Ben, the boy with pink-tipped spiky hair, before correcting herself. "Or *nearly* twelve."

"Like it matters," Lewis said. "Come on, let's play. Jordan, you're on my team with Shane, Dave and me – Danny, you're with them. Put Sophie's cardigan on so we know who's who."

A look of disgust crossed Danny's face as Sophie handed over her pale knitwear cardigan. Instead of slipping his arms through the sleeves, he tied it round his waist and then the game kicked off.

Both sides were easy on us at first, but it soon became clear that I was on the winning team. Lewis, Shane and Dave were like pro players: score, score, score, save, score, score ... I was starting to think that was probably why Danny's team had more players – to at least give them a chance.

The rules were vague and the game was dirty. I'd never seen so many fouls go unnoticed. It was worse than our away games with sleazy Slatershill. And to make matters worse I kept getting sand in my eyes.

"You all right, Jordan?" Shane or Dave said when we had a moment to catch our breath (I still couldn't remember who was who). We were watching Lewis tackle Ben from the imaginary goalpost.

"It's hard to run on sand," I admitted.

Shane/Dave smiled. "You get used to it –"

"ARGHH!"

He was interrupted by my brother's scream. I looked up. Danny was on the floor, clutching his leg. The sand wasn't a problem anymore as I ran over to him.

"Danny! Are you okay?" I said.

Nobody else moved.

"I'm –" He grimaced as I helped him to his feet. "I'm fine. Just a bad tackle."

Lewis closed the short gap between us and put an arm around Danny's shoulders, knocking me out the way. "You all right, Dan?"

"It's Danny," he reminded him bluntly.

Lewis didn't seem to hear, though. "Tell you what, we won't count that last goal. D'you think you can take a penalty?"

Danny shook his head.

"Maybe we should go back to the hotel," I said. I wasn't sure how bad his leg was but Mum and Dad would know.

Lewis turned to Sophie and Leanne. "You two take him back. Make sure he gets there okay."

They agreed without question. I was about to follow when Lewis put his arm out in front of me. "Where are you going?"

"With Danny," I said.

"Oh, come on … Can't you two be apart for

more than a few minutes?"

"I need to check if he's okay."

"Calm down, he's fine. The girls will take care of him. Besides, I've been through tougher scrapes than that." Lewis gave my arm a friendly punch. "Don't worry about it. Shall we play on?"

I hesitated.

And then I nodded.

CHAPTER SIX
WEDNESDAY - PRESENT DAY

It was dark in my room, and I could hear the patter of rain starting up against my window.

I couldn't sleep. Not after what Danny had told me last night. After seeing his first message, that he knew who had murdered him, I'd immediately asked him who it was.

Danny then rearranged the letters to form the name he was after:

$$C_2 \quad I_1 \quad L_2 \quad L_2 \quad I_1 \quad A_1 \quad N_1$$

$$O_2 \quad H_2 \quad A_1 \quad G_2 \quad A_1 \quad N_1$$

My heart had thumped fiercely against my ribcage, as though wanting to break out and hunt the monster down itself. I'd been desperate to know the truth since the moment I'd heard that my brother had been murdered. And now I knew.

Cillian O'Hagan was my brother's killer.

"Tell me where to find him," I'd said. I needed to hear him confess and then make him suffer the way he'd made my brother suffer. I needed to make him *pay*. "God, he's going to get what's coming to him."

The fact that Danny didn't object reassured me of one thing: my brother wanted revenge. The only problem was, he wouldn't tell me where I needed to go.

I rolled onto my side and checked the time on my phone. 5:07am.

There was no point in trying to fall asleep now. Besides, I still had so much to plan, if I wanted to track down Cillian and avenge my brother today.

I brought my laptop over to the bed. Dad would be up for work at half past, so I didn't bother switching on the lamp. He'd see the light from under the door and, since I was ditching school today, I didn't want him to know I was awake. He'd ask questions and I didn't need the hassle. He and Mum would hardly believe a word I said about Cillian, and I had no evidence to involve the police yet. So, this was the plan so far:

To avoid suspicion, I was going to leave the house at quarter past eight like I usually would for school. Instead of catching the school bus, though, I would follow Danny and hunt down his killer.

And that's it.

Vague, I know. That's why I was so worried. Since Danny had spelled out Cillian's name, all I'd found out was that Danny was going to lead me. I had no idea where to or how I was getting there – he refused to say anything else. If it hadn't been for the wall of cold moving around me, I would've thought he'd left.

I sat up, propped my pillow against the headboard behind me and rested my laptop on my legs. Maybe he'd tell me more this time. I could hardly leave without a sense of direction, and I needed to be sure that I'd be back in time for when school ended.

I dimmed the laptop screen and opened a word document. Danny knew the drill. He often typed out his responses for me.

"Danny?" I whispered into the dark. "Where will I find Cillian?"

I shuddered as the room became cooler; my forehead was tingling from new energy. I could sense him. He was at the end of my bed.

"Where does he live?" I tried again.

I felt him move around my bed, the cold coming closer. I stared at the empty word document, but Danny said nothing. I wasn't giving in so easily, though.

"Who is he? Why did he kill you? How do you know it was him?"

I kept firing questions at him but, like last night, he didn't answer a single one.

By the time Dad's alarm clock rang out, I'd made no progress whatsoever.

I listened to Dad's heavy footsteps on the

landing as he made his way to the bathroom. That was the end of that, then: I couldn't speak to Danny in case he overheard. Instead, I tried googling how to catch a murderer. All that came up was the same science articles and psychology reports that I'd read a million times before, and a few reviews on the TV series *To Catch a Killer*. I re-read a couple of articles and then, as a last-ditch effort, I typed in the name "Cillian O'Hagan" …

"Jordan, time to get up." Dad knocked on my door like he always did before leaving for work, making sure I was awake. I switched on the lamp and told him I was just getting out of bed.

My shoulders sagged. I knew it was a long shot, but I was kinda hoping I'd find *something* useful. The only relevant thing I found was variant spellings of his name and a list of different Cillians on Facebook, Twitter and Wikipedia. None of them had the same surname, though.

I sighed, sitting up straighter. "I'm not getting anywhere here, Danny. You need to start giving me some answers. How am I supposed to find him if you won't tell me anything?"

I checked the time on my taskbar. 7:40am. I needed to get ready. If I wasn't out the door in my school uniform with my satchel in half an hour, there'd be no chance of ditching school – Mum would end up giving me a lift like she always did if she thought I'd missed the bus.

I was just about to close my laptop lid and get out

of bed when letters began to appear on the screen in front of me. He was cutting it close.

I watched each key sink down as Danny typed out his response:

I will take you there

I leaned closer to the screen. "Okay," I said slowly – but he'd already told me this. "Can you give me a rough idea where I'll be going?"

I waited but he didn't answer.

There was only one place I could think of that made any sense. "It's got to be somewhere in Devon, surely? Near The Brookston Manor Hotel? That's where he found you."

The keys sank down again:

I will leed you to him

Stubborn git. Why did he have to be so secretive?

I closed my eyes for a moment, suddenly feeling very tired. When I opened them again I saw that Danny had typed something else:

Trust me

I rubbed my face. "Of course I trust you. I just have no idea how to go about this!" I paused for a moment before changing tactics. "If you won't tell me where I'm going, can you at least tell me which train to catch so I can book the tickets and work out times?"

More typing. Faster this time.

No trains or buses. They won't stop at the right places.

"Well, I can hardly ask Mum or Dad for a lift!"

Taxi

"This is going to cost me a bomb, isn't it?" I muttered, fully aware of the £168 I had to my name. "You do realise the driver will want to know the location before we even set off, right? What do I say?"

There was another pause. This time I knew it was Danny thinking.

Head towords Deven

Devon. I knew it. (*I'd definitely need to borrow some cash ...*) "Are you sure I can't just catch a train?"

Taxi is better. Pleese trust me. Theres more than one stop you will need to take.

"What do you mean? What other stops?" The more he told me, the more confused I became. I knew I wouldn't get an answer, though. And now another question began to weigh on me. If he answered nothing else, I at least wanted to know this: "Why now, Danny? Surely you've known your killer for years! How come it's taken you so long to tell me?"

He was done with my questions. The chill left; I was by myself.

Staring back at the word document with all his brief statements, I tried to organise my trip — it was impossible without knowing all the information. I searched the number for Richmond's taxis (the only taxi company in Woodlock), but ... what the hell was I meant to say to them? I couldn't get picked up from home and I still didn't have a specific destination to give them. The only alternative was walking down to the taxi rank, jumping in one of the cabs there and hope that they'd follow the vague direction I'd been given.

But then what?

I was seriously considering delaying the mission when, out of nowhere, I pictured something horrific —

I was looking down on the scene: strong hands were holding a child's head under water ... the thrashing of someone fighting to breathe. He couldn't free himself. The flailing slowed. Just when the burning pain of suffocation was too much to bear, the man brought his head up. Coughing. Spluttering. And then the man slammed him into the rocks at the bottom of the stream. There was no more thrashing; no more flailing. Bubbles ceased in the red water. And then the boy was left there. Dead.

I'd had that exact scene play through my head before. I didn't know if it was part of Danny's memory or something my own brain had conjured up, using the few facts the police had given us. That's what made it worse though, not knowing if I was watching something that really happened.

I unclenched my jaw and when I loosened my fists, I saw the tiny marks my nails had left on my palms.

I set down my laptop and fetched my money-box from under the bed. I knew Danny would have my back, but would Cillian O'Hagan try to kill me too? Most likely, once he knew who I was and why I was there. First, I needed to record his confession on my phone for Mum, Dad and the police. Then, it was payback time. If Danny wanted to finish him off, so be it – if not, he was mine. Either way, in my mind he was a dead man walking. I just needed to make his death look like an act of self-defence (which, to be honest, will probably be the case anyway). The police wouldn't take down a kid for killing a murderer in self-defence, surely? Especially if that kid was a Police Constable's son – right?

The idea of school was laughable now. I emptied my faded satchel of any books, pens and paper and re-packed it with my phone, wallet, the bottle of Coke

I'd brought from school yesterday break-time, and the rest of the cash from my money-box. I decided I'd find a weapon at Cillian's house — it would make it look more believable when I told them I had no intentions of killing him. Also, I didn't know how long I'd be carrying my bag for, so I didn't want to weigh it down. Instead, I stuffed in one of my hoodies to bulk it out in case Mum got suspicious with how little I was taking. I slid my books under the bed and headed downstairs just before ten past eight. Right on time.

Most of my rage had worn off now, replaced by nerves that made my jaw chatter. I kept it under control, though, when I popped into the kitchen to say bye to Mum.

"I'm off now," I said, trying to sound casual.

Mum looked at me. Instead of wishing me a good day like she usually did, she said, "Promise me you won't get into any more trouble."

I had to fight to keep a straight face. *If only she knew ...*

"I promise." It was easier lying to her when I thought about how grateful she'd be when I caught Danny's killer.

I knew I was being irresponsible, but I couldn't carry on as normal now that I knew who'd murdered my brother. And nobody would take my word for it if I told them who did it. So, without looking back, I made my way down the hall and let myself out and the front door.

CHAPTER SEVEN

The rain was worse than yesterday – just my luck. I pulled up my hood and headed the way I always went to get to the school bus stop, in case Mum was watching. I turned left at the end of the road, but instead of going straight on I took the first left onto Trueway Drive, doubling back down Kendal Drive's neighbouring street. It was the quickest way to Richmond's Taxi Rank.

Danny wasn't with me anymore. There wasn't much he could do while I was still in Woodlock but he'd appear again soon enough.

Traffic was hectic up ahead. Cars were gridlocked while pedestrians bustled past with umbrellas clenched firmly in their cold hands. So much for spring. I shoved my hands deep inside my jacket pockets and kept my head down against the wind. I was walking through a crowd of sullen faces with a backing track of car horns and angry voices.

The weather was good for one thing: everybody was staring at the ground, making it less likely that I'd be spotted by anyone from school.

Once I'd reached the end of Trueway Drive, I crossed over and cut through the park that brought me close to Woodlock town centre. After crossing about five other roads and passing what seemed like a hundred mothers and their pushchairs, I finally reached Richmond's Taxi Rank. Usually there were at least three cabs parked up in the bays – but of course the day I actually *want* to hire one out, there are none. Maybe I should have phoned up first after all.

I stood under the roof of the taxi rank, checking up and down the road for any sign of a cab. I couldn't wait there long, though. The wind was blowing rain straight at me, so even beneath the shelter I was still getting soaked. After maybe five minutes, I decided to go inside the taxicab office.

I closed the door behind me and had to resist wringing out the sleeves of my jacket. Then I pulled down my hood. The rain had soaked through it, so my hair was dripping water onto the black-and-white tiled floor.

I'd passed this place hundreds of times but never once been inside. The room was tiny, probably no bigger than our garden shed. After three small steps I'd reached the front desk, where two women sat behind a glass panel smeared with fingermarks. One of them was on the phone, yapping a bunch of

"Yeah"s and "Uh-huh"s, so I approached the one staring at a computer screen instead.

"Excuse me," I said.

She didn't look up.

I cleared my throat and tried again, louder this time. "*Excuse me.*"

Again, she didn't respond. For a moment I thought she might've been deaf. After a few seconds, though, she opened her small mouth and said, "What do you want?" So she wasn't hard of hearing. Just ignorant.

"Do you know when there'll be another?" I asked, indicating out the window with my thumb.

There was another long pause before the woman responded. This time, though, she raised her head from the computer screen and fixed me with a look of complete irritation. She could've been in her fifties but her hollow cheeks and sagging, dried-out skin made her appear ancient. Her upper lip twitched when she noticed the water I was dripping onto their floor; then she turned back to her computer screen.

"Next taxi should be here in ten minutes," she said.

That wasn't so bad, I guess.

"Thanks," I muttered, then headed back to the door.

There were no chairs, so I leaned against the wall, listening to the rain hammering on the roof as though it was being peppered with bullets. It clearly wasn't a waiting room but it's not like anyone else was queuing up. I knew I'd made the wrong call standing here, though, when the second woman finished her call. She wore the same lifeless expression as her colleague, only instead of ignoring me she stared daggers. It was like having a snake size you up to see if you're small enough to eat. Maybe it was because of the water I was still dripping onto their floor.

I decided I'd rather freeze outside.

I pulled up my hood before stepping out into Hurricane Inconvenient.

* * *

I checked the time on my phone for what felt like the millionth time. I must've been standing here at least twenty minutes and yet there was *still* no sign of a taxi. Either the cab was late or Ignorant-woman had lied. A lump formed at the back of my throat when I saw that it was almost nine o'clock – my tutor would be taking the register any minute now and I hadn't even left Woodlock!

I dried my phone screen on the shirt beneath my hoody and jacket before putting it away. I was surprised the rain hadn't seeped through all my layers yet.

The wind kept pulling at my hood and my nose was dripping like the broken showerhead in the boys changing room. I was ready to storm back in the taxicab office to give the two receptionists a piece of my mind when I heard a screeching sound at the end of the street. I looked up just in time to see a taxi skid around the bend.

At the same time, a red Peugeot on one of the drives opposite me began pulling out onto the main road. They seemed to spot each other at the same time but I couldn't tell if it was too late. The Peugeot driver stalled in panic halfway off the drive, his rear end sticking out in the middle of the road, while the approaching taxi screeched to a halt. Surprisingly, they didn't hit, but the two cars were only a whisper of a millimetre apart.

The man in the black cab blared his horn. Then he unwound his window, stuck out his head and swore like a maniac at the Peugeot driver.

I took a step back without realising.

Whoever was in the Peugeot quickly restarted the engine and pulled onto their drive again. The taxi driver wasted no more time, revving the cab's filthy engine for added measure. Being the only one here, that same taxi then pulled into the bay in front of me. Was this really where my journey began – in the back of this madman's cab?

The driver was clean-shaven with a faint scar running along the side of his face – a pink, jagged indentation from his temple to just above his jawline. I could only imagine how he'd got it. Fighting? A car accident? His hair was the colour of wet mud, cut short enough not to need any product. If I had to take a guess, I would say he was in his mid-thirties, with crows' feet and worry lines etched deep into his face — although he didn't strike me as a particularly worried person.

Through his still open window, he called out to me. "You waitin' for a cab?"

I nodded. I'd almost forgotten why I was standing here.

"Well, get in then," he said, jerking a thumb in the direction of the back seats. "I ain't got all day."

As he wound up his window, I briefly considered turning him down. He seemed short-fused and had an offputtingly large build to match. Just pure muscle piled on top of thick arms and broad shoulders. I wasn't sure how long I'd be waiting for the next cab to turn up, though, and didn't want to ask the two ignorant receptionists. So I took a breath and climbed in. Hopefully I wouldn't end up regretting this.

I slammed the door shut, blocking out the wind and rain and trapping myself with the mad taxi driver and the smell of boot polish — a stark contrast to the cab's otherwise grubby appearance.

"Where to?" he asked.

"Uhhh..." Danny still hadn't given me any new instructions and the vague directions I'd intended to give him no longer seemed enough.

The driver turned in his seat. "Are you 'avin' a laugh?"

I shook my head.

"Good. 'Cause I 'aven't got time for your games." He was watching me carefully, and then his eyes narrowed. "Shouldn't you be at school?"

I swallowed. He wasn't the sort of man you'd want to mess around and yet, before I was fully aware of what I was saying ... "I'm seventeen. I finished school about a year ago."

Seriously, Jordan? My voice was a giveaway but maybe he'd buy it ...

"And how do I know you're gonna pay?" I guess he was only interested in his money. Should I tell him I'd have to pay most the fare when I was back in Woodlock?

I pulled two crumpled twenty-pound notes from my wallet and held them towards him, implying I had enough.

He was silent, wondering whether I was worth his time. In the end he said, "Tell me where to drive you or get out." He wasn't kidding.

He clenched his jaw, waiting for me to reply, his large gorilla hands gripping the steering wheel. All I had to offer, though, were my vague directions.

"I ... know how to get there," I said. Which was partially true. Danny was going to lead me. These senses aren't easy to describe. It's like a gut instinct or a niggling feeling, telling you to choose one thing over another – only I knew that these "feelings" were coming from my brother. Basically, as long as I kept my mind empty, Danny could always reach me. "I just don't know the name."

I held my breath.

Luckily, after what felt like an age, he set the

metre and put the car in gear. There was no turning back now.

I fastened my seatbelt as he pulled out of the taxi bay and felt my stomach knot. Danny better make an appearance soon ...

"Well?" the driver snapped.

We were nearing the end of the street.

"Left," I quickly said. I thought back to what Danny had told me before leaving the house, about heading towards Devon, and passed on what little information I had. "Head for the M5. I'll lead you from there."

The driver grunted, switching on his indicator. I was glad he wasn't much of a talker. It gave me time to think.

CHAPTER EIGHT

Getting out of Woodlock was a nightmare and the M5 was backed up for several miles: a lorry had crashed into the back of someone during rush hour so two of the lanes had been closed off, making what should've been a half-hour drive take almost a couple of hours.

I'd already switched off my phone. School would've rung home by now and I didn't want to face Mum's calls and messages demanding to know where I was and why I wasn't in school. Plus, I needed to reserve the battery for when it was time to record Cillian's confession. Instead, I looked ahead at the increasing price on the taximeter. It was distracting but not enough to stop me thinking ...

I wanted everyone to know the truth about Cillian, but I also wanted to hurt him, to make him suffer. To *kill* him. But how was the best way to go about it? I wasn't exactly strong – my fight with Matt proved it. The only obvious way for me to win was by having the element of surprise. But how could I kill him by surprise when I still needed a confession? Not to mention, that would also rule out any sign of a struggle for the "self-defence" story I planned to give the police. I guess I just needed to turn up, assess the situation and take it from there, trusting that Danny would protect me the entire time.

I leaned back in my seat, watching the raindrops bead down the window. We were finally moving at a steady pace. I was beginning to think we might still make it to Devon around midday when the taxi driver heaved a sigh. I didn't ask him what was wrong.

"I'm low on petrol," he told me anyway. He had an edge to his voice, as though he blamed me. Then I remembered he always had an edge to his voice.

He indicated left and slowed to change lanes, following a slip road that took us off the M5. "Just goin' to fill 'er up," he said, jabbing a button on the taximeter with his stubby finger to pause the timer. "Won't be long."

The lane twisted and turned, and it was clear from the number of potholes he had to dodge that the road had been neglected for many years. We passed a car heading back onto the motorway, and then I saw another car just off the main road. It had been left in a low ditch, burnt out and orangey-brown with rust. Nobody had bothered to move it. Taking a quick glance around, I saw that there were no other vehicles, no other people.

"Is there even a service station down here?" I asked.

I gathered it was a stupid question by the look on his face in the rear-view mirror, but I couldn't help feeling a little on edge. I was on my own out here with a hundred dodgy Uber-driver stories in my head.

After a couple more turns, though, a dusty petrol station finally came into view. Only two of the six pumps looked like they were working and the small shop behind it was just as desolate. The final letter of the sign was missing and the window spanning the length of the front wall was filled with a desperate amount of sale advertisements, even though there was nobody around to persuade. It was difficult to imagine this place up and running in a year's time.

"I'm just going to stretch my legs," I said, as the driver pulled up at one of the working pumps. I needed a change of scene from the back of his cab.

"Make sure you're back by the time I'm done," the driver warned as we both stepped out.

The rain had stopped but the air was humid. I made my way over to the shop, stepping over water-filled potholes.

A tiny bell rang as I opened the door. There was nobody at the front counter – or anywhere in the entire shop, for that matter. Newspapers, map books and magazines lined the shelves at the back; refrigerated snacks and drinks were opposite the till, and along the final wall was a variety of chocolate bars, crisps and sweets, as well as three revolving stands filled with second-hand DVDs and an out-of-order ATM machine.

I didn't have enough to buy anything but at least the films were something to look at.

I made my way over to them and started scanning through the sticky DVD cases when a voice piped up from behind me. "Can I help you?"

I jumped, quickly turning to face whoever it was. A man with tanned skin and grey hair was now standing behind the counter. His thin lips were smiling but he looked almost confused.

"Uh … No thanks. I'm just waiting," I said, indicating the taxi outside.

The man nodded, looking at me as though I was going to say more. I didn't. I smiled back, cleared my throat and turned away. I couldn't tell if he was still watching me or not and I didn't look up to check. I picked up the first DVD I came across—

"Ah! So you're into sci-fi," he said.

I glanced up at him. "Sorry?"

He gestured to the film in my hand. "Used to be one of my favourites back in the day. Have you watched it before?"

I shook my head.

"You won't be disappointed." Then he pointed to the "3 for 2" sign above the DVD stand. "If you buy another two films—"

"I don't have any money." I put the film down

before he could try roping me into something.

He opened his mouth again but the bell above the front door cut him off. He turned, beaming at his next customer. It was my driver. "Good morning, Mr Butch," the older man said. "How are you this fine bleak day, hm?"

"Not too bad, Pete," the driver – Mr Butch – said. "How's business?"

I was taken aback by his friendly tone – and was that really his name? I half wondered whether Pete had made it up.

"Far from booming," Pete said.

Mr Butch made his way over to the fridges along the side wall. "I dunno," he called back, rifling through packets of sandwiches for a particular filling. "I saw another car drive off when I turned onto your road. Don't forget about me when your store hits the roof."

"Yeah, well … you're one to talk! I heard you're on the verge of being sacked!"

They both laughed, as though failing at their jobs was the funniest thing in the world. Was that what adult life was like? Mum and Dad never laughed about work. Dad complained about it most dinner times, and even though Mum's gained an extra twenty-four pounds she seems so much happier since being on maternity leave.

As the banter between them continued, I noticed one of the wine bottles beside the counter begin to edge forwards.

Don't you dare, Danny, I thought, inching towards it. The bottle tilted and a replay of yesterday with my lamp flashed through my head. I reached out and caught the bottle. Another lucky save.

It was the first time Danny had showed himself since earlier this morning. He was getting impatient and wanted me to get going.

"I don't care how badly I need the money," Pete said. "I can't sell you that." He was staring straight at me with a humourless look on his face.

I looked down at the wine bottle in my hands and realised what he meant.

"And if you thought I was gonna let you drink that in the back've my cab –" Mr Butch glared at me "– you'd better think again." He placed two packets of cheese sandwiches and a can of Pepsi on the counter before taking out his wallet.

"I was just reading the label," I muttered dumbly, putting the bottle back on the shelf.

Satisfied with my answer, Mr Butch turned back to pay Pete for the fuel and food. Danny was still close by, though, so I was on edge until Pete handed over the receipt and said bye.

When we left the store, heavy drops of rain were again starting to fall from the blanket of grey that covered the sky. It was either the aftermath of one storm or the beginning of another. As we hurried back to the car, I pulled up my hood and was hardly surprised to find that it was still damp from this morning's downpour.

Mr Butch put the key in the ignition and started the cab. He didn't resume the metre, though, until we were back on the M5. The only time we broke our usual silence was when Danny told me to take a certain exit – a niggling feeling pulling me in a certain direction.

I told Mr Butch where to go and he signalled left, following my instructions without a word. Danny's directions soon led us onto winding country lanes, similar to the one leading to Pete's petrol station. The scenery changed from monotonous grey to towering grass and overgrown bushes.

Mr Butch had to slow down. The roads were waterlogged, and he didn't want to risk any of it splashing into the engine. "You still know where you're goin'?" he asked. This assured me that he had no idea where we were either.

"Yep," I lied with a convincing smile.

"You better have enough cash, kid." His voice hardened right there. "Those twenties ain't nothin' to what you owe me now."

I couldn't look at him. Once we were back in Woodlock, Mum and Dad would have to pay what I couldn't cover in exchange for about a year's worth of weekly allowances. The only thing that mattered was reaching Cillian. "Don't worry, I've got enough."

"Me? Worried? *Ha!* That'll be the day."

* * *

It was coming up to two o'clock. I wasn't sure how close we were to finding Cillian, but I knew I wouldn't be home until late now. I could feel my phone in my trouser pocket, pressing into my leg like a constant reminder. Should I switch it back on? Probably. But I couldn't bring myself to do it.

I took a breath.

Everything looked the same out here; it felt like we were driving in circles until we approached a fork in the road. I relaxed a little.

"Kid, which way do we –?"

"Right," I said, before he could properly finish his question. Danny had been signalling this for the past fifteen minutes, so I knew there must've been a turn coming up at some point.

Not long after the turn, Mr Butch let out a fed-up groan. "No way," he remarked, glancing at me through the rear-view mirror. "I know *exactly* where we are. Down there's Linley Road which takes you back on the M5," he said, gesturing with a terse nod at the passing lane. "Travellin' with you is like listenin' to a bloody sat-nav! I could've got you here in half the time."

I said nothing. I still didn't know where we were or where I was going, so it was pointless for me to comment. At least we weren't completely lost.

I reached into my bag for the bottle of Coke I'd packed from home and took a few swigs. It was lukewarm and flat, but I barely noticed. I didn't realise how hungry I was, though, until Mr Butch brought out his cheese sandwiches.

My stomach growled and Mr Butch glanced back at me with accusing eyes.

"Didn't you bring any food?" he snapped.

"I'm fine," I said.

I tried to ignore the dying sounds my stomach continued to make, but he could only take so much.

"Kid, if you —"

I cut him off there. "My name's Jordan," I stated. I didn't like being called *"kid"*. It was only a step away from being called "it".

Mr Butch paused and then continued as though he hadn't heard me. "If you know how to get there, then you should know how long the trip'll take. So why didn't you bring any food? Or buy somethin' back at Pete's?"

"There's been more traffic than usual."

He sighed as my stomach let out another low growl. I clutched my belly and willed it to shut up but it was out of my control.

"Here!" Mr Butch grunted, tossing one of his four sandwiches back to me.

"You sure?" I asked, taking a humongous bite before he could even answer. I knew better than to think of this as an act of kindness. It was only to stifle the sound that was irritating him beyond all measure. Not that I cared. I was just glad for some food.

CHAPTER NINE

Mr Butch switched on his headlights. The rain was torrential and the grey clouds were darker than ever, making the three o'clock sky look like dusk. Back at school, everyone would be waiting for the final bell to ring.

I took out my phone, my finger resting on the power button. I knew I should call Mum, or at least send her a text telling her I was okay. I bit my lower lip. There'd be a build-up of voicemails and messages the instant I switched it on, though, and the thought of listening to them all made my stomach lurch.

Five o'clock, I told myself. Five o'clock and I'll ring home.

I put my phone on the seat next to me, blocking it from my mind.

The beads of water on the windows made the world look disjointed and ugly. Mr Butch slowed to a crawl whenever we came across puddle-filled dips in the road. We were still following flooded country lanes. The fields were waterlogged and the road we were on was so narrow that it would've been impossible to fit two cars past each other. So far, that hadn't been a problem. It must've been at least twenty minutes since I'd last seen another car.

Thunder boomed above us. I leaned back against the headrest and closed my eyes. I could feel the beginning of a migraine pressing. Danny was telling me to go straight on and I couldn't see any turn-offs ahead to distract Mr Butch, so I let my mind wander …

I was ten, bursting into our hotel room: "Have you seen Danny?" I'd asked.

"I thought he was with you."

Then I was on the beach, with Lewis and his mates: "Relax. He can't be too far …"

"He's in trouble. I just know it."

"Kid?"

"Where's your brother?" Dad asked.

"I don't know!" –

"Kid!" Mr Butch interrupted my thoughts. It was the same gravelly voice I'd heard all day but for some reason I now found it aggravating.

"Jordan," I corrected.

"Which way do we go?" he said.

The car slowed to an idling stop. I opened my eyes. We were at a crossroads. All three turns were identical. I didn't have any niggling feeling telling me to turn left or right, so I assumed Danny wanted me to continue straight on.

"Uhhh …" I waited a moment longer, just in case Danny was still deciding. Or was he just as lost as I was? How did he even know where we were supposed to go, anyway?

"Straight on," I eventually said. I wished Danny would stop wandering off. I could've done with some reassurance.

Mr Butch didn't move. "You sure?" he said, studying me in the rear-view mirror.

I nodded.

"You absolutely *positive*?"

"Yes!"

Mr Butch reached for the gearstick, hesitating for just a moment before setting off.

This was getting ridiculous. I was still waiting for Danny's guiding pull to assure me that I'd made the right decision, but he wasn't in the car with us.

Lightning tore through the sky, lighting up everything around us for a short second.

"Bloody weather," Mr Butch complained. And then there was another trembling wave of thunder. I didn't mind the storm; it was actually the perfect distraction from all my worries about school and money and facing Cillian.

The moment lightning flashed across the sky, I began to count – *one … two …* – until thunder sounded out. I did this a few times until the ground beneath the tyres changed from asphalt to a stony dirt road.

Mr Butch glanced at me. "This seem familiar to you?"

"Uh-huh." I said, swallowing discreetly.

As we began heading uphill, I leaned back in my seat again, gripping the door-handle like a nervous flyer would just as they were starting to take off from the runway.

Lightning pierced.

Thunder growled.

Rain poured.

Mr Butch moved down the gears. Minutes passed and the only thing that changed was the hill's growing altitude. That, and Mr Butch's frustration. "How much longer is this bloody hill? It's still gettin' steeper and I don't know how much this thing can take. It's a taxicab, not a Goddamn Land Rover!"

Outside my window was a towering dirt wall. We seemed to be making our way up a cliff-side.

I bit my tongue.

"Oi! You listenin'?"

I tightened my grip on the door-handle. "It's not much further," I said, hoping I was right. It wasn't enough to shut him up, though. As he went on about "damaging the engine", I began my counting game with the lightning again. The storm was practically on top of us so there was hardly any time to count before thunder sounded out.

"I'll tell you somethin' else!" Mr Butch was still going on. "If you think that —"

Another flash of lightning lit up our path. He

slammed on the brakes and the seatbelt cut into my neck.

"What's wrong?" I asked, rubbing the skin that had just been caught.

Mr Butch yanked up the handbrake. He stared straight ahead but said nothing, leaning over the steering wheel to get as close to the windscreen as possible. His squinting reflection mirrored back. The headlights were already on full beam but I couldn't see anything.

"What's wrong?" I asked again, more urgently this time.

Lightning flashed again, and when it did, Mr Butch lurched back in his seat.

He turned back to me, wearing a look I hadn't seen on him before. Confusion? Concern? Maybe a mixture of both.

"Wait here," he said, and unfastened his seatbelt.

"Are you nuts? Where are you going?"

"There's someone out there. They might need help."

Seriously? We were in the middle of nowhere! Who else would be out here?

Mr Butch opened the door and a gust of rain rushed in with the wind, slapping me in the face. He heaved himself out the car, shutting the door behind him.

The headlights were still on full beam. I unfastened my seatbelt and leaned through the gap between the two front seats to try and get a better look. Other than Mr Butch, I couldn't see anyone.

The road curved ahead, zig-zagging up the cliff-side that was inches away from my window. To my right was a low wooden barrier that ran alongside the road. Over the top of this, I could just make out the tops of trees being beaten by wind. They were level with us, so we must have been pretty high up.

I turned back to Mr Butch. His hands were cupped around his mouth and I could hear his muffled shouts as he called out to whoever he saw. I still couldn't see anyone, though. In the end, wet and defeated, Mr Butch trudged back to the car. I sat back in my seat.

He slammed the door shut behind him and wiped the rain from his face.

"No sign of 'em," he said.

"Maybe it was just a trick of the light," I suggested. "It's pretty dark out there."

"I know what I saw. They probably got scared and ran off."

I didn't believe that for a second – and I'm not sure he did either. He would never admit to being wrong, though, especially since it'd meant leaving the car and getting drenched. He was still defensive when he turned in his seat and snapped, "Where the *hell* am I takin' you, kid?"

I gave him the same tense glare he was giving me. "The name's *Jordan*," I corrected, for what felt like the millionth time. "And I don't know!"

It wasn't until I saw Mr Butch's reaction that I

realised what I'd said. His brows furrowed so low that his forehead appeared to be made of nothing but wrinkles. "You don't *know*?" he repeated. "What d'you mean you don't know? Why didn't you tell me that before – like when we *wasn't* up on a bleedin' mountain somewhere!"

"I didn't know I was lost then!" *Stupid* – I was digging myself a deeper hole to climb out of. "I mean … I'm not lost. I just don't remember coming up here …" I cursed in my head. Where the hell was Danny?

Mr Butch rested his forehead against the steering wheel and sighed heavily. "Great …" I think I heard him mutter; the sarcastic tone, at least, was easy to detect.

I kept my mouth shut this time.

"Right," Mr Butch said. "We're not goin' any further up this thing. It's too bloody dangerous in this weather."

I didn't know what to say to that. He had a point, though, and I wasn't even certain this was the route I was supposed to take. God knows where I should go from here, but I didn't object as Mr Butch put the car in reverse. Well, not at first, anyway.

As soon as we began to crawl back down the unlit road, the empty space beside me turned cold. Ice cold. Danny was back, which meant we must now be going the wrong way.

"Uh, actually Mr Butch," I quickly said. "I *do* remember going this way."

Mr Butch braked. "What?" He was leaning against the passenger seat's headrest with one arm, his body turned so he could see through the back window. He looked straight at me.

"We need to keep heading uphill," I said. Danny didn't move. If he'd wanted me to stay on track, he shouldn't have left me.

"There's no way I'm drivin' us up there! Can't you see how dodgy this is?" Mr Butch swore before continuing downhill.

Danny grew even colder.

"Mr Butch —"

"I'm takin' you to the nearest town. You're gonna pay up and then we're done. Find someone else to take you to Neverland!"

My phone started to levitate beside me. I grabbed it from mid-air before Mr Butch spotted it and shoved it in the side compartment.

"Mr Butch, *please* ..." I tried again.

"No. Unless you tell me exactly where you want me to take you, this journey is over. That's hardly unreasonable."

"But I —"

"But you don't know." Mr Butch sped up. He was focused on the back window. "Forget it, kid. I'm done." Danny disappeared that very instant. Where to, I wasn't sure, but I knew that unless Mr Butch changed his mind and started listening to me, something bad was going to happen. "I suggest you prepare yourself better next time, instead've goin' on some Mickey Mouse adventure –"

BANG!

The cab lurched as the back tyre under me blew out. The noise and sudden jerk startled Mr Butch, making him turn too hard on the wheel and hit the cliffside next to me.

I gripped the door-handle again, realising I'd forgotten to re-fasten my seatbelt.

Mr Butch counter-steered too much. The tyres skidded and the back end of the car knocked through the low barrier.

"Shit!" he yelled.

The back wheel went over the edge, leaving the car suspended.

Neither of us moved. My heart was hammering, my breathing laboured. We were stuck, hanging over a cliff in the middle of a storm.

"You okay?" he eventually said. He sounded calm but he looked like he wanted to kill me.

I nodded. "Yeah. You?"

Mr Butch sighed. "Bloody fantastic." He turned his head slowly to the right, looking back at the tyre dangling over the edge. The cab was leaning into the sheer drop. I didn't dare follow his gaze.

"We need to get out," Mr Butch said, pointing out the obvious.

The taxi shook with every gust of wind. I wasn't sure how much longer the car was going to hold out for, but I knew why we hadn't moved yet.

"Won't the car tip over the edge if we move?"

Mr Butch didn't answer straight away. He must've known it was a possibility – not that we had a choice. It was either we climb out and risk tipping the car over or stay inside and wait for the inevitable. "As long as we're careful, we should be fine," he said. I guess he didn't want to worry me.

Mr Butch undid his seatbelt and climbed across to the passenger seat; I was reaching for the door-handle next to me when the taxi gave another sudden lurch. We froze again. Staring wide-eyed at one another, we knew time had run out.

"Out! *Now!*" Mr Butch ordered, abandoning our original plan of caution.

I swung open the car door just as Mr Butch opened his. I didn't feel the cold that rushed inside. I didn't feel *anything*, except sheer panic and fear of death.

The abruptness rocked the cab even more, but we didn't bother waiting for it to settle. We moved quickly. I was almost out when the taxi jolted again.

Mr Butch fell face first onto the muddy ledge, but I wasn't so lucky. I lost my footing and fell back inside the car, landing hard against the other door.

The impact should've been enough to tip the cab over the edge, but it didn't. Danny must have been holding it up – there was no other explanation. He only had so much energy, though. How long could he keep it from falling?

The car was at such an angle now. The open door above me wavered, caught in the gale. I knew that when it came crashing down, sealing me in the cab again, the impact would be enough to send me over the edge.

I wasn't going to make it.

A gust of wind rocked the car and it shuddered from the strain. It wanted to fall ...

"Come on! Get out!"

I looked up. Mr Butch was holding the door open against the gale. He must have caught it just in time.

I didn't need telling twice. I started climbing up along the back seats. I didn't get far, though. Something was holding me back. I peered down and realised my shoelace had got snagged on something.

"I'm stuck!" I called up to him.

"Well get yourself bloody *un*stuck!"

It was caught around the window crank. I pulled the lace, but it was only making it worse. My hands were shaking and moist from a combination of sweat and rain. I heard Mr Butch's voice but I wasn't listening. If the door slipped from his fingers, I'd had it. I began unwrapping the lace – twice around the crank and then a final tug from the groove it was trapped in. That's when I heard Mr Butch's words: "Take off the bleedin' shoe!" But I'd already freed myself.

The car gave another lurch.

I grabbed the two headrests closest to me and hauled myself up, trying hard not to slip on the wet seats as the rain poured into the car. Just as I reached the top, the car gave a final jerk and this time it didn't stop.

"Aahhh!"

I lost grip and was about to fall back into the cab when Mr Butch grabbed my arm, heaving me out onto the ledge.

There was the sound of metal grinding against rock. I turned in time to see the front end of the taxi go over the edge and out of sight, crashing through tree branches on its way down. My throat tightened with every *crunch* and *snap;* the sound seemed to go on forever until it eventually became lost in the howl of the storm. Another second or two and I would've still been in there, plummeting to my death. That's when I realised, with a horrible, sinking feeling: my phone and satchel were still in there. I had no way of getting in touch with Mum or Dad ... No way of recording Cillian's confession ...

Goddammit.

I got to my feet, my body shaking from too much adrenaline as I stared down into the dark pit the car had just fallen into. *I'm still alive though,* I told myself. I'd call Mum when I got to a payphone somewhere in town. And if Mr Butch didn't want to lend me any change (because why the heck would he?) then I'm sure a local bar or café would let me borrow their phone. As for Cillian – I just had to pray I'd find something to record him with before then.

I turned to look at Mr Butch. He was breathing heavily through his nose. "I'm in deep shit now," he said, his eyes fixed on the darkness below. When he turned to me, his face was filled with so much rage that I had to look away. "I hope you're happy! *'I'm lost ... no, wait, now I'm not lost ...'* You're a bloody *joke* is what you are!" He went on cursing and mimicking me for a good few minutes. I thought he might change his mind and throw me over after all.

When his rant came to an end, he went back to breathing heavily while staring after his taxi. Without the headlights and brief flashes of lightning, it was difficult to make anything out. But it was down there, battered and broken – one of Richmond's taxicabs: a firm Mr Butch would no longer be welcome at.

I wasn't in a position to argue. Danny had blown the rear tyre. I knew he'd meant no real harm, he just wanted to stop us from backtracking. If Mr Butch wouldn't drive us further, Danny wanted to make certain that he at least didn't drive me back and make this a wasted journey. He hadn't expected Mr Butch to react the way he did.

Mr Butch raised his arms before dropping them to his sides again. "Now what?" he spat, as though I had planned for this to happen and was fully prepared for what to do next.

"I don't know!" I could see beads of rain dripping off the end of his nose and tried to focus on that instead of his glare.

Mr Butch shook his head. "We need to find shelter," he quickly decided. "There's not much else we can do in this bleedin' storm."

"Where?" I asked, because there wasn't anything around for a good couple of miles.

Mr Butch stared up at the cliff. I wasn't sure what he was looking for, but I knew he'd found it when his eyes widened. He pointed up the muddy bank a few short feet above us. "There," he said, and I spotted it instantly in what little light we had. There was a small opening that looked just big enough for the two of us – if we crawled and didn't mind tight spaces.

Mr Butch barged past me, grabbing hold of a few wet shrubs to pull himself up with.

I groaned under my breath. I wasn't good at climbing. I never had been. When me and Danny were little, I always found excuses to avoid playing in the treehouse in our grandad's garden.

I looked up – Mr Butch had almost reached the den. It wasn't too high up, but the sides were thick with mud. I found it pretty much impossible to keep my footing; every time I started climbing, I would slide back down to where I started. Eventually, though, (and I wasn't quite sure how) Mr Butch managed to get up onto the narrow ledge outside the entrance to the den.

He turned around carefully and dropped down onto his stomach. Then he reached out a hand for me to take.

It took me several attempts, and every time I slipped, the side became even trickier to climb. The second Mr Butch was within reach, though,

I grabbed his hand and he pulled me up onto the ledge.

"Thanks," I mumbled. This was the second time he'd saved me, in the space of maybe fifteen minutes.

The entrance was low and narrow. We crawled inside, squeezing to the back where it thankfully widened a couple of metres. Even hunched over, though, the stone ceiling would've been too low for us to sit up. We lay on our backs, listening to the storm building around us. It was pitch black without the lightning but in between flashes I saw scattered patches of grass and weeds. Something must've taken shelter here not long ago.

"How long's this storm s'posed to last?" Mr Butch asked.

"I'm not sure."

"Bloody ace. And I don't s'pose you 'ave any signal on your phone either, do you?"

"I wouldn't know. I lost mine over the cliff." *And I still couldn't believe how stupid I was for letting that happen.*

"Seriously?"

Then it struck me: if I let Mr Butch think I'd lost all the money I owed him – the money I didn't even have to begin with – he'd never know I lied about it and might even give me a break. I didn't expect him to wipe the slate clean; I just wanted him to shut up about it until I'd figured out how I was going to pay him. "Yeah. My phone, my wallet ... literally everything. My entire satchel went over."

"You *what?*" I couldn't see much in the dark, but I heard him shuffle as he turned onto his side to face me. "Listen, I don't give a damn where your wallet is, you're *not* gettin' out've payin' – understand? You owe me almost seven-hundred quid!"

"I know," I said, trying to keep my voice steady. It was difficult, though, because I'm not even sure Mum or Dad had that kind of money lying around, especially with the baby on the way. I was screwed, to put it simply, completely and utterly, and I hope Danny knew it. "Once I'm home I'll get you the money."

"You'd better," he said. "For *your* sake." He pulled up the sleeve of his fleece. A tiny blue light on his wrist lit up from what I guessed was his watch. He sighed again. (I had a feeling I'd be hearing that a lot tonight.) "Even if the storm finished by seven, it'll be getting' dark by then."

I said nothing as he summed up the obvious.

"So we're stuck 'ere, basically," he concluded.

"I guess so."

We were quiet after that. Our clothes were saturated and caked in mud, Mr Butch would obviously be fired, and I'd hit a financial crisis at the age of only fifteen – so neither of us felt like talking. Our negative energy was probably detectable from the deepest depths of Hell – which might explain why Danny wasn't here. He wouldn't wander far now that I was stranded but he must have sensed my mood and decided to keep away. Besides, we couldn't go anywhere in this weather, so it's not like he needed to guide me just yet.

So we lay there, with our bodies shivering, jaws chattering, noses dripping … I had no way of keeping track of time and the storm showed no sign of abating.

I closed my eyes, trying not to think of home, focusing instead on the rhythm of the rain hitting the den's stone entrance.

FiVE YEARS EARLIER

"Cutting it pretty close, aren't you?" Dad said from the living room area when I walked in. The door had been left unlocked for me. "Did you have fun?"

"Yeah, I played football with some kids we met on the beach," I said, dumping the carrier bag with our buckets, spades and toy dinosaurs in by the door. I didn't know where Mum or Danny were, but I was starving. "What's for dinner?" I asked, because I knew I wouldn't be allowed to snack on anything, and I could hardly steal a packet of sweets since there was no wall separating the kitchen area from the living room.

Dad gestured to a pile of leaflets on the chair next to him. "Take your pick."

I headed over and began flicking through them. There were a few hotel-organised day-trips: zoos, farms, a sea-life centre, three different theme parks;

the rest were takeaway menus. I spotted my favourite straight away. "Can we order from Papa John's?"

"As long as Danny's okay with it."

"I'll go ask him. Where is he?"

"In your bedroom." He pulled a face. "Have you two fallen out?"

Now it was my turn to pull a face. "No." *What made him think that?*

I left the buckets and spades in the living room with Dad and carried the leaflets and bag of toy dinosaurs to my room. I opened the door and found that Danny had already claimed his bed. He was sitting on it cross-legged, playing on his iPad.

"Hey," I said, shutting the door behind me. "How's your leg?"

"What do you care?" he snapped, not even bothering to look up. He'd fallen out with me all right.

I knew I should've followed. I'd *wanted* to follow … I don't know why I didn't. Instead of telling him that, though, I settled with a line I took from Lewis. "Sophie and Leanne were with you – it's not like you were by yourself. Can't we be apart for more than a few minutes?"

That got his attention. Danny stared up at me. "Since when did you care about having time away from me? You're the one who can't go anywhere on your own." He turned back to his game again, frantically tapping and swiping the screen.

I went to argue but couldn't think of anything

to say. He was right, after all, no matter how much I hated it. Besides, the walls were paper thin – I could hear the TV show Dad was watching in the living room – so I knew he and Mum would hear us if we started fighting. It was better to let Danny's comment slide.

I crossed the room towards the window in four strides. There was hardly any floor space. It made our room back home look huge. The two beds were up against either wall, leaving only a slim aisle to walk down. Beneath the window was a bedside table we'd have to share, fitting snugly in the gap between our beds. I put the menus there and emptied the bag of dinosaurs next to my pillow.

"What d'you want to eat?" I asked glumly, changing the subject.

"I don't care," he said. A few seconds later, though, he glanced at the leaflets. "Is there a Papa John's?"

I rifled through them and handed him the menu.

As he looked over the different pizza toppings, I asked, "Do you want to play dinosaurs while we wait for them to deliver?"

Danny sighed. At first I thought he was going to say no, but he surprised me with an "Okay," and quit the game on his iPad.

Once we'd decided what to order, Danny leapt the short distance from his bed to mine and I began sharing our dinosaurs between us. Dad would be in soon to ask what we wanted.

"Hang on a minute," Danny said, tilting his head to one side. He made a quick count of our toys. "One's missing!" He leaned back and figured out almost instantly which one it was. "Where's Timothy the Tyrannosaurus?"

I twisted my hands in my lap. "I, um … I let Lewis borrow him. When he saw our toys, he said his little sister loved dinosaurs too."

Danny sulked.

"Don't worry!" I jumped in before it turned into an actual argument this time. "He's going to give him back tomorrow."

"What d'you mean?" Danny sounded wary.

"We're meeting them at one on the beach again. Mum and Dad shouldn't mind. He'll give back Timothy then. He promised."

Danny shook his head. "I'm not going."

"What! Why not?" I didn't think he'd be overly happy about seeing Lewis again, but I wasn't expecting a straight-up refusal.

"I don't like them."

"Come on," I begged. "Lewis is really sorry about hurting your leg. He wants to make it up to you."

"I don't care. Anyway, it's not about my leg. They just seem …" Danny struggled to find the words. In the end he settled with, "They're not like us."

"But they're loads of fun, honest. When you left, Mike put a crab in one of the girls' bags —she only found it when they were about to leave!"

Danny looked disgusted. *Maybe you had to be there to find it funny,* I thought.

"You go then," Danny said firmly.

"But I don't want to go by myself. *Please,* Danny! I wouldn't've let Lewis borrow him if I thought you wouldn't come."

"*I* thought you wanted time away from me."

"That's not fair! Listen, we don't have to stay there long. Only for like an hour or something. And then I promise I'll never ask for anything from you again."

Danny fell back on my bed. I was only going to keep begging, and he knew it. He covered his face with my pillow to muffle his long, exaggerated groan. "Fine."

CHAPTER TEN
THURSDAY - PRESENT DAY

I woke during sunrise. My eyes hurt, my clothes were still damp, and the cold had seeped into my bones like poison. I couldn't have slept more than a couple of hours. The sun was up, though, so we could finally get going. It would've been impossible to feel refreshed anyway, crammed against mud and rock without a dry set of clothes, no matter how much extra sleep I gave myself.

I winced at the knots in my back and neck. It felt like parts of my muscles had formed into stone. When I tried to rub away the stiffness, I noticed aches in other parts of my body. I groaned, disturbing the empty silence.

Mr Butch stirred beside me. He wiped the tiredness from his face and yawned, his mouth wide enough to swallow the entire planet. Once he clocked that I was awake, he muttered something with a thick tongue. It was either an insult or a

"Good morning".

He rolled over onto his front and backed out the cave like an overgrown bear. I waited until the exit was clear before following.

"Bloody freezin', ain't it?" he said once I was outside. He was breathing into his hands, trying to warm them.

"Yeah," I said, waiting for the pins and needles in my legs to fade.

The wind was a gale this high up and almost threw me over the edge. It cut through me like a sheet of ice, carrying the smell of wet dirt. It wasn't enough to cover the lingering stench of two guys' stale sweat, though. My clothes were ruined, and I needed a shower as badly as Dad needed his morning coffee.

I shielded my eyes against the rising sun. Red light bled across the sky, staining the clouds pink. "What time is it?"

Mr Butch glanced down at his watch. "Just gone half six."

"Don't suppose you have anything for breakfast, do you?"

He turned on me and I found myself wishing I'd kept my mouth shut. It was a long shot anyway. What was I expecting him to say?

"I lost everythin' over the cliff – includin' my job! So *no*, Jordan, I do *not* have anythin' for breakfast. Do *you?*"

I looked away, resorting back to silence. At least

he'd called me by my name.

Mr Butch peered down at the trees beyond the narrow ledge we stood on, and the pathway that zig-zagged downhill beneath us. Then he looked up at the rest of the cliff towering above us. "Right, no point waitin' around," he said. He coughed up a gob of phlegm and spat it out on the ground behind him. The gooey mess landed with a solid *splat* as he began making his way towards the slope that would lead us down to the main path again. "Let's get goin'."

He was heading the wrong way again.

"I'm not going back," I said, when he tried pushing past me. I still didn't know where I was going so I couldn't give him a reason.

Mr Butch stared at me blankly. Once he realised I was being serious, his expression changed to a look that could melt steel. He squared up to me, his shoulders almost double the width of my own. "You best be jokin'."

"We're really close!" I hoped I wasn't far from the truth.

"I don't care! I want my money and then you're explainin' to my boss that —"

"I'm explaining *what* exactly to your boss? How you almost got us killed?" I tried to keep myself from shaking — it was either the cold or more adrenaline. He could easily throw me over if he wanted. It'd be stupid to make him angry while we were this high up, and nobody would be able to hear me shout for help if he really did decide to finish me off.

"Don't," he said, taking another step closer to me. "Don't you *dare*. It's *your* fault we're in this mess, not mine. And you know it."

"Look, you can go back. Just give me your address and I'll post you a cheque."

"As if you'll pay up. That'd be a perfect turnaround for you, wouldn't it? Gettin' a free lift to Devon after about a day's worth've travellin'? No chance, mate."

"Well," I shrugged. "I need to keep going. You can do what you want."

"That's not how it's gonna work, kid."

"Yes it is." I sounded more certain than I felt. "Why should I pay you a penny if you end up dragging me back to where I started? I'm heading on. I'll pay you extra for your trouble, though, and I won't even sue you for almost killing me."

I could tell he wanted to hit me. His fists were clenched and his nostrils flared. He knew I wasn't budging. The way Mr Butch saw it, though, was that if he let me go, would he even see his money? There was only one easy solution …

He turned on his heel and trudged to the other side of the ledge. He'd decided to come with me.

Facing the muddy cliff that our small cave was set in, he hoisted himself up. "You're payin' extra for this," he snapped. I followed him up to the dirt road, one level closer to the top. "Just because I've got no cab doesn't mean I'm chaperonin' you for nothin'."

I was about to tell him that I didn't need

"chaperoning" but then I figured this was the best deal I was going to get.

* * *

My body ached with every step. It wasn't raining anymore so maybe my clothes would finally dry out. I wish I could say that moving did at least warm me up, but it didn't. The wind was a whiplash across my face. I suppose it's to be expected really, when you're two hundred feet or more from the ground.

Mr Butch led the way the entire time. There were no breaks and no attempt at conversation. And the further we walked, the more the road narrowed. It looked dodgy as hell. No way would the taxi have fit along here – *if we didn't lose it over the frickin' cliff* – especially when, after what felt like an hour, the road became too narrow to even walk along. Turning back wasn't an option so we side-stepped instead, our backs pressed against the rocky wall.

"This is ridiculous!" Mr Butch spat. I didn't argue with him. He stopped and I did the same. Then he peered up. "Not too far from the top now – look."

"That's okay. I believe you." There's no way I was looking up. If I lost my concentration, I knew I'd lose my balance.

Mr Butch shrugged and then we set off again, side-stepping for another few minutes before coming to another standstill. Mr Butch turned to me. "I think we'll 'ave to start climbin'."

I froze. *"What?"* It wasn't until I properly took in the quizzical expression Mr Butch was giving me that I realised I'd taken my eyes off the path. My head felt light, like it'd been filled with helium, and coloured dots began to dance in front of my eyes. I breathed heavily, trying to convince myself that I wasn't standing on the edge of a two-hundred-foot drop.

"You okay?" Mr Butch asked.

I ignored him.

"Here, you go first and I'll help you up," he said.

"What's wrong with the path?"

"What's wrong with it is that there ain't one. It's all broken away." He slowly manoeuvred himself until he was facing the cliff's wall, ready to start climbing. "Come on."

He held his hand out towards me. It was an odd gesture coming from him, especially after our disagreement earlier, but I took it. He helped me turn on shaky legs until I was facing the right way.

"Right," Mr Butch said, his voice steady. He pointed to a groove in the wall – "Put your foot in there. It should hold you."

I did as I was told, grabbing a fistful of weeds to help hoist myself up.

"Check that the weeds'll take your weight before lettin' go, okay?"

"Uh-huh," I whimpered.

Just don't look down … just don't look down … Don't even look up, just focus on climbing. Focus on *anything* if it helps, just *don't look down.*

By the time I reached the top, my muscles were burning. I was taken aback at first by the sight of flat land stretching out before me; land that wouldn't crumble beneath my feet.

Mr Butch climbed up beside me, his face as red as mine surely was. "I'll climb up and then I'll pull you over."

There was no need, though. I wasn't going to stay dangling off the edge of a cliff for another second. I heaved myself up and rolled onto the side with some hidden strength. Then I crawled away from the edge and lay spread out on the uneven ground. I grinned, resisting the urge to laugh as a surge of adrenaline pumped through my veins. I'd actually made it to the top. *On my own.* Why was I ever afraid of climbing our old tree-house?

A shadow fell across my face; Mr Butch was staring down at me. The relief I'd felt only seconds before vanished in an instant. Just because we'd made it to the top didn't mean our struggles were over. And I still needed to find out why Danny had led me up here in the first place. I scrambled to my feet.

The only thing around was some structure that must once have been a castle but now lay in ruins. It had probably been built for some long-ago billionaire who had had the same "people-hating" attitude as Mr Butch. Why else would someone build a place so inconveniently high up, if not to look down on enemies and those they detested?

The castle couldn't have belonged to anyone important. I mean, if this was ever home to royals or any great military leader or whatever, surely somebody would've made an effort to preserve it. Most of the structure had collapsed and a lot of the bricks were missing from the walls that remained.

"What is this place?" I asked.

"What makes you think I'd know? You're the one who's s'posed to've been 'ere before." His tone was harsh. I found it difficult to imagine him ever believing another word I said.

I made my way over to the crumbling ruins. Ancient debris was scattered everywhere, with knotted vines and roots entwining every piece. Mr Butch followed me, no doubt thinking I still knew where I was going. I didn't, though. I needed Danny to point me in the right direction.

"Oi!" Mr Butch piped up. I turned to face him. "Wait 'ere a minute. I need to go take a leak."

"Okay." His timing couldn't have been better.

"If you try and run, I'll track you down."

I held up my hands, signalling that I wasn't going anywhere. Like I stood a chance anyway. We were in the middle of nowhere.

Mr Butch started making his way towards the nearest intact wall for some privacy. Now that I was alone, I really hoped Danny would show. I didn't know how much time I had on my own.

CHAPTER ELEVEN

My chest tightened with every step. There was something off about this place ... Or maybe I was just losing my nerve.

I could make out some of the room partitions but most of the castle was gone. All that remained were loose bricks and broken stone walls. High windows were set in a few of the outer walls, and there was a wide staircase leading up to a second floor that no longer existed, with steps missing and ugly roots and vines lacing the banisters. It was clearly once an impressive structure, but not anymore.

I checked behind me – Mr Butch was nowhere in sight. I took this chance to talk to Danny.

"Where do I go from here?" I said.

I could sense him. Different from the cold that carried with the howling gale, this chill came from inside me; that's how I recognised Danny was close in the dead of winter. It was something supernatural.

This time, I also felt something else. Something colder, something unfamiliar … a close-by presence that wasn't Danny.

My neck creaked as I scanned around me. I didn't know who else or what else I sensed, but it definitely was not my brother. As far as I could see, though, I was completely alone.

I decided to keep going, venturing further into the ruins in search of answers. As I did, the colder I felt and the tighter my chest became. I stopped. This didn't feel right. There must have been others like Danny wandering about. A presence you couldn't see but a presence nonetheless.

That thought didn't sit well with me. I had no idea if whoever I sensed was friendly or not. Maybe I was intruding.

I was about to sprint in the opposite direction back to Mr Butch when I caught a glimpse of someone half hidden behind one of the broken-down stone walls.

I crept forward to get a better look.

It was a young girl. She was sitting with her back to me. Thank God we weren't the only ones up here …

I made my way towards her, treading heavily now so that she would hear me coming and wouldn't startle. As I got closer, I saw she was cradling a tatty-looking doll. I could hear her humming to it, lost in her own innocent little world. She must have been about eleven. Her blonde hair was pulled back in a high ponytail, two butterfly clips on either side of her head pinning back stubborn strands of hair. Was she the one Mr Butch saw yesterday? If so, how the hell did she get up here? I couldn't see her parents anywhere.

I turned to check on Mr Butch, but he was nowhere to be seen.

Danny, I thought, *make sure you give me a sign before he shows.*

Then everything was silent: the little girl had stopped humming.

I looked back and found her staring straight at me. That's when I noticed how pale she was, as though she'd been shielded from the sun her entire life. And her eyes – they were sunken and shadowed.

I tried to smile, even though her stare made me feel like I'd committed a crime I hadn't considered. "Hello," I said, giving her a shy wave. She smiled back so I took another few steps towards her. I rounded the low wall that separated us and saw that she was sitting cross-legged by a pile of rocks. "What are you doing here?"

She twirled her doll's hair, unsure whether to answer me. I hadn't meant to freak her out.

"What's your name?" I asked instead. "I'm Jordan."

"Julie Davis." She actually replied. Her voice was soft enough to make boring stuff sound poetic.

"That's a pretty name," I said casually, trying to keep her calm. "Are you here by yourself?"

Her smile faltered. She lowered her head, focusing on the tufts of grass poking out from the pile of rocks. "They left me."

"Who left you?" I asked. "Were you here with your parents?"

She didn't answer. *(I guessed not ...)*

"Your friends?"

More silence *(Nope ...)*

Then it struck me. "Are you lost?"

She stared up at me. Although she didn't say anything, her gaze told me everything: shadowed, troubled, suffering ...

A kid should never have to wear that look.

How long had she been here?

I looked behind me. Still no Mr Butch. I'd have to deal with Julie on my own for now. I smiled back at her. She didn't need to worry anymore, she was safe with us, and that's exactly what I told her. "My friend is somewhere over there," I said, pointing behind me. "He's nice." (Or rather, he was blunt, stubborn and extremely opinionated, but I knew he'd take care of her.) "If you come with us, we'll take you to the police and they'll find your parents in no time."

She tilted her head to one side, as though she didn't quite understand. We couldn't just leave her here. But what if she didn't want to come with us? Would it still be considered as kidnapping if we were taking her straight to the nearest police station?

I was about to say something else when Julie cut

me off.

"You're the one, aren't you?" she said.

I blinked. "What d'you mean?" Did she think I was the person who left her?

"You're here."

"Julie, I think you might be confused. Why don't you come with me? I'll keep you safe."

She was still staring at me when she smiled that same smile from earlier. It made her look like the kid she was supposed to be. I held out my hand for her to take – and then she disappeared.

Holy ... *What the hell?*

I rubbed my eyes but it made no difference. Julie was gone, faded to nothing.

I thought back through the entire conversation we'd just had. *Was she even there to begin with?* I'd had a really rough night, and I hadn't eaten for hours ... Maybe I'd imagined her?

No. She'd been there, I knew it.

That's when I noticed the tightness in my chest had also vanished. Were they related? Was Julie Davis a ghost?

She couldn't have been. She was so real.

But nobody can just *vanish.*

I had to strain my jaw to keep my teeth from chattering. I'd never sensed another spirit before, and I'd definitely never come across anything like this. Danny was a spirit, after all, but I'd never actually *seen* him.

I didn't want to stick around in case Julie returned,

so I started heading back the way I'd came. That's when I felt another chill. *Damn supernatural senses.*

At first I thought it was Julie, but then the feeling shifted to a more familiar one.

I was safe.

"Took you long enough," I muttered.

In response Danny yanked the hood of my jacket up over my head.

I pulled it down. I wasn't in the mood for playing games. "Where've you been? I've been calling for you all morning. You almost got us killed last night!"

I knew it was an accident and I knew he didn't need reminding. I was just pissed off.

He picked up a handful of leaves and moss and threw them at me. Then he threw some more. And then some more. And even more ...

"All right! I'm sorry, okay?" I glanced over my shoulder. Mr Butch was approaching from a distance. We didn't have long. I lowered my voice, even though there was no way he'd be able to hear me from where he was. "Where do we go from here?"

My wrist was seized by an invisible vice as Danny began dragging me.

"Hey, slow down! I can't walk through everything like you," I said, as I stumbled along.

Danny led me to the edge of the cliff near an overgrown thorn bush, and behind the bush were some hidden cobblestone stairs. They twisted and turned down the side of the cliff until meeting up with an empty road at the bottom. The steps looked just as ancient and brittle as the castle behind us.

A cluster of leaves began to swirl around my feet, a mixture of dull reds, yellows, and browns. They moved forward, guiding me away from the cobblestone steps. I followed until they eventually dispersed at a metal lectern tangled with weeds. I pulled at them, making the stand just about accessible. It was a map of the area. A red arrow pointing to the top of a mountain read: *You are here.*

I grinned. "Perfect."

Using the map, I worked out the journey I'd taken so far. The crossroad was in the top left-hand corner. The left turn shortly fell off the map whereas the right continued in a straight line until joining with "Marshland Road" – the road I'd just seen at the bottom of the cliff. The final turn, the one we took, continued straight over and led up the cliff we now stood on. Apparently, Saint Edward's Castle used to stand here. The name didn't ring a bell, and I'd already figured the castle couldn't have been of any importance. Somebody would've made an effort to preserve it otherwise, rather than letting nature bury the evidence of its existence.

I placed my finger below the faded red arrow and let Danny guide it across the page: down the cobblestone steps and then along Marshland Road, until stopping me at what looked like a bus stop. I drew my eyes away from the clear path my finger had made through all the filth and grime that stained the map and checked the key at the bottom of the page. It had a list of several nearby towns. Danny used my finger one last time to circle the penultimate town on the key: Brookston.

The same Brookston we visited all those years ago. I *knew* it had to have been there. Why did Danny make me go cross-country before he told me? It wasn't like him to keep secrets. He couldn't have been thinking straight.

"Okay," I concluded, wiping the ill-green dirt from my finger on my already filthy school trousers. "Let's get going."

Danny disappeared.

I looked behind me – Mr Butch was close. I waved him over and gestured to the map. "Huh. That's convenient," he said, examining it just as I had done. Relief was only half evident in his voice, though. He was good at hiding emotion that wasn't anger or distaste.

"I told you I knew where I was going," I lied.

"Where am I takin' you then?" Mr Butch folded his arms. "Or, better yet, when am I gettin' my money?"

"Brookston." I pointed to the town on the map. "Just get me to Brookston and we'll work out how much I owe you."

"Well, there's the taxi fare – not to mention all my wasted time ... We're easily talkin' over five hundred quid."

He had to be bluffing. There was no way I could

afford that. Surely he knew it.

"Was it really worth it?" he continued. "Where you're goin', I mean? You could've booked a couple've flights to Florida with that, instead've *Devon*."

I sighed. I wish he would stop going on about it. I knew I'd have to fix up *some* payment arrangement with him, since I couldn't give him money I didn't have. He'd either have to wait a few years, or Mum and Dad would have to pay the bulk of it. Either way, I was going to be dirt poor for the next few years.

"Don't worry," I told him, knowing he'd still find it hard to believe me. "I'm not trying to scam you."

"Me? Worried? That'll be the day."

I was about to point out that he seemed pretty worried yesterday when the car was falling off a cliff, but I decided against it.

"Let's get this bloody thing over with," Mr Butch snapped.

I showed him the cobblestone steps hidden behind the thorn bush. We cut our way through and then I let Mr Butch lead the way again.

CHAPTER TWELVE

The narrow steps seemed to go on forever and Mr Butch's dark mood only made time drag. Weeds and branches spilled onto the path and occasionally we found ourselves having to push through stinging nettles. A lot of the steps were chipped and weather-beaten like the zig-zagging road on the other side of the cliff.

By the time we reached the bottom I had small cuts all over my hands and shins and my trousers were torn in several places. I stared up at the cliff, measuring how far I'd climbed. It made me dizzy.

Now that I'd stopped moving, my aching legs began to stiffen. I sat down on the bottom step, wishing I still had my half a bottle of flat Coke.

"Come on," Mr Butch said. Taking a break was clearly not an option. "The bus stop is over there –" He pointed to a sign that stood about forty metres away. No seats, no shelter; just a sign.

"I'll meet you there." I couldn't bring myself to stand just yet. We'd seen a bus drive by maybe half an hour ago, but nothing else. It was a very remote area, so I was sure I'd hear it coming if I wasn't already at the stop.

"Don't be pathetic," he sneered. "What's up with you? It's only a few feet away. You can rest over there."

I said nothing. Despite being out of breath and red in the face, I wasn't any warmer. I'd sweated through the only dry layer I had on.

Mr Butch stared at me, his expression similar to the one Dad wore whenever he was trying to complete a difficult crossword puzzle. Did he think I was planning to do a runner? Right now, I didn't care what he thought. There wasn't much he could do other than carry me, and he was hardly going to do that. He'd just have to believe that I was true to my word – or that I was as unfit as I probably looked. Afterall, it's not like I could get far without him noticing. Either side of us were open fields filled with wrapped haystacks, browning wheat and electricity pylons. He'd be able to spot me a mile off.

Mr Butch must've felt pretty confident that he'd be able to chase me down, because he began making his way to the bus stop with nothing more than his signature heavy sigh.

I watched him go. The road ahead of him stretched for about half a mile before curving left out of sight behind a small wooded area. The further he got, the more relaxed I felt.

Yesterday's storm had left dinosaur footprint-sized puddles everywhere. In fact, some parts of the field looked completely flooded. If I'd wanted to ditch Mr Butch, there's no way I'd be able to cross even the first field without slipping over.

I stared across the road at a group of blackbirds, feasting on the worms that had surfaced. I wish it was that easy for us to find food.

I licked my cracked lips, but my tongue was drier than the hay inside those plastic bags, and my stomach sounded like it was digesting itself. (Come to think of it, it kinda *felt* like it was digesting itself, too.) All I wanted to do was guzzle back a full bottle of Sprite, with thick beads of condensation dripping down the cool plastic …

A few stones trickled down the cliff and landed by my feet. I kicked them away. Without thinking, I turned to see where they might have fallen from and –

"Aahh!"

– There she was. Julie Davis. About ten steps above me.

I fell back and nearly landed in a puddle. *She* had caused the stones to fall.

There was no trace of a smile on her face and her doll was missing, but her shadowed eyes were very much the same. She stared down at me, her limp arms hanging by her sides. Why was she following us?

I looked over at Mr Butch. He was almost at the bus stop, oblivious to the girl in front of me. When I turned back to her a second later, though, she was already gone again.

I swallowed. Her absence didn't make me feel any less on edge, especially now I knew she could appear at any moment. What if she followed me on the bus? What if she followed me back home? What if she never left me again? Surely Danny knew she was here. He'd get rid of her for me, right?

I couldn't stop looking at the spot where Julie had just been standing.

I tried to calm myself, taking measured breaths, when the bushes at the edge of that same step began rustling.

Shit. She was coming back ...

I wanted to get up and run but my body was locked in place. All I could do was watch as the bushes rustled more and more until ... a grey squirrel scurried out onto the cobblestone steps.

All my limbs seemed to loosen at once. If I hadn't been sitting, I would have fallen.

The squirrel stared at me from Julie's step. It took me a moment to realise that *that* must've been who knocked the stones.

But that didn't mean Julie wasn't watching me.

I got to my feet and barely noticed the aching in my legs as I hurried over to the bus stop.

"All rested up, are you?" Mr Butch quipped the instant I reached him. He was sitting on the wet ground, leaning against the pole of the bus stop. And why not? Our clothes were already ruined.

I rolled my eyes, deciding not to fuel him with a response. "How long until the next bus gets here?" I asked.

"Four hours."

"What!" I forgot about Julie and turned to the bus schedule, just to double-check. "What's the time?"

"Almost quarter past eight."

I skimmed over it but – "Goddammit!" – I don't know why I bothered. I suppose I was just hoping he'd read it wrong or something. He hadn't, though. Even more annoyingly, we'd only missed the last bus by about twenty minutes.

I puffed out my cheeks. We had two options: wait four hours for the next bus to Brookston, or keep walking.

I could already feel blisters on my heels and toes; no way could my feet manage another hour's walk, let alone the entire ten miles to Brookston. Maybe if I had my old Nike trainers instead of my crappy school shoes, I could've done it. "I guess we wait," I said.

Mr Butch grunted.

I sat down just a bit away from him, and then we settled into our familiar silence. My legs still ached but I could already sense the numbness that would set in after four hours of waiting.

CHAPTER THIRTEEN

"Bloody Brookston," Mr Butch said for the umpteenth time.

The half twelve bus never showed up. If we had known that was going to happen, we would've just walked it, blisters or not. By the time we realised it wasn't coming, though, there was only another two hours until the next bus was due. And what was a couple of hours when we'd already wasted – I mean, *waited* – five hours? So we'd decided to wait for the half three bus.

During that time, not a single car passed us – and the blackbirds from earlier had taken to the grey skies hours ago, bellies full of juicy worms. *All right for some,* I thought.

Even though my mind was constantly flitting between the idea of food and a cool drink, I couldn't stop thinking about Julie, about Cillian, about Mum, Dad and the baby, about the money I owed

Mr Butch ... I could tell the latter was playing on Mr Butch's mind too. He was silent for the most part but whenever he looked my way it was with a cold glare. He didn't trust me to pay up and he knew he must have been fired.

I didn't want to bother him, but he was the only one with a watch. I cleared my throat. "How long until the bus gets here?" Last time I asked it was almost three — that could've been half an hour or five minutes ago.

Mr Butch sighed, pulling up the sleeve of his fleece. "Fifteen minutes," he grunted. "If it even bothers to turn up this time." He went over to check the timetable again, using his finger to follow the schedule. If his mind was anything like mine it would be wavering, making it difficult to focus on any small print. He was quiet for the time it took him to find what he was looking for. "Oi, how about we stop off at Charbonville first?" he said. "It's the closest town from 'ere and I'm bloody starvin'."

"Sounds good to me!" My mouth watered at the thought. If Danny had a problem with this, he could go trash our room back in Woodlock. Buses will be more regular in town, so there wouldn't be much of a delay if we stopped for a bite to eat. I'd pass out way before I reached Cillian otherwise.

* * *

It was just gone half past when we saw the bus

round the corner at the end of the road. Nothing had passed our way for almost an hour, so it was strange hearing the rumble of an engine in the empty silence.

The bus stopped with a hiss in front of us and the doors snapped open.

"Two singles to Charbonville," Mr Butch said as we climbed on board. He paid for me without question, adding it to my tab. Guess he was just eager to get out of here.

As the driver printed our tickets, Mr Butch complained about the bus that never showed, like anything could be done about it now.

He tore the tickets from the machine and then we made our way to the back of the bus. The doors slid shut and, at long last, we were on our way again.

I felt a lot better now that we were moving – especially with the promise of some food and drink. Once I settled into my seat, though, I noticed some of the other passengers glancing back at us. That's when I became very self-conscious about the muddy rags I was wearing and how badly I stank. They must've thought me and Mr Butch were hobos or something. I stared out the window and pretended not to care. It's not like I was going to see these people again.

Thirty minutes later and we were back on the main roads. I was sick of looking at open countryside and welcomed the dull faces of ignorant city-dwellers going about their lives, even though the scenery was nothing spectacular. We passed too many streets of rough-looking flats and council houses. Some of the windows were boarded up, others had paint-chipped bars welded in front of them like some sort of cheap prison. Small shops and fast-food outlets were dotted between stone terraced houses, and a construction company I'd never heard of had boarded off a run-down warehouse. After a few more graffitied streets, we passed a sign that said we were now entering Charbonville.

"Finally," Mr Butch mumbled. It had taken nearly an hour to reach this place. As we got closer to the town centre, people began arranging their coats and bags, readying themselves for the next stop.

Over half the passengers stood up as the bus pulled into a bay opposite a memorial clock tower. They shuffled down the aisle, mumbling apologies to anyone they knocked with their bags as they made their way off the bus. Me and Mr Butch got off last. As soon as we stepped onto the pavement, the double doors closed stiffly behind us and the bus pulled out onto the main road again, kicking up a dust trail.

"Come on then," Mr Butch called out, walking ahead of me.

"Hold on," I said. I was still standing under the bus shelter. As hungry as I was, I knew I had to think practically. I scanned the timetable. Now that we were in civilisation, there was another bus route that went to Brookston.

I checked the time on the clock tower: it was coming up to twenty to five. That meant the next bus left in less than ten minutes. After that, there would be one every half an hour until seven. That made things a lot easier. I told Mr Butch.

"That's great," he said. "Now come *on*." He turned on his heel and I had to run to catch up.

More people stared as we walked by and most of them weren't exactly subtle about it. Mr Butch didn't seem fazed, but I was.

We made our way past a row of market stalls that were being packed away for the day. One woman was still haggling over a snake print design handbag. It looked like the one I remember Mum using a few years ago.

As we carried on down the street, being jostled by people trying to get home from work, it was difficult not to notice people carrying steaming fresh coffee in paper cups or snacking on crumbling pasties ...

"Where d'you want to eat?" Mr Butch asked.

I scanned the storefronts. There were so many places to choose from. In the end, I settled for some American-themed café. It looked the least busy so hopefully we'd get quicker service.

"How about there?" I said, pointing to it up ahead.

Mr Butch followed my finger and his face lit up. "Great idea," he said, and set off towards it.

I walked with him, matching his fast pace until he passed the entrance. He showed no sign of stopping.

I was about to call him back when I realised where he was heading – across the road to a busy-looking pub called 'The Yonder Square Inn'.

I rolled my eyes. *Typical.*

I caught up with him at the pedestrian crossing just as the green man lit up. The pub was a little further down on the other side, with a busy beer garden at the front.

As we crossed over, I saw a pale young man stumble out of the pub doors. He couldn't have been older than twenty. All the smokers huddled around heat-lamps and picnic benches ignored the man as he staggered past them. When we passed him halfway up the garden, he lurched sideways and almost fell into me. I shuddered. The man looked ill; he was drunk in a way I'd only ever seen on telly.

I looked over my shoulder, watching the man sway and stumble. By the time we got to the pub doors, he'd somehow managed to reach the road without falling over. He stood close to the curb, a few feet away from the pedestrian crossing. He looked like he was about to fall onto the road. I stopped.

"Now what?" Mr Butch snapped, when he realised I wasn't following.

I didn't answer.

The drunk guy swayed again before stepping into the road.

"WAIT!" I called out.

I ran towards him without thinking, but it was

too late. The van heading his way didn't have time to react. It slammed straight into him and I knew there was no way he could have survived the impact.

His body was scooped up by the bonnet, crumpled against the van's windscreen and fell as a bloodied, mangled heap at the side of the road. I was expecting the driver to pull over, but he didn't. Instead, the van sped up to get through an amber light before they changed back to red. It was a hit-and-run.

"Jordan!" I heard Mr Butch call after me.

I didn't stop until I'd reached the man lying at the side of the road. My stomach lurched. His body was bent at an impossible angle, and the blood ... it was everywhere. How can people hold that much blood inside them?

"Jesus ..." My voice caught. I swallowed and tasted vomit. What should I do? I didn't have my phone so I couldn't call for an ambulance. It was too late for him to be saved anyway. I looked around but everyone seemed confused by my reaction, oblivious to the dead man oozing blood.

Mr Butch was making his way towards me. Even he looked confused. *Surely* he'd seen what'd happened though.

I turned back to the man lying dead by my feet ...

But he was gone, and not a single trace of blood remained.

The lights changed to green and traffic passed

over the spot where, moments ago, a man had just been killed.

I looked up at the people around me. They couldn't have seen the man. They wouldn't have been staring at me, otherwise, with the same bewildered expression. It was a look I'd been given a thousand times before; a look that meant they thought I was crazy.

But why would I imagine such a horrific thing?

Mr Butch walked up alongside me, but I turned away before he could say anything. That's when I saw it, a few metres up the road … Bunches of flowers, glossy-eyed teddy-bears and a cascade of bows and ribbons tied to a metal barrier next to the pedestrian crossing. Cards and plaques were lined up beside photographs of the drunk young man I'd just seen, with water-bled words that were impossible to miss: *R.I.P.*

CHAPTER FOURTEEN

"Are you all right?"

Mr Butch's voice cut through my thoughts. What the hell had I just seen? It couldn't have been my imagination. Not when it was so vivid, so real … Besides, I didn't know that anyone had died on that road, let alone what the victim looked like, so there was seriously no way I could've made it up. And then he'd disappeared, just like Julie. Something strange was happening to me – and I was making a complete spectacle of myself as it got worse.

I couldn't meet Mr Butch's eyes.

He cleared his throat. "You're probably just hungry," he said, aware of the looks people were still giving us. "Didn't sleep well last night either. Come on, let's get some grub in you."

For argument's sake, I agreed, letting him lead me back to the pub. I knew these 'outbursts' had nothing to do with lack of food or sleep, though.

They were something supernatural, and I needed to ask Danny about it the first chance I got.

I followed Mr Butch inside, ignoring the frequent glances he cast my way. It wasn't hard to do, since the place was completely rammed with loud-mouthed locals. I stayed close to Mr Butch, walking in his shadow as he prised through the crowd.

It wasn't like the family-friendly pubs I went to with Mum and Dad – although this place did have its perks: the shouts and laughter of drunken men made me feel invisible, which right now was a blessing.

Glasses clinked and cheers erupted when England scored a try on the many flat-screen TVs around the room. I barely noticed the game, though; my mind was focused on the food we passed as we squeezed by tables to get to the bar.

"You save us a table," Mr Butch said. "I'll get the drinks. Tap water good for you?"

I nodded. Usually I'd have a Coke, but right now anything would do.

I made my way through the pub alone, past an old jukebox and several "Quiz Night" posters, until I came across a free table. There were still a few empty pint glasses and some spilt lager on it, but nobody had claimed the spot. I avoided the mess and took the double seat lining the back wall. Some of the cover was torn at the seams, yellow stuffing spilling out of the top like foam dripping from an overfilled pint. The lumpy chair wasn't the most comfortable, but that didn't bother me. Not after the couple of days I'd had.

I was about to reach for one of the grubby laminated menus when a barmaid came over to clear the table. She wore skin-tight trousers with a frilly white shirt, her dyed-blonde hair held up by a hundred or more grips like so many of the girls from school had their hair.

"Hey," she said, because she wasn't ignorant like Mr Butch.

"Hey," I said back.

She stacked the glasses with one hand and pulled out a cloth from her belt with the other to mop up the spilt drink. She gave me a brief smile before making her way back to the bar.

I watched her walk away, weaving between burly men and collecting more glasses as she passed other tables. *I'd hate to work in a place like this,* I thought. It was bad enough sitting here.

Through the crowd, I could see Mr Butch at the front of the bar being served. He shouldn't be long now.

I picked up one of the menus and started flicking through. The pictures were faded, and the plastic curled at the corners, but it didn't make the crappy two-for-one pub meals fall anything short of five stars in my starving mind. As I began eyeing up starters I wouldn't be ordering, a loud voice called out, making me jump.

I looked up to check what had happened. A small

table of five leering men were starting a fight with someone. They were in their late twenties and as scruffy as you'd expect a group of thugs to be: one skinhead, another with dreadlocks, one short and podgy with a round nose, a gangly guy with tattoos and varicose veins, and a man with flushed cheeks and thick-rimmed glasses.

It was Skinhead who had called out, and with a pang in my gut I realised he was talking to me.

"Whut you lookin' at?" he said. His posse sniggered.

Their table was filled with used glasses, their recent drinks dotted wherever they could fit them. The barmaid clearly didn't want to approach them, and I couldn't blame her.

I shrank into my seat, using the menu to cover my face. There was no reasoning with people who were rat-faced …

My body immediately tensed at the sound of a chair scraping the wooden floorboards. Skinhead was out of his seat.

I groaned. Why did he have to come over?

Skinhead was soon joined by one of his cronies. I looked up: it was the podgy man.

A sharp chill raced down my spine. Skinhead and Podgy had almost reached me, but Danny was here too.

Without warning, an empty stool from a neighbouring table skidded across the floor on its back legs. It crashed into Podgy, toppling to the floor by his clown-sized feet.

"*OW!*" Podgy yelped, cursing and rubbing his shin. Being in front, Skinhead had missed all the action. He looked over his shoulder and I saw the glimpse of a scowl cross his face. I tried not to laugh, wondering what Danny had planned for him too.

When Skinhead turned back to me, I didn't look away. He swaggered over alone. The idiot was going to lose big time if he wasn't careful. He stopped in front of me and leaned forwards, resting his hands on the table.

"Why was you starin' at 'Olly?" Skinhead said, his voice ugly and slurred.

"Who's Olly?" I asked.

"HOLLY!" Spittle left his mouth. "The barmaid. Blonde, long legs ... You chattin' 'er up?"

"No! I was just reading the menu –"

"But you *looked* at 'er, though, di'n't you."

I didn't know how to answer that. Of course I'd looked at her. She was standing right in front of me. I couldn't just blank her.

The table began to shake. I held it steady. Danny was getting ready to defend me.

Skinhead leaned closer. His breath smelt foul and his clothes reeked of stale cigarette smoke. Not that I smelt any better, I guess. "You keep away from 'er, all righ'?"

The table shook harder. Luckily Skinhead's attention was fixated on me.

I tightened my grip, trying to still the table.

"Is there a problem?" That was Mr Butch. I hadn't notice him come back.

He stared down at Skinhead, easily half a foot taller. Even holding a glass of water and a pint of whatever – with a couple packets of Walkers crisps wedged between his fingers – Mr Butch didn't look like the kind of guy you'd want to mess with. He wore a face as though somebody had tried fobbing him off before paying his taxi fare – an expression I recognised all too well.

Skinhead stood to his full height. He was bitter and drunk but obviously not dumb enough to pick a fight with Mr Butch. His scrawny frame didn't stand a chance. And although Mr Butch was outnumbered if Skinhead's posse stepped in, he wasn't worth their time.

"Nah, mate." I could tell it took all the pride Skinhead had to say that. He gave a false smile – one that only an idiot would believe – before making his way back to his table.

"What was all that about?" Mr Butch asked, taking a seat on one of the stools opposite me. He set the drinks down and I immediately reached for mine.

"Nothing," I said, and then chugged back my water. Mr Butch only sipped his cider; he must have downed a few glasses of water before coming over.

We opened our smoky bacon crisps and munched through them in under a minute. Hopefully it would hold off the noises our stomachs kept making until our dinner was served. I'd already decided what I was having, and it didn't take Mr Butch long to make up his mind either. He went up to order for us both and I tried draining whatever water was left in my glass. I'd never been this excited about food in my life.

As soon as Mr Butch was back to watch the table, I wanted to go wash my face and underarms in the men's room. And if I could just scrub off a few mud patches, that'd make me feel a hell of a lot less self-conscious.

I leaned back in my seat. There was a torn quiz-night advert stapled to the wall behind me. I was just reading the small print when the table started shaking again.

"Danny, stop it," I muttered, trying to hold it still. But of course, he didn't listen. "Do you want me to get my teeth kicked in or something?" I looked over at Skinhead and his crew, making sure I hadn't drawn their attention. They were pulling on their jackets, getting ready to leave.

Good riddance, I thought.

Danny stopped rocking the table, but he didn't go away. Instead, he started tugging the hem of my trousers – he wanted me to follow him.

"Not yet, I'm starving!" I hissed. "If I follow you now, I'll pass out before we even reach Brookston – and where will that leave us?" Just because *he* didn't need to eat.

He stopped tugging on me but the temperature

stayed the same.

"I'll go with you after I've eaten, okay?"

Danny knocked over the salt pot. I looked around to check that nobody had noticed. The room was so loud, though, and everybody was so enthralled in the match that I don't know why I bothered. When I turned back, Danny had written something in the spilt salt.

I sighed. "What about Mr Butch?"

He underlined the message he'd just written.

"I owe him a *lot* of money because of you. Do you really think he's going to let us go our separate ways before he gets paid?" It wasn't just the money: I *wanted* him with me. I knew Danny would protect me but having Mr Butch around was kind of reassuring. I'd seen the way Skinhead and his posse had looked at him. I was keeping Mr Butch close for as long as I could.

I saw him leave the bar, pushing his way through the crowd carrying two fresh glasses of water. I swiped the salt onto the floor, closing the matter with Danny. We'd be on our way to Brookston soon enough. He just had to be patient.

But Danny didn't do being patient. He began rocking the table again. I held onto Mr Butch's cider to stop it from spilling.

"All right already! Just stop," I said. And for once he actually listened. I put Mr Butch's drink down. I knew Danny's patience wouldn't last long so I quickly added, "I'll go by myself." I needed to talk to him anyway. I didn't know what I'd seen outside, with that man from the memorial, but I had a feeling Danny knew.

When Mr Butch reached the table, he set the drinks down and sat back on his stool. "You owe me for this, too, you know," he said, making a show of slipping the receipt in his wallet.

Danny was still lingering. I knew he was going to wait around until the very last forkful.

CHAPTER FIFTEEN

Mr Butch took another swig of his drink, glancing at the game on the TV screen closest to us. Time was ticking. I hadn't even been to the toilets yet to clean up – I was too busy wondering how to tell Mr Butch that I'd be popping out for a while. He wasn't going to be happy about it, I knew that.

"So what you got planned in Brookston? Must be pretty important," Mr Butch said, and because he was still staring at the TV, it took me a moment to work out that he was talking to me.

"Um ... I'm meeting my brother." It was the first thing I could think of. I brushed some of the remaining salt grains off the table to give myself something to do.

"And he'll pay me, will he?" That's when Mr Butch looked at me. He seemed to relax a little when I nodded. "Still don't know why you di'n't just catch a train. Would've been so much cheaper — and a hell've a lot quicker, too."

As long as he got paid, what did it matter to him how I got to Brookston?

I was about to take the plunge and tell him that I needed to head off alone soon when Holly came over with our food: steak and kidney pie for Mr Butch, and a cheeseburger for me. We both had a generous portion of chips to go with it. I said thank you to Holly but this time I didn't look at her, even though Skinhead had left some time ago.

I picked up my burger and took a huge bite, too hungry to faff around with ketchup or vinegar. Grease from Mr Butch's pie dribbled down his chin and some of the chips fell off his plate as he shovelled food in his mouth.

It didn't take us long to devour what was in front of us. Once our plates were empty, I finished the rest of my drink and watched Mr Butch do the same.

"Right," he said, checking his watch. "D'you want another drink or shall we make a move?"

"Um, actually ..." I could sense Danny next to me. It was now or never. "I saw a payphone outside — I ... I'd best ring my brother, tell him about the whole money situation ..."

"I'll come with you then."

"No —" I knew he'd say that. How was I supposed to stop him from following me? "I mean ... it's okay. I won't be long. I'll come back as soon as I'm done."

Mr Butch frowned. "You're not thinkin' of doin'

a runner, are you?"

"Of course not —"

"Because I'd track you down. You *will* pay up."

"I'm not scamming you!" I knew he had no reason to believe me but I was getting sick of reassuring him. "Look, I was supposed to have turned up last night. He's going to be wondering where I am. I'll ask him to write you a cheque for when we arrive, okay?" I don't know why I said the last part. I suppose it just sounded better but I'd really hammered the nail in the coffin with that one. Eventually he was going to realise there was no cheque.

Mr Butch crossed his thick arms over his chest. The stool beneath him suddenly looked far too small for him.

"Just give me half an hour," I added. "I'd rather have some privacy while I talk to him."

I stood up, and so did Mr Butch. Since I was against the wall, it meant I'd have to pass him to get around the table but there was no way he was letting me by.

"Sit back down, kid." Mr Butch's voice was grave, just like on the cliff outside the den — only this time he wasn't changing his mind. But I could hardly do as he said. I stepped forward and he moved to block me.

Danny was growing colder, feeling less certain. I knew that if he panicked or thought I was in danger, things could go really wrong really fast. "Please, Mr Butch. Just let me pass."

He laughed in a way I'd never quite heard before. "You think *manners* are gonna make me change my mind? I'm not lettin' you leave me jobless *and* penniless!"

"But I'm coming straight back —"

"If you leave, I'm coming with you. It's as simple as that. Only a guilty mind would find that unreasonable."

The temperature around me continued to dip lower and lower until the cold made me shudder. Whatever Danny was about to do, he was going to do it soon. Unless I beat him to it.

I tried to barge past Mr Butch and, as predicted, he seized my arm, pulling me back to face him. That's when I put my off-the-cuff plan into action. There was no guarantee it would work but it was all I had …

"GET OFF ME!" I shouted. Loud.

Heads turned and I felt myself blush from the attention. Holly stood nearby, her eyes wide with alarm. "Excuse me," she said, looking from me to Mr Butch. "What's going on?"

Mr Butch stared at Holly, instantly letting go of me. His cheeks burned a deep shade of red. He knew exactly what I'd done. "Nothin'," he said, and then tried explaining. "He owes me money … I was just sayin' … Look, never mind, okay. It doesn't matter."

Holly still looked uneasy.

I stepped around him. Most people had lost interest now but there was still far too much attention on us for Mr Butch to try and stop me.

"I'll be back in half an hour – one hour max," I told him. "I promise. I just have a few things I need to sort out with my brother." That was no lie.

I felt terrible about what I'd done but it was better than the alternative. Danny could be dangerous.

"If you don't come back, I'll track you down," he said again, quietly this time as Holly was still watching.

"I know. Just … have a couple of pints on me." I quickly turned to make my way back through the pub before he could grab me again. The place seemed even fuller now. I squeezed past drunk, sweaty men and tipsy women, trying to ignore Mr Butch's burning glare piercing the back of me.

Once outside, I took a deep breath. The fresh air felt good on my lungs. I hadn't realised how stuffy it was in there.

Everyone in the beer garden was oblivious to the scene I'd made inside, but I was still half expecting Mr Butch to come rushing out at any moment. I continued walking, following my brother back to the crossing.

I stared at the memorial by the side of the road. The bows and ribbons tied to the metal barrier rippled in the wind, but I was drawn mainly to the photographs. It was weird: the man looked so happy, so relaxed, so clear-headed and very much alive. Had I seriously seen a replay of his death? Once I was somewhere more secluded, I knew exactly what

I was going to ask Danny first.

He guided me away from the town square and led me down a wide country lane. A tractor was parked at the side of the road next to a padlocked gate and a wooden 'public footpath' sign. In front of the gate was a small crate of apples that had *help yourselves!* scrawled on the side in black marker. I think my stomach had shrunk because I wasn't even tempted, still feeling full from my cheeseburger and chips. Where was this offer when we were stranded?

We carried on down the road, passing large detached houses that were visible through the branches of the leafless bushes at the foot of their massive front gardens. Opposite them were even more fields. I checked behind me. The busy streets were out of sight now and there was nobody else around. I turned my focus to Danny.

"I need to ask you something," I said, still following his pull. "On the cliff I saw a little girl – Julie Davis – and I think she followed me down. She literally disappeared though! Was she a ...?" I didn't want to say it but there was no other way. "Was she a ghost ... or did I just imagine her?"

Danny didn't respond, so I continued.

"And before we went into the pub I saw a man get knocked over by a van. No one else saw him but me! And there was a memorial at the side of the road – *his* memorial, Danny. He was already dead, but I *know* I saw him. How could I have imagined him when I'd never even seen his picture until then?"

Danny seized my arm, leading me further down the road made up of old five-bed houses. I knew he'd heard me, but he showed no signs of answering. I was sick of his selectiveness.

Once we'd passed all the rich homes, walking alongside a seven-foot-high grey brick wall, I stopped dead and yanked my arm free from Danny's grasp. The trees growing on the other side loomed above me. As far as I was aware, nobody was watching.

"You either answer me or I'm going back to the pub," I said. For a horrible second, I reminded myself of Mr Butch. I didn't like being this stern with him, but he was giving me no choice.

I think Danny realised I wasn't fooling around. He moved a stone from the side of the road and began scratching a reply onto the path by my feet:

I LET THEM IN

What?

I furrowed my brows. "Why?" Did that mean he'd stopped them from coming through to me before, or was this all new to him?

TO HELP YOU

I shook my head. "I don't get it. How are Julie and that man going to help me?"

He took my arm and I let him pull me further down the road, wondering what he could've meant.

Up ahead, the brick wall ended at a set of black iron gates. At the top read *"Charbonville Cemetery"*. I stopped again. I didn't need any clues or supernatural senses to know that this must be where Danny was taking me.

I also knew that I was about to meet more spirits in there – spirits that Danny would "let in". It was the same reason he'd led me up the cliff yesterday: to find Julie. That's why I couldn't go straight to Brookston: *"Theres more than one stop you will need to take"*, he'd told me ... I hadn't understood at the time but now it made sense. He was introducing me to other spirits along the way. But why? Were they going to help me get back at Cillian?

"Who am I going to find in there?"

In the mud at the side of the road, he spelled out the name:

I was right: I was meeting more spirits. *God, why was I suddenly so nervous?* "How is she going to help me?"

Danny swiped away the last message to make room for his next one:

Ask her and find out

Clever little git. Why couldn't he at least give me a clue?

Whatever. I had a funny feeling that this 'Melissa Cundille' girl ... *ghost* ... was expecting me, anyway.

I walked through the open gates of the cemetery and along the main pathway. It was wide enough to fit a car down it. Conifer trees lined the perimeter, with smaller trees and other plants dividing the many rows of graves. Most of them looked abandoned: limp weeds tangled over a lot of the headstones and the lettering had faded so much that I could barely read the inscription on some.

Danny didn't follow me in. I'd be facing Melissa alone. She couldn't be dangerous, I kept telling myself, or Danny would've come with me – in fact, he wouldn't have led me here *at all* if he sensed even a hint of trouble.

Reassured, I made my way through the cemetery, sticking to the main path. I didn't know where she'd be, but that wasn't a problem. Before I could get halfway around the cemetery, my forehead started tingling and goosebumps formed along my arms. Then, something materialised by one of the graves on my right. I turned to look – a pale, thin, translucent figure of a little girl, her colour desaturated. Like Julie, she seemed to be around Danny's age.

Melissa had found me.

"You're here," she said, just as Julie had.

Even though I was expecting it, even though I'd seen it before, my heart still pounded and my mouth went dry. I knew I was safe – it was just my body responding to the abnormality of it all.

I swallowed. "Melissa Cundille?" I asked, though I was already certain it was her.

She nodded, and I couldn't help noticing her hand passing through the gravestone of a Victor Salter as she swayed, levitating maybe half an inch from the ground.

Going against my instincts, I took a step towards her. The air was colder, thicker, the closer I got. "You know my brother, don't you?"

"Yes," she said, staring up at me. "He died a year before me."

My gut knotted. She said it so casually … did it not bother her?

"He, um – he said you were going to help me. Is that true?" I hoped Danny had already run it past her. If not, I was going to sound very presumptuous.

"We can help each other," she said. "Cillian murdered me as well."

Wait ... *What?*

The same Cillian I was going after? The same *monster* who ...

I needed a second to take this in, but Melissa carried on. "And he got Julie. She was killed two years ago. She's very shy – you've probably noticed she doesn't speak much."

Shit ... He was a *serial killer?*

I finally got it. *That's* why Danny led me here. They wanted revenge too! "And what about the man from the memorial?" I asked, waiting for clarification.

Melissa tilted her head. "What man?"

"I saw a man – er, I mean *ghost* – get run over outside the Yonder Square pub back in town. Has he got something to do with Cillian as well?"

She shook her head. "I don't know anyone connected to a pub." Then, seconds later, her face lit up. She leaned forward, as if she was about to share a secret. Instead of adding something more about the man, though, she asked, "Do you want to know how I died?"

I almost took a step back. Where the hell did that come from?

I'll admit a very small part of me was curious, but the answer was still no. She looked kind of excited, though – like she was looking forward to telling me. For Danny's sake, I played along. I needed Melissa on my side, and I didn't know if she'd be offended if I turned down her story. "Uhh ... sure," I said, and I could sense her energy start to buzz. It never occurred to me until now, but I must have been the first person she'd shared this with.

She walked behind Victor's gravestone and said, "He grabbed me right here —" She held a clump of matted hair at the back of her head, imitating what Cillian had done. "Then he did *this* —"

She slammed her head into the stone and I cringed at the impact, watching her skull crack open. My stomach flipped; it was way more gruesome than the memorial guy being run down. Melissa didn't stop. She looked possessed, slamming her head against the same spot, over and over again.

I was transfixed. There was no sound of her skull smashing against stone, but I imagined it regardless. Same as there wasn't any blood spilling from her head like there would've been during the real event — my brain pictured it anyway: spattering the graves like paint flicking off a paintbrush, streaks of dark red dripping down Victor's headstone and pooling in the dewy grass …

And my imagination didn't stop there.

We were alone, just me and Melissa, and yet I could see Cillian gripping her hair, smashing her ten-year-old skull into the stone. Despite never having actually seen Cillian, my mind had formed an image. This Cillian had a twisted mouth, narrow slits for eyes and claws instead of fingers; he was a hybrid of rogue, ugly animals.

I'd lost count of the number of times she'd hit

her head, but eventually, Melissa slumped to the ground. Soundless. Still.

Dead.

Her body looked rigid in that horrible corpse-like way. I couldn't breathe. This was reality at its most horrific. Cold-blooded murder.

I squeezed my eyes shut, trying hard to block out the image. It didn't help. I started picturing Danny being drowned in a stream, thrashing, panicking ... *And I wasn't there to save him –*

"They don't know."

"Huh?" I opened my eyes. Melissa was standing next to Victor's grave again.

"The police," she said. "They don't know it was Cillian. So even after all these years, none of our families know the truth. It's still hurting my parents, but I can't get through to them like Danny can with you."

"I'm really sorry. I know how difficult it must be. The police haven't told us anything for the past three years, and Danny only told me two days ago. How's Cillian getting away with it?"

"He had help." Melissa looked older now; her shoulders tensed and her mouth became taut, as though she tasted something bitter. "My mum still cries – she never *used* to cry. They don't know who killed me and it's ..." She broke off and her face screwed up with what I can only describe as pure rage. "IT'S DRIVING ME CRAZY!"

I jumped back. She was even more terrifying

when she shrieked. I didn't know what to say. Was this the equivalent to Danny throwing things? "It's okay," I settled for. "I'm going to –"

"DON'T TELL ME IT'S OKAY! I'VE HAD TO WATCH THEM MOURN FOR FOUR *YEARS!*"

She started hyperventilating – well, it *looked* like she was hyperventilating. Spirits didn't actually breathe, though, did they?

I was about to remind her that she wasn't the only one who'd suffered. Sure, I wasn't dead, but I'd watched Mum and Dad grieve for five years – knowing Danny was here, and yet, unable to convince them … It'd messed me up big time, and I was still dealing with the repercussions.

I kept this to myself, though. Melissa wouldn't care and I didn't expect her to.

I waited out the silence. When she'd finally calmed down, she tilted her head to one side and said, "Are you going to talk to April?"

Was she another one of Cillian's victims?

"To be honest," I said, "I don't know what I'm doing but I'm definitely going to get him to confess. Then, one way or another, I'm going to make him suffer for everything he's done – I just haven't figured out how to go about the last part yet." He wasn't walking out alive, though. *That,* I knew for certain.

"We'll help you," Melissa said.

I now knew why she was so willing; why Julie

was as well. It was in their interest for me to reach Cillian and survive to tell their families the truth.

Without another word, she turned and began making her way down the muddy aisle behind Victor's headstone, flanked by another row of old graves. She disappeared before she reached the end of the pathway, exactly like Julie had done.

I stared at the spot where she'd just faded and felt the tiny hairs on the back of my neck stand on end. It was going to take a while to get used to that.

The buzzing energy left with her; I was alone now, with a billion and one thoughts echoing in my head. How, exactly, were Melissa and Julie going to help me? And who was the memorial guy?

I doubled back through the cemetery, my mind racing. Now that I had answers, I was more determined than ever to get going.

Danny met me outside the gates and kept me company as I ran back to town. I wanted to catch the next bus to Brookston. With Danny, Melissa and Julie on my side, there was no way Cillian could harm me. I just hoped Mr Butch had taken me up on the drinks offer, and that the couple of pints had softened him up a little.

CHAPTER SIXTEEN

The clock tower in town read half six. Only fifteen minutes until the next bus. The stop was just up ahead but I needed to fetch Mr Butch from the Yonder Square pub. If I was fast, we might still make it.

I was about to turn down a side street that would lead directly onto the road with the memorial crossing when I spotted a familiar-looking large figure standing at the stop we needed to wait at.

Mr Butch was already there.

That saved some time, I thought. But the relief I felt was short-lived, for even from this distance I could tell Mr Butch was pretty narked off. He had a face like a prison guard, all stony and miserable and prepared for shit to hit the fan. He must've been cursing me something fierce while I was away.

He kept checking over his shoulder and across the road towards town, no doubt on the lookout for me. I made my way to him, thankful for witnesses. I didn't want to dwell on all the ways he could get back at me for showing him up earlier.

His steely eyes met mine as I was crossing the road. I forced a smile, my insides squirming. "Told you I'd be back," I said when I reached him.

There were others waiting at the stop, too. A couple of them glanced my way and I immediately worked out why. Mr Butch had managed to clean the dirt from his clothes and face. Now that I was the only one who looked a mess, it made me feel even worse. It was going to be another self-conscious bus ride for me.

Mr Butch grunted. "Where the hell d'you go? I've been out 'ere almost forty minutes and the phone booth's been empty the entire time."

"Someone else was using it when I got outside. I found another one not too far away."

"And some spare change on the floor, I take it?" he scorned.

"I had a few quid left over in my pocket."

"Sure you did. What did your brother 'ave to say then?"

I shrugged to buy myself some time before expanding the lie I'd already started. "He was annoyed. I'd rather not talk about it."

"I'm not bleedin' surprised he's annoyed. Understatement if I ever heard one. He's still payin' me, though, yeah?"

I nodded.

Mr Butch was about to say something else when the bus rolled up early, sparing me from whatever accusations or insults he surely would've thrown my way. We got in line, fifth from the front, and waited for the doors to slide open.

This driver was much cheerier than the first one we'd met. His bald head and big-framed glasses seemed to exaggerate his personality. He chatted and smiled to everyone who boarded – the complete "anti-Mr Butch". I wondered whether it was even possible for his smooth, wrinkleless face to frown.

Mr Butch paid for our tickets and then, because we could, we made our way up to the top deck. Most the seats were empty, including one at the very front. I took that one and Mr Butch sat behind me.

We weren't waiting long. As soon as everybody else had boarded, the double doors closed and the bus lurched onto the main road. We were finally on our way again, even though it was already dusk. I couldn't believe another day had passed! I'd be facing Cillian at midnight at this rate. Then again, maybe that wasn't such a bad thing. I'd have the advantage if I got to him while he was asleep. Maybe I could find a way of restraining him before he woke ...

I still had nothing to keep track of time, but I know I spent a good chunk of the journey scheming and being jolted by the bus's harsh braking. We seemed to pull up at every stop. Mr Butch had complained about his job as a taxi driver but at least in a taxi he could take the most direct route – except, of course, when he was driving me. It'd taken us almost forty minutes to reach the edge of town, by which point we'd become the only passengers on the top deck. Probably the entire bus. Mr Butch had switched places as soon as the other front seat became available.

The neon signs in town were gradually replaced by dim streetlights in narrow built-up areas, and pretty soon the setting sun disappeared below the horizon. Charbonville looked different at night, kind of ... unsettling. Maybe someone else had died out here –

Shut up, Jordan, I immediately told myself. *Stop thinking like that.*

I couldn't help it, though.

My stomach clenched when the streetlights ended, plunging the world into complete darkness. I gave up trying to look past the interior's reflection and propped my feet up on the seat instead.

"I don't like this place," I mumbled to myself.

Mr Butch glanced at me. "It's just another place in the world. Just because it's dark doesn't mean all the ghosts and ghouls come out."

I thought about Danny, a ghost himself. "Yeah," I replied, with masked uncertainty. Then I thought about Danny five years ago, alone in the forest – that too was 'just another place in the world'. "What about murderers?" I said.

I turned back to the window, trying again to peer through the dark when Mr Butch's reflection came into focus. He was looking straight at me.

"What's the matter with you?" he asked.

I turned to him. "What d'you mean?"

"All this rubbish about killers?"

I shrugged. "I dunno. I'm just tired."

As the bus pulled up at yet another stop, Mr Butch shook his head and turned away, giving up on the conversation. I was glad. He never had anything nice to say.

The double doors opened and then I heard the low mumble of a man's voice outside. I couldn't make out what he was saying.

I closed my eyes, leaning against the unevenly padded seat. I hated buses. The school one was bad enough, but this was taking a lifetime to reach the next big town.

The man stopped talking and laughed: deep, gruff and irrepressible.

I turned to Mr Butch. "I wonder what they're talking about," I said. I didn't know if the guy was on the bus yet, but he was sure taking his time buying a ticket.

"What?"

"That man downstairs," I said. "Listen."

But the guy had finally shut up.

"Never mind." I settled back into my seat. I was about to let myself drift off for a few minutes when I heard him speak up again, much clearer this time.

"I know where you are," he said, in a menacing, sing-song tone. "I know what you're planning and

I'm coming to get you …"

I sat upright. Who was he talking to? The driver? Or was he on the phone?

I looked across at Mr Butch. Something didn't feel right. It wasn't just the threats or the mocking voice, it was the fact that Mr Butch didn't react to any of it. He was drumming his fingers against the window frame, oblivious to the voice downstairs. It wasn't because he didn't care; it was because the voice didn't exist. Not to him, anyway. The threats were inside my head, which could only mean one thing …

Danny? I begged him to make an appearance. I didn't feel safe without my brother close by.

I knew the threats were aimed at me. Why else would the man project his voice into my head? Whoever he was, he was not like the spirits I'd come across yet.

I took a deep breath and let it out slowly through my nose. Who'd have thought Dr Ashton's stupid breathing exercises would come in handy? I tried to ignore everything around me and focused on reaching out to Danny. Surely he was close; surely he knew what was happening …

I was halfway through asking him a question when the bus rocked sharply, almost knocking us out our seats.

"Ah!" I reached for something to steady myself.

"What the blazin' 'ell was that?" Mr Butch said. He let go of the railing he'd grabbed hold of for balance and I did the same.

The man's voice had disappeared now. Instead, the lights above us had begun to flicker. It only lasted a few seconds but it was enough to completely freak me out. When they returned to normal, I looked at Mr Butch.

"We need to get off," I decided.

"What?"

The lights above us flickered again until finally deciding to stay off. Everything was pitch black.

"Now!" I said, getting to my feet. I headed towards the stairs, using the backs of seats to guide me. I wanted to leave but I knew I wouldn't go anywhere without Mr Butch. Why was I such a coward?

"Sit back down, kid," he said. He had no intention of leaving. "It's most likely just faulty wiring, so if you're worried about those 'murderers' you were goin' on about before, then just forget it."

I swallowed. He didn't know what he was up against. Whoever this guy was, he'd made the driver pull over, got in my head and tampered with the lights. It didn't take a genius to figure out he had a lot of energy. Either way, Mr Butch had clearly decided he was staying put – and because I was too afraid to go anywhere by myself, it meant that I was stuck here too, against my better judgement.

I felt exposed standing halfway down the bus in the dark, so I went to sit at the front with Mr Butch again. Then the engine cut out. The vibration stopped and the silence was piercing. *Crap.*

My heart pounded against my ribcage; I was half expecting it to burst out of my chest.

"What's the driver playin' at? We're not in Brookston yet," Mr Butch said, mostly to himself. "Probably the bus breakin' down again, knowin' our luck."

I heard Mr Butch get to his feet and make his way down the aisle. When he reached me, he gave my shoulder a reassuring squeeze. "Wait 'ere," he said.

I listened to him trudge blindly down the narrow staircase. He was leaving me alone up here. "Are you kidding?" I muttered, before following him down to the lower deck.

I moved silently, listening out for anything strange. By the time I reached the bottom, my eyes had adjusted to what little light the moon gave. I crept up behind Mr Butch and noticed him staring towards the front of the bus. I followed his gaze, squinting through the darkness until I saw what was holding him up.

"Where's the driver?" I whispered.

Mr Butch jumped. Spinning round to face me, he snapped, "I thought I told you to wait up there."

"He's gone," I said, ignoring his comment.

"Stop workin' yourself up, Jordan. He's probably just gone to take a leak."

I wasn't convinced. And I wasn't convinced that he was convinced, either. Perhaps he was trying to be logical. After all, he didn't hear the voice upstairs.

A crisp breeze drifted through the open door. I peered around Mr Butch, this time looking in the direction of the ignition. The key was still there.

When I pointed this out to Mr Butch, his face lit up. "You see!" he said. "He's obviously comin' back. Let's take a seat down 'ere." He gave me a knowing look before passing me. "Told you there's nothin' to worry about. You kids overreact —"

Thud!

I froze, and Mr Butch stopped mid-stride. I thought I was going to throw up from shock.

"What was that?" Mr Butch asked. The fact that he'd heard it too did not make the situation any less terrifying.

Something had hit the window.

"I don't know. It sounded like it came from over there." I pointed towards the windows on the right-hand side, halfway along the bus.

Mr Butch didn't hesitate. He made his way down and squeezed between the seats to peer outside, cupping his hands on either side of his face. I held my breath in anticipation until he eventually moved away and sighed. "Can't see a damn thing from in 'ere."

He brushed past me, heading for the door. "Stay here," he said. "I'll be back in a minute."

"Wait! Where are you going? You know what happens in films when everyone splits up."

"Yes," he said slowly. "But we're not in a movie,

are we?"

"That's not the point."

Mr Butch sighed again. It was too dark to see but he probably rolled his eyes as well. "Don't you dare leave this bus," he warned, stepping outside anyway. I listened to his footsteps fade to nothing as he walked away. He called out twice to anyone nearby but there was no reply. I couldn't decide if he was being brave or stupid.

I'd already made up my mind to follow him. No way was I waiting here by myself. Not when that horrible voice could come back at any moment. His words were already echoing in my head: *"I know where you are. I'm coming to get you ..."*

I took a breath and then stepped outside. This was probably a dumb idea.

I didn't know if it was the cold or fear or that menacing spirit that caused me to shiver, but it took an effort to keep my jaw from chattering. The slightest sound, movement or shadow put me on edge. I rounded the front of the bus and immediately froze at the sight of someone lurking in the distance. My legs were pent-up with adrenaline; I was ready to run if I needed to. Once my eyes had properly adjusted, though, I realised it was only a signpost.

God sake, Jordan – keep it together!

Stepping off the pavement, I glanced around just to make extra sure no one was around. There were trees either side of the empty road, casting a darkness that concealed the rest of the forest. I had to force my imagination to a standstill before I started picturing all kinds of crazy stuff.

When I reached the other side of the bus, I spotted Mr Butch at the opposite end, towards the back. He was hunched over, peering around the other corner. I made my way to him, treading lightly so I didn't make a sound. Had he found something? Was it the creepy spirit I heard a few minutes ago? Maybe it was that April girl.

Mr Butch straightened up, turned back around to face me and —

"Ahh!" He covered his mouth the instant he realised it was me. I jumped at the noise and then watched him curse. "What the hell are you doin' 'ere?" he hissed. "I bloody told you to *wait on the bus.* Do you 'ave a problem followin' instructions or somethin'?"

I was too afraid to care how mad he was. "What did you find?" I said quietly.

Mr Butch shook his head. "Nothin'. I *thought* I saw somethin' but there's nowt to worry about, all right?"

"If there's nothing to worry about then why are you so jumpy?" I asked.

"I'm not bein' jumpy. I was just …" He broke off, unsure how to finish his sentence. He rubbed his face with the palms of his hands, removing them only when he was ready to start again. "Right, get back on the bus. I'll meet you there in a couple've minutes, and then we'll —"

"I'm not going back there by myself."

Mr Butch gave me an exasperated look. He opened his arms, gesturing to our surroundings. "There's no one here!"

"Then who are you hoping to find, peering around corners like that?"

"For the love of ..." He barged past me. "Come on! We'll 'ave to continue on foot. I don't see the driver around anywhere."

He couldn't have disappeared, though, I thought, being careful not to say it out loud. I could tell I was beginning to irritate Mr Butch – even more than usual – and I didn't want to wind him up further. Instead, I asked, "How long d'you think it'll take to walk to Brookston?"

"A couple've hours. Maybe less." When we got to the front of the bus, he pointed to the sign that had startled me earlier. "Says there that Brookston's only five miles away. We should make it by nine-ish."

Without another word, he stepped onto the path and started heading towards Brookston with his stupid long strides. He needed no time to prepare.

I jogged to catch up, then felt a familiar chill sweep over me. I didn't know where Danny had been all this time. Had he tried keeping that other spirit away? Maybe he'd gone to get Julie and Melissa? I don't know, but I was sure glad that he was finally here.

CHAPTER SEVENTEEN

"Keep up, will ya?" Mr Butch called back to me.

"I am!"

"No you're not. You're somewhere behind me."

Why don't you slow down then? I thought, jogging to his side again. I was trying not to limp whenever I put too much weight on a split blister. It felt like we'd been walking for hours. There was still a forest of trees either side of the road and the only light we had was the occasional car that sped by, their tail lights fading in the distance as quickly as they had appeared. I didn't know how much longer we had left but pain erupted from my feet with every gammy blister-bursting step I took.

I'd already decided that I couldn't face Cillian tonight. I was shattered and I could barely walk – surely Danny could sense that. Besides, even if Cillian was asleep when I found him, I still had to wake him to record his confession. Julie, Melissa and Danny would help keep me from getting killed, but I only had one shot to get everything I'd need. I didn't feel ready. If I was going to do this right, I needed my wits about me, which meant staying the night to catch up on some sleep.

More money, more lies, I thought.

I hoped Danny would be okay with this; I knew Mr Butch wouldn't.

Eventually, I spotted the soft orangey glow of streetlights up ahead: Brookston. It was an ugly blessing to have finally reached here. Instead of feeling relief, though, my stomach dropped. This was the place where it had all happened.

The forest ended as civilisation began, with parked cars, community noticeboards, and overflowing dustbins outside plain houses. Danny was still with me when we passed the lit-up sign that said "Welcome to Brookston", but his presence couldn't reassure me this time. Everything was starting to feel very real.

"So where does your brother live?" Mr Butch asked.

"On the far side of Brookston. It'll take ages to walk though. At least another hour."

"Can't he bloody come pick us up?"

I bit my lower lip. (*Why couldn't he pick us up?* Because …) "He can't drive," I said. I knew it wasn't enough, so I added, "He's really ill – that's why I'm visiting. But he said he'd put us up at a B&B if we didn't reach his by tonight."

"So he's booked that in advance, has he?"

"Uh ... no. I mean, we need to find one first — and put the charge on his tab."

Mr Butch laughed but he was far from amused. "I don't believe this!" He picked up the pace, making my aching feet want to scream. It was better than him stopping or heading the other way, though. "You're 'avin' me on. I just know it."

"I'm not!" I knew there was nothing I could say to convince him, but silence would sound like defeat. I was so close to reaching that scumbag-Cillian; I just needed one more night. We'd be home by tomorrow afternoon. "You don't understand how important this is. I know you'll never believe me but, I promise, whether you stay with me or not, you'll get your money."

Mr Butch was weighing up everything I'd just said. It was getting late, though, and I guess he must've felt as spent as I did for him not to question me. "You're damn right you'll pay me — I'm not lettin' you out've my sight 'til you do." He shook his head. "What would you do if I left, anyway? Sleep on the streets? Can't get mugged I s'pose. You ain't got a penny to your name!" He grunted, still walking briskly. "Well, come on then. I'm not turnin' down free digs. Bet it'll be pricey at such short notice. Your brother better be rich. Then again, he must be if he can afford to make mistakes like this. *Pft!* Some people just have money to burn ... Don't know they're born … Don't cost nothin' to use your brain … Bloody Brookston …"

Terraced houses with drawn curtains lined the streets, and local shops were dotted few and far between, their shutters down and neon signs turned off. The streetlights made the parked cars on the kerbs look the same dull shade of orangey-grey. It was a pretty ordinary-looking town and I didn't recognise any of the streets. This must have been a residential area rather than the tourist side of Brookston I'd visited. I knew it was only March but there didn't seem to be any room here for the bouncy castles, no massive fields or empty patch of gravel for a mini-funfair, and the grand building of the Brookston Manor Hotel (with its many flags billowing on top) would've looked ridiculous in the middle of all these tiny shops and houses. Sure, the hotel could've been torn down and built over, for all I knew, but there was no moving the sea. Me and Danny had been able to see the beach from our hotel room – I couldn't even smell the sea around here.

Mr Butch continued to rant until we came to what must have been the town square. Maybe hotels and B&Bs would be harder to come by than I thought.

I was just getting used to the idea of sleeping in somebody's doorway when Mr Butch gave my arm a sharp nudge.

"What?" I asked.

"What d'you mean *'What'?*" He pointed to

a detached house on the corner across the road. The front garden was a mess. Weeds were growing through the stone driveway, coiling around a half-filled skip and a row of empty flowerpots, and the hedges were wilder than my nan's frizzy hair ... I bet my dad could've sorted it in a single cider-supplied afternoon. Sellotaped to one of the downstairs windows, though, was a printed sign on A4 paper:

> **Bed & Breakfast**
>
> **Vacancies**
>
> **From £35 a night**

I wasn't getting my hopes up. It could've been an old sign that the landlord forgot to take down. And who was to say they'd put us up at such short notice anyway?

We crossed over and made our way up the drive, stones crunching under our feet. A tiny light came on above the door as we approached the house, revealing paint-chipped wood and a faded brass number 1. There was no doorbell, so Mr Butch gave four solid knocks.

It wasn't difficult to picture the type of person who lived here. The place was probably a drug den, and the sign merely a ploy to fool the police. Even the *Welcome* mat we stood on looked somehow half-eaten. Mum would've had a fit if she'd had to stay in a place like this.

We waited a few seconds but nothing. Mr Butch knocked again. I was starting to think that nobody would answer when, suddenly, the hall light came on inside and we saw a figure in white approach through the textured window in the door.

There was the sound of several locks being undone and then the door opened a couple of inches, restricted by the chain that had yet to be taken off. Even through such a slim gap, I felt the warmth from inside and was struck by the smell of fresh paint.

The person who stood in front of us was nothing like I'd imagined. She was in her late twenties, wearing a white dressing gown and faded grey slippers with a teddy bear printed on them. Her wavy black hair flowed over her shoulders but didn't reach much further. She looked uneasy at the sight of us. Even though Mr Butch had at least tried to clean himself up, he still looked like a man who'd spent a rough night outdoors.

"Hello," she said. "Can I help you?" Her voice was soothing and her tone polite, but there was little doubt she was capable.

"Hi there." Mr Butch cleared his throat and pointed to the sign in the window. "Uh ... it says there you run a B&B. Don't suppose you have any room, do you?"

Her eyes widened with surprise. I was right. She'd forgotten to take down the sign.

"Yes, there's still room," she said, making me eat my words. I had to fight to keep a straight face. Talk about luck. I couldn't believe I'd be sleeping in a bed tonight!

It took her another second to decide to undo the chain on the door. "Is it just the two of you who'll be staying?"

"Yeah. I'm Leslie – this is Jordan." Mr Butch jerked a thumb in my direction before adding, "He's my nephew."

We passed the woman and the glare he gave me told me to keep my mouth shut.

Plastic transparent sheets covered the carpet. It creased beneath our feet, making it impossible to be quiet. Empty paint tins stood by the door and a few unopened rolls of wallpaper lay at the foot of the stairs. The skirting-boards looked freshly painted and the walls were stripped bare, ready to be re-papered.

"Sorry about the mess," she said. "As you can see, we're in the middle of re-decorating." When she'd re-locked the two chains and three bolts, she turned to us and smiled, holding out a hand for us to shake. "I'm Natasha, by the way."

Mr Butch's hand was like a bear paw against hers. When she shook mine, I was surprised by how firm a grip she had.

She led us through the door on our left, into the living room. I decided the room at the end of the hall must have been the kitchen.

Her living room was very minimalist – the complete opposite to mine. It seemed to have a wood and velvet theme, from laminated floorboards and the gas fireplace, to the soft maroon curtains and matching cushions. It gave the place a very sophisticated look.

"If you'd like to take a seat," she said, gesturing to the two settees by the door. They were identical, positioned opposite each other with a glass-topped coffee table between them. Natasha made her way to the other end of the room, passing a bookcase, sagging armchair and a second door that I thought must lead back round to the kitchen. "I won't be a minute," she said, opening the bottom draw of a fairly new-looking oak cabinet. "I just need to sign you in."

Me and Mr Butch sat on the settee against the wall. My legs turned to lead. I sank into the chair, fighting the urge to curl up against the velvet cushions and sleep.

"Do you live here alone?" Mr Butch asked.

"No ..." She pulled the drawer out completely, placing it on the floor to continue rummaging until she found what she was searching for: a thin leather-bound book with tattered edges and bits of paper poking out. "Here we are! You can probably tell it's been a while since we've had guests."

Natasha came back over with it. Taking a seat on the settee opposite us, she and Mr Butch began talking through the booking. Their words washed over me. I could feel my eyelids growing heavier and heavier until a biting chill cut through me. I didn't care what Danny had to say, though. I needed sleep.

I sat up straight, trying to pay attention to

Natasha and Mr Butch. It was no use. Sleep was inevitable when you were as dog-tired as this. I was just beginning to drift off when I saw an elderly woman shuffle into the room through the end door. She was so quiet that I probably wouldn't have noticed if I wasn't looking right at her. Naturally, Natasha and Mr Butch were both oblivious.

She must have been in her seventies, but she acted much older. It was the pain that had aged her; I could see it on her face, in her movements ...

She was about to lower herself into the sagging armchair when she suddenly clutched her chest and started gasping.

Oh God ...

"Guys?" I said, but Mr Butch cut me off with an abrupt 'Sshh!'

The other two hadn't noticed.

They continued talking as though nothing was happening and then the left side of the old woman's face began to fall, like gravity had become stronger on that side.

Oh *shit* ...

The woman wavered on the spot before silently collapsing in a heap. "Nuh ... Nuh-taaash-aaaah!" she called out, her frail voice loud enough to be heard this time. But still nobody acknowledged her.

I went to give Mr Butch a whack on the arm to get his attention when I realised what I was watching. I could see through her, like a hologram. And yeah, she was pale, but it was only now that I noticed just *how* pale: it was the same thing I'd seen outside the pub ...

The old woman wasn't talking anymore. She whimpered. She cried. Her body twitched and flailed. She was having a stroke. And there was nothing I could do to save her because it had already happened.

When she was still, it only took a couple of seconds before she faded away, leaving me, Natasha and Mr Butch alone in the living room. I couldn't move. I couldn't speak. There was no way she was related to Cillian's case, surely? So why the hell was I able to see her?

A few minutes later, she shuffled into the room through the end door again, approached the same sagging chair by the bookcase, and the whole thing started over ...

"Jordan?"

I blinked, turning back to face Mr Butch. He was standing now. They both were. Natasha looked a little concerned, glancing back at the armchair I'd been transfixed by. Mr Butch looked (surprise, surprise) as annoyed as ever, now holding a key with a large metal disc attached to it. I guess it was to make it harder for people to misplace.

"Sorry, I was miles away ..." I muttered, getting to my feet.

"What were you goin' to say?"

"Huh?"

"Earlier. You said somethin'. What did you

wanna say?"

"Oh yeah ..." I'd forgotten that I'd tried to get their attention. I was hardly going to tell them what I'd seen, though. I shrugged. "Can't remember."

Mr Butch sighed but Natasha smiled sympathetically. "You must be tired," she said. "Here, I'll take you to your room."

I followed her over the threshold and immediately felt warmer. I hadn't realised how cold the room had become with that older spirit constantly appearing.

With Natasha in front, the three of us made our way upstairs, the plastic covering crinkling under our feet. "Natasha?" I asked. I was still trying to make sense of what I'd seen. "Who did you say you lived here with?"

"My husband, Ethan" she said.

"Does he always leave you to answer the door at night?" Mr Butch added snidely.

Oblivious to – or touched by – his show of concern, Natasha ignored the negative tone directed at her husband. "To be honest, we rarely get visitors – let alone at this hour. Besides, he has to be up early for work."

"Did anyone else use to live here with you?" I jumped in, before Mr Butch hijacked the conversation.

He frowned at me, but I couldn't help myself.

Natasha nodded. "Yes, actually. This was my mother's house. We moved in with her when she fell ill."

"What happened to her?" I asked, and for that Mr Butch elbowed me hard in the ribs. We'd reached the top of the stairs but none of us moved down the landing.

"It's okay," she reassured him, before turning to me. She swallowed; retelling the story seemed to take her a great deal of effort. I almost felt bad for asking, but my curiosity outweighed whatever guilt I felt. "She had a stroke six months ago, when I was out hanging the washing. It happened so fast. The doctor said there was nothing anyone could have done."

"Oh my God ..." I said.

"I know," Natasha said – but she really didn't. I'd watched her mother die twice only a few minutes ago. I'd seen what Natasha had missed when she was in the garden hanging clothes out to dry ... heard her last words ... saw her final struggle ...

How ...? Why had I seen that?

Natasha cleared her throat and tried to carry on as normal. "Right," she said. "I, uh ... guess I better show you to your room." She pointed out the bathroom as we passed it on the landing and then unlocked the end door with her own copy of the key Mr Butch was still holding.

"It's not much," she admitted, opening the door to the room we'd be staying in. She switched on the light, but it was one of those energy saving bulbs that took a while to brighten. "I haven't started decorating in here yet."

Even in the dimness, the room seemed perfect to me. There were two single beds (which, let's be honest, was all I was really interested in) with matching purple bedspreads. A chunky 90s TV was set on a wooden chair in the corner, a portable antenna balancing on top, with a built-in video player beneath the slightly curved screen. Despite her claiming that nobody had stayed here for some time, there was not a trace of dust in sight.

"It's great," Mr Butch said. He had never been more right. And the smile he gave her was so genuine, so *nice,* I didn't think it suited him.

Before she left, Natasha offered us teas, coffees and biscuits but really all we wanted was sleep. "I'll leave you to get settled in then," she said, with the kind of smile only beautiful women can give. "Goodnight." She closed the door softly behind her.

Mr Butch wasted no time. As soon as the door clicked shut, he clipped the back of my ear.

"*Ow!* What was that for?"

"You're too damn nosey for your own good!" he said, and then made his way over to the bed closest to the window, leaving me with the one in front of the radiator. I was too knackered to take a shower, so I peeled off my muddy clothes to my boxers and climbed into bed. It was like lying on a giant marshmallow. The duvet was thick, the pillows plump. I wrapped the covers around me so that only my eyes and nose were visible, and inhaled slowly, savouring the moment. The sheets smelt of lavender.

I looked over at Mr Butch. He was sitting on the edge of his bed, his large hands cupped, staring at the floor while lost in thought. "You okay, Uncle Leslie?" I mocked.

Mr Butch shot me another glare. I wish I could say I was used to it, but it cut just as deep as the first time, back in his grubby cab. "I had to tell her we were related in *some* way," he said in a low voice. "It'd be a bit weird otherwise, a man like me accompanying some kid."

"True," I said.

He made his way over to the light switch and turned it off. Now all I could see was a strip of light from the landing seeping under the door.

It was dark but I still looked away when I heard the rustling of fabric as Mr Butch took off his jeans and jacket. He asked me about tomorrow while crawling blindly into bed, and then instantly started yammering about "bloody Brookston" again and "people with money to burn". I left him to it, giving in to the blissful oblivion of sleep.

FiVE YEARS EARLiER

It was cloudy but still hot when me and Danny left the hotel. Mum was less worried about letting us go this time, but she still gave us her "Stay On The Beach" lecture and told us to be home again by four.

When we were in the lift, Danny gave me a look. "I want to be home well before then, Jordan."

"I know." I shouldn't have let Lewis borrow Timothy the Tyrannosaurus. It was almost half one. Once we got him back, we could leave whenever we wanted.

The lift *pinged* at ground floor and the doors slid open. It would've been a waste not to race each other across the empty lobby, so that's exactly what we did, skidding on the newly waxed floor, zooming past the fancy engraved front desk and sprinting into the packed car park. Danny won, but only just. When we reached the sandy steps, Lewis and the others were already there, waiting at the bottom like a pack of wolves. They spotted us and Lewis grinned broadly. "What took you so long?"

"We were finishing our lunch," I said, climbing down to join them.

"Fair dos." He dug around in his frayed denim shorts pocket and pulled out the Tyrannosaurus figurine.

Mission accomplished, I thought as he tossed the plastic toy over to me. Now all we had to do was wait for an opportunity to leave.

"Cheers, Jordan," Lewis said. "My sister's *obsessed* with those giant lizards!" Then he turned to Ben and indicated Danny. Ben was holding an unopened packet of Haribo. On Lewis's order, he threw the sweets over to Danny, who caught the packet with ease and a look of puzzlement.

"They're yours," Lewis said to him. "Sorry about your leg. Is it any better?"

Even though Danny wasn't limping, I knew he was still annoyed about it.

He nodded anyway. "Yeah ... Thanks."

I didn't know how long it would take for either of them to drop in a snide remark, so I cleared my throat and changed the subject. "What are we playing?" I asked. They didn't have their football with them today.

"I was thinking hide-and-seek in the old woods. It's not too far from here. Only about a twenty-minute walk. You guys up for it?"

I turned to Danny.

"What?" Lewis said, seeing the hesitant look on our faces. To them, going to the woods was no big deal.

"Our mum told us to stay on the beach," Danny said, not seeing me cringe. He seemed glad of the excuse to turn Lewis down, but I knew how lame it must've sounded to them guys.

Lewis just laughed. "And my mum told me I was grounded this morning. Jordan, what d'you say? Wanna come with?"

Everyone turned to me. I swallowed. "Why don't we play football instead?"

Lewis crossed his arms. "We played football *yesterday.* Come on, it's not like your mum's gonna find out."

He had a point. As long as we were back on time, she and Dad would never know the difference.

I could feel Danny looking at me, trying to warn me against what I was about to agree to. The way I saw it, though, was if we played hide-and-seek for an hour or so, Lewis wouldn't care if we left early.

"I guess we could play ..." I said.

Danny gave a quiet sigh next to me. I promised myself that I'd give him my dessert this evening to make it up to him.

Putting an arm around my shoulders, Lewis began leading us back up the concrete steps. My chest tightened with the fear of being caught. All Mum or Dad had to do was peer out our bedroom window. It was only when we passed the hotel and started heading down Brookside Street, blending into the crowds outside shops, restaurants and arcades, that the suffocating feeling went away.

We went left at the end of the street, onto an empty old road. There was no pavement and the white divider line had all but faded on the cracked tarmac. Overgrown hedges filled with thorns and berries grew either side of us, blocking the many miles of farmers' fields.

The busy sounds of Brookside Street gradually faded to countryside silence beneath Lewis and his mates' joking and laughter. It was kinda nice to listen to; it distracted me from looking over my shoulder every ten steps.

Eventually, the forest came into view: a towering thicket of trees sectioned off by a tall chain-link fence that seemed to go on forever in both directions. As we got closer, I saw that it was set behind a steep ditch in which a thin stream trickled at the bottom, turning the mud thick and gooey. I scanned up and down the fence; there didn't seem to be an opening. I hoped we didn't have to climb it.

"Are you sure we're allowed in there?" I said, trying to make it sound like it was no big deal. There were no signs telling us to stay out, but fences were put up for a reason – especially giant ones with no gates.

Nobody answered. I didn't ask again.

The nine of us stopped at the ditch. Danny looked just as moody as I thought he would.

"Follow me," Lewis said, and leapt across. He pulled back some of the chain-link fence and squeezed through to the other side. I didn't know who had cut it or when it was done but I had a feeling it'd been like this for a while now. It wasn't difficult to picture Lewis as the culprit.

A couple of the others – Mike and Sophie – followed him, jumping across like pros. They'd clearly all done this before. When they began inching through the gap, the others got ready to join them. There wasn't much room between the bank and the fence on the other side, so we had to wait for each person to squeeze through.

Once Ben had jumped, I knew it was our turn.

"We should make a run for it back to the hotel," Danny whispered so only I could hear.

Now Ben had squeezed through the gap and all eyes were on us.

"What are you waiting for?" Lewis called out.

If we went home now, Mum and Dad would wonder why we'd left early, and I didn't want to raise their suspicions. I already felt guilty for coming here. Besides, we still had another six days in Brookston – what if we ran into Lewis after we'd ditched them? He was bound to say something to us. He might even tell Mum where we'd been, since he knew we weren't supposed to have come here.

I whispered a quick apology to Danny before leaping across the gully. I stumbled a little, but managed. I didn't need to check if Danny was still behind me.

Lewis held the fence open for us as we squeezed inside. Specks of rust were visible at the exposed ends. I'd never done anything like this before.

CHAPTER EIGHTEEN
FRIDAY - PRESENT DAY

It was early morning, at least a couple hours before sunrise. I couldn't lie in bed knowing my brother's killer was so close. He needed to be taught a lesson, to die painfully at my hands; every second that passed was a second he was getting away with what he'd done. I didn't wake Mr Butch because I knew he'd try to stop me, so I left Natasha's house alone.

Outside was dark and bitter cold. I zipped my jacket up to my neck and walked with measured strides; the faster I got there, the faster this was over. My footsteps echoed and the wind howled around every corner. Aside from stray cats and hooting owls, the village was deserted. Everyone was still in bed, their alarms set to go off for work in maybe an hour or two, but for now they were warm, safe, and oblivious of me.

Or so I thought.

Something moved in the shadows across the road.

I turned to look, thinking it may just be a street cat. Instead, I spotted the silhouette of a tall, hooded figure that actually reminded me a lot of Slenderman, leaning against the side of a semi-detached house. God knows what he was doing but it made the hairs on the back of my neck stand on end.

I tried to appear casual, like I was used to walking the streets at this time. I picked up the pace a little and went down the first street I came across. Only then could I begin to relax. What a creep.

I glanced over my shoulder to check that nobody was around …

And there he was, standing across the road beneath a streetlight with a flickering bulb. It was easier to see details now. He wore a long trench coat that fell to the ankles of his thick work boots. His hood was up and his hands were buried deep in his pockets. Was he following me?

My body felt hot and cold at the same time. I hoped I was overreacting, but my gut was telling me otherwise. I wished I'd woken Mr Butch.

Turning down another street, I set into a sprint until I rounded a second bend, giving the man the slip. I tried to stifle my heavy breathing as I peered around the wall to check if I'd been followed.

I hadn't.

Letting out a quiet sigh, I turned back to continue my journey and …

He was in front of me.

It was definitely the same man. He was under another streetlight only this time he was on my side of the road, the orange-grey beam shining a spotlight down on his dull figure.

Shit. *Was he stalking me?*

I crossed over. It was too dark to tell if he was watching me but he didn't move. At least, not until I'd passed him on the other side of the street. That was when I heard footsteps. *His* footsteps.

I quickened my pace and he quickened his. I broke into another run and so did he.

Adrenaline pumped through my veins as I sprinted down street after street. There was no way I'd be able to find my way back to Natasha's place now. I shouldn't have left the house. I should've waited until daylight. I should've brought Mr Butch along.

Behind me I could hear the *thud-thud-thud* of someone chasing me, and then, suddenly, suspiciously ... nothing. I didn't stop to check what had happened; I just kept running, going down streets I'd never seen until I could run no more.

I stumbled around another corner and then I had to stop. My heart was pounding so hard it was making me feel sick. I leaned over, my hands resting on my knees as I tried to regulate my breathing. I listened carefully and even though the footsteps never returned, it still took me a moment to muster the courage to check around the corner. Luckily, the man was nowhere to be seen. Thank frickin' God: I was alone again.

When I faced forward, my heart practically leapt out of my chest. He was there: under another streetlight on the other side of the one-way street. He was directly opposite me now, the closest he'd been. His face was hidden in the shadow of his hood but I could feel him staring me down.

How did he get there without me noticing?

His coat swayed in the wind that ruffled my hair and made the town creak. No matter where I ran, I knew he'd find me.

He took a step closer. I somehow managed to back into the wall behind me but my legs wouldn't listen to the simple command my brain was screaming: *Run, you idiot! He's going to kill you! RUN!*

I had nowhere to escape to, though. The streets behind me had disappeared and two brick walls had suddenly appeared either side of me, boxing me in. They were too high to climb so all I could do was watch the man in the trench coat advance on me.

Everything was silent; even the howling wind seemed to have died down. There was only me and the man in this moment together.

He was on my side of the road now. "You look like him." His voice came out as a hoarse whisper.

Who? I wanted to ask, but I was too afraid to speak.

"Do you want to be with him?" he continued.

My body was shaking uncontrollably. I opened

my mouth, but the words didn't come easy. "Wh-who do I w-want to be with?"

He stopped in front of me. His warm, liquorice-smelling breath made my skin crawl. "Your brother!" he said, no trace of a whisper left in his scratchy voice. He pulled down his hood to reveal the hideous face of a man I didn't recognise. A scar like Mr Butch's ran down his left cheek, his hair looked like it was falling out in clumps and his mouth was twisted, lopsided, with a set of mangled teeth that reminded me of a rabid dog. I'd never met this man and yet I knew exactly who he was. He was a different version of the man I'd pictured with Melissa.

Cillian O'Hagan.

I wanted to run but my legs gave way, making me crumple to the ground. I then found myself sprawled on dry mud and grass instead of the concrete I'd been standing on moments before. Nothing made sense anymore.

I stared up at Cillian. The buildings and three high walls boxing me in had vanished. In their place, trees had appeared all around us and I could hear rushing water behind me.

"Accept it, Jordan," he said. Stooping down, he grabbed the front of my jacket and pulled me towards him. "Accept it like your brother did."

"No ..." My hands were a lot smaller now as I struggled against him. "NO!"

Everything looked bigger somehow: the molehills, pinecones, tree trunks, boulders ... and the low-hanging branches were now out of reach. It took me a while to realise that the world hadn't grown; I was just smaller: I'd shrunk to the size of a child.

"Accept it!" Cillian hissed a third time. He dragged me away, my feet scuffing the ground as I tried to resist, until the sound of rushing water filled my ears and I could hear nothing else. I knew what was about to happen next …

I thrashed and screamed louder than I'd ever screamed before. My body was finally responding. I dug my nails into his arms, thrust my head into him and kicked out for all I was worth. None of it had any effect on him …

He forced my head close to the fast-running stream, and then I was under.

Lungs burning. I couldn't breathe.

He brought my head up for maybe a second and I spluttered, choking. Then I was pushed under again.

I needed air.

He held me under longer this time – long enough for me to feel myself slipping into darkness. Then, when I'd given up all hope of escaping, he heaved me out the water again. As he turned me around to face him, I knew this was the end.

Just do it, I thought. *Just get it over with.*

"Accept it, Jordan," he said again, grabbing my arms and shaking me.

I have!

"Accept it! Are you listenin'?" More shaking.

"Look at me, kid. Jordan? *Jordan!* Wake up —"

My eyes snapped open.

For a moment I thought I was still staring at Cillian, but as I took in the rest of the room, lit by the dim bedside lamp, I realised it was actually Mr Butch. It was Mr Butch who was gripping my arms, who had been shaking me awake.

"You were dreamin'," Mr Butch said, quietly, so that he didn't disturb Natasha or her husband.

I sat upright, catching my breath. I tried to focus on something, *anything,* that wasn't to do with the nightmare I'd just had, but my mind kept flashing back to my invented Cillian's grotesque face.

Was that how Danny had felt? That raw feeling of panic, fear, desperation … Was that what he'd felt in his final moments before death? Or could it have been way, *way* worse?

My mouth was dry and it took an effort not to vomit.

The covers were damp from cold sweat and my vision was blurred with tears.

"Are you okay?" Mr Butch was still looking at me but I couldn't meet his eyes. I nodded anyway. Then he asked if I'd like to talk about it, and to that I shook my head. I was afraid that I'd break down if I opened my mouth.

Mr Butch understood. He gave my shoulder a firm squeeze that I wished could've given me the strength to pull myself together. It was nothing, though, just a touch. Danny was still dead and I hadn't saved him.

I balled my hands into tight fists under the covers so Mr Butch couldn't see. I needed to be left alone and that's exactly what I told him, in a cracked voice that should've embarrassed me.

I was used to taunts from kids and prying questions from Dr Ashton, so I was taken aback when Mr Butch stood silently and headed back to bed. He must've been confused, maybe even a little concerned, but he knew enough to know not to go on at me.

He climbed into bed, facing the other way to give me some privacy. "Wake me if you need me," he said, as an obvious last-ditch thought.

I couldn't have replied even if I'd wanted to. My jaw was quivering so much – I was just concentrating on keeping my teeth from chattering. I switched off the lamp and rolled onto my side, facing the wall to hide the tears that were now rolling down my cheeks and wetting my already damp pillow. I let the dull ache in my stomach eat away at me. I deserved this pain. Like that feeling at the hotel – when I heard Dad come home without Danny, and Mum fall to pieces – it was suffocating.

I stuffed the corner of the duvet in my mouth to try and stifle whatever pathetic noises escaped me. I don't know how long I lay there like that, but I remember at some point Mr Butch started snoring. Sunlight eventually bled through the curtains, and then I heard movement in another room upstairs –

Natasha's husband getting ready for work.

By the time he left the house, I figured there was no hope of me falling back to sleep.

There was shuffling from that same room as Natasha got ready herself. I waited for her to go downstairs before pulling back the covers and heading to the bathroom.

CHAPTER NINETEEN

I showered quickly but savoured the feeling of the hot water and soap running down my body. It loosened my stiff muscles for the first time since sleeping in that den. I'd already scrubbed the dirt from my clothes, leaving them on the radiator to dry, but when it came to putting them back on, everything was still drenched. I looked in the mirror. Even with the cold fabric clinging to my skin I felt more myself again.

I unlocked the door and headed to the bedroom. Mr Butch was still fast asleep – on his back, mouth open, snoring loudly. It was time to make a move.

There was a cheap A5 notebook on my bedside table. I took it and found three ballpoint pens tucked away in the drawer beneath it.

My arm turned cold and I felt a pressure around my wrist. Danny was trying to pull me away.

"Hold on," I muttered to him. My chest was so

tight with nerves.

I grabbed one of the pens, clicking the top of it. Although I felt safer travelling with Mr Butch, it would be better if I did this part alone. Mr Butch would only slow me down. It was hard enough leading him to Saint Edwards Ruins, Charbonville and this B&B in Brookston; he'd never follow me into some stranger's house and there was no way he'd believe that Cillian was a murderer – especially since I'd lost all his trust. What kind of protection would he offer then? No, I'd go out, do what I had to do, and then come back for him – before he hunted me down for the money I owed him.

So, despite the warning I'd been given in my dream, I turned back the cover of the notebook and scrawled:

Popped out for some air.

Be back by noon.

– Jordan

Being careful not to wake him, I placed the note on Mr Butch's bedside table and left the room. Danny was buzzing, his energy level higher than usual.

I made my way downstairs, the plastic sheet crinkling under my feet. It was a wonder nobody heard me.

The muffled tune of BBC Breakfast was just

starting up as I reached the final step. I tried listening out for Natasha. It sounded like she was in the kitchen; the kettle was boiling, and crockery clinked as though she was making breakfast or putting away clean dishes.

I peered around the banister; the kitchen door was closed. I wasted no time in heading to the front door. Turning the latch, I pulled down the handle and stepped outside, silently locking myself out.

The street was quiet and a lot less scary now that I could see everything for what it was instead of as distorted silhouettes. I switched my focus back to Danny, letting him guide me again.

We cut through a small park and then he led me around the back of a church with scaffolding above the entrance. As I passed by, a feeling of sadness swept over me – or was it longing? – like I could feel the many years of mourning that'd taken place here. It was weird, but the sensation soon passed when we were off the church grounds.

I walked down an alley that passed the back of a primary school before coming out the other side onto a clipped-grass, tidy-hedged neighbourhood. I quickened my pace, still following my brother's pull until, a few turns later, Danny grew colder. Much colder. We were there.

I didn't know what I was expecting Cillian's house to look like. Old? Isolated? Creepy? None of that was the case. Instead, I was staring up at a tiny terraced house in the middle of a street of narrow houses with net curtains and stone bird baths.

I opened the low picket fence gate to Cillian's front garden and made a point of not closing it behind me. The garden was well-kept; tiny wisps of green were poking out of the flowerbed. It would've been easy to forget that this house was home to a monster. Before I knocked on his front door, I snuffed out his plants.

"Okay," I said. Goosebumps ran along my arms. I clenched my fists, took a deep breath and straightened up to my full height. Danny was by my side. "Let's do this."

There was no doorbell or knocker, so I rapped on the pane of glass set in the front door, loud enough for it to echo around the street.

The noise immediately set off several dogs inside. At least three of them had rushed to the door barking, their shapes distorted in the frosted glass. The sight of them made me take a step back. Usually I didn't mind dogs, but these were over waist high and had a bark that sounded deeper than Mr Butch. That's when I spotted a sign in the living room window: **Beware – Irish Wolfhounds.**

There was no point in knocking again. The dogs would draw Cillian's attention.

I waited as long as it took me to realise nobody was home, and then cursed under my breath. I'd been through too much to have it all count for nothing. If Cillian wasn't home, I'd just have to poke around and find some evidence in the meantime. In fact, I may even be able to find something to record his confession. Now that I thought about it, this was actually turning out to be pretty convenient. I'd confront Cillian when he came back, far more prepared than I would've been.

"Danny?" I said quietly. "Can you get me inside?" I'd never broken into anywhere before. Not like this, anyway. My palms were moist, and my hands were shaking.

I heard the lock turn from the other side – Danny never failed to impress me.

The dogs' barking changed to a low, menacing growl. The thought of their bared teeth would've been enough to stop me going in, but through the window I saw them backing away. They could sense Danny. Now it was all up to me.

I glanced around just to make certain nobody was watching. The street was silent and empty. I pushed the door open, and the growling immediately changed to whining.

Here goes, I thought, and walked in.

Three pairs of dopey brown eyes stared back at me from behind long hanks of wiry fur. They had shaggy brindle coats and their long tails curled at the end just before touching the floor. They were as big as Shetland ponies – easily over half my height. I was expecting to get mauled or trampled on at the very least, but they were keeping their distance. I closed the door behind me and made my way into the first room I came across. The dogs moved aside and followed me through, still whining.

As soon as I stepped into the living room, I was greeted by the foul, unmistakable smell of dog shit. It was frickin' rank. I watched my step as I crossed the room, but I didn't see any turds.

I could deal with the stench for now – the house was small so it wouldn't take me long to search the place – but the three crying Wolfhounds were impossible to ignore.

"Shut up!" I hissed. This only seemed to make them whine louder, though. I couldn't search the house with them trailing at my heels and making such a racket.

Their silver, bone-shaped tags jingled against the metal tips of their collars. I managed to catch an engraved name on one of them: "Kasper." I held out my hand without needing to stoop down to reach him. I figured that if they were going to attack, they would've done it already.

Kasper backed away, pushing past his two brothers. The direct approach was clearly not an option. I made another plan.

I knew they'd follow me, so I made my way to the only other door, currently ajar. I could see through the gap that it led to the kitchen. If I could just shut them in there, I'd be free to search the rest of the house alone.

When I nudged the door open fully, though, I was hit by a wall of absolute stench, far stronger than what I'd smelt in the living room. I covered my nose with my jacket sleeve and almost gagged. The tiled floor was glistening with a layer of urine, and huge dollops of crap were spread everywhere.

The three dogs stood behind me. Their whines were lessening but it suddenly occurred to me that they might not have been let out in days. Cillian must not have been home for some time – and their filthy empty dog bowls, fastened in raised stands, only confirmed this. What made Danny think he'd be back today?

I waded through the kitchen, trying to step over the worst of the mess, until I reached the back door. The key was already in the lock, so it was just a matter of turning it and flinging the door open. I moved aside as all three dogs bounded out of the house and into the garden, and then I headed back into the living room. I closed the kitchen door behind me, keeping the foul smell and three Wolfhounds away from me.

"This is ridiculous," I said, rubbing my forehead. The lack of sleep had finally caught up with me. "When's he coming back?"

Danny gave me a light shove in the back – it felt like an ice cube being wedged into my spine.

"What? I don't know what you want from me!" I turned to face him and spotted letters on the coffee table addressed to *Cillian Iollan O'Hagan*. I definitely had the right house. We were just too late. "We've missed him, Danny. Help me find some evidence so I can at least involve the police. Maybe they'll have more luck tracking him down." I'd wanted to confront him myself … but if that was no longer an option, I at least wanted him to rot behind bars.

Danny pulled my arm, his grip freezing as always.

I sighed, letting him drag me through the living room, along the hall and to the stairs. Framed photographs lined the pale green walls along the staircase. I looked at them all in turn as I made my way up: a man outside some museum; the same man in an open field with the three dogs I'd just let outside; him dressed in overalls in a sunny garden, holding a battered watering can with soil on his hands and kneecaps … As I reached the final photo at the top of the stairs it dawned on me that the happy, balding man in all these photographs must have been Cillian.

"Hold on," I said, pulling my arm free.

I swallowed. My tongue felt thick and I had to hold onto the banister rail to keep myself from falling backwards. It was him. The man who killed my brother.

I stood on the final step, staring at the last picture on the wall. It was winter in this photograph but the people in it didn't look cold, with their wide grins and woolly hats. I found it weird, seeing him with his family. I'd always figured he'd spawned from Hell. I didn't take any interest in the others around him, though; I was drawn to Cillian, standing in the middle of the group with his arm around a beaming young girl's shoulders.

It was the first time I'd ever seen him. Now I finally had an image to go with his name. He looked nothing like the monster in my dream last night. The real Cillian was an average height with a lean build and round face. He was clean-shaven (or at least, he was at the time these photographs were taken) and looked somewhere in his early thirties. He seemed ... *ordinary.* It was the smile that got me, though. His thin lips were stretched wide, revealing a set of coffee-stained teeth. You could even see it in his bluish-grey eyes: he was happy.

My body stiffened. He had *no right* to be happy. If he wanted to run away, so be it. I'd find a way to prove what he'd done and then make him pay. Even if the police found him first, I'd be there on the court date. As long as he saw me ... As long as Danny got to take his revenge ... My brother could stop his heart or make him choke as easy as bursting a taxicab's tyre. We just needed to find out where he was.

Danny began tugging my arm again.

"I'm coming," I said. There was nothing else to see anyway.

As we headed across the landing, a chill raced up my spine. It was so abrupt that it made me stop in my tracks. "Are you okay?" I whispered to Danny. But it wasn't my brother. I didn't know *who* I'd just sensed.

I was about to take another step when I heard

children laughing from one of the rooms upstairs.

"Um ... Danny? Who else is up here?"

He was leading me towards the sound.

My legs wouldn't respond straightaway and it was difficult to keep my breathing in check. I knew they weren't actual kids; they were ghosts ... spirits ...

Heart hammering, I followed Danny's pull towards the very door I was hoping to avoid – the one I could now hear snippets of conversation coming from.

I placed my hand on the door-handle. "Promise you won't leave me."

It was Danny who pushed my hand down, opening the door. I could still feel his presence by my side as I entered the room.

CHAPTER TWENTY

The voices stopped as soon as I entered. I scanned the narrow room: broken, outdated junk was piled high either side of me, but there was nobody here.

Weird.

I let the door swing closed behind me – I didn't want to risk moving something to prop it open in case the whole lot came crashing down.

This room was much colder than the rest of the house and smelt of rotting wood. The place needed a proper clean and airing out. Black mould was growing on the ceiling and around the window, with paintings, video cassette tapes and vinyl records stacked in front of the worst of it.

There was a sort of pathway through the mess that led from the door to the window. I made my way along it, unsettling dust that had quite possibly been undisturbed for years. As well as the ugly fur growing on the walls, I figured the smell was heightened by the antiques that were dotted around the room. I spotted an actual typewriter on the floor, with a few discoloured sheets of paper wedged in the top, and a rotary phone with wires poking out of the end of the cable, balancing on a stack of tattered books. A lamp without a shade lay on its side by a faded floral armchair. The armchair, I noticed, had a spring poking out of the sunken seat, and a clock I couldn't see was ticking somewhere to my left.

Now that I was further in, I could feel a draught from the window. There were no curtains or blinds and the metal frames had been painted over with gloss, sealing them shut.

Through the cloudy glass I could see all three Wolfhounds in the garden, sniffing plants and plodding along with their big heavy paws. The kitchen door had closed but none of them seemed to have noticed.

Like the front of the house, every plant, stone and slab seemed to have been positioned with great care. There was a gap in the line of small trees along the back fence, leaving access to a gate that led onto an overgrown playing field. That must've been where Cillian walked his dogs – before he disappeared.

I wasn't sure why Danny had led me here. Maybe he knew there was a phone, or even a camcorder, hidden somewhere in all this junk?

I turned away to start my search – and then I saw them: three ghost children stood side by side in front of the closed door. Two boys and a girl, pale and translucent, their colour desaturated. Again, they looked similar ages to Danny, the boy in the middle maybe slightly younger. They were watching me. I should've known the cold was something more than a draught.

The older boy at the end smiled but it didn't reach his eyes. He was slightly overweight and had short, curly hair. He'd been an ordinary kid, one that used to find humour in everything, I bet. "Danny said you'd come," he said.

All I could do was nod. At least this time I didn't feel the urge to run away, and not just because they were standing in front of my only exit.

"Don't be scared," the girl said, as if it was that simple. She had curly hair too, only hers reached past her shoulders. "We can help you. Just be our voice and we'll protect you from Cillian."

"What do you mean?" I asked. "Are you going to possess me or something?"

"No, nothing like that. None of us have the strength to possess anyone anyway. I just mean you have to tell people what happened to us and where we are. Nobody knows we're here."

The penny dropped. And honestly, I don't know why it'd taken me so long to figure it out: "You three were murdered by Cillian." It wasn't a question. I already knew. As if killing Danny, Julie and Melissa wasn't monstrous enough ... the guy was definitely a psychopath. "What are your names?"

"I'm Emily Porter," the girl said.

"I'm Aaron Boid," said the overweight boy at the end. He gestured to the small, thin kid in the middle. "And that's Brett Miller."

I looked at the three of them – I mean *really* looked – and felt that same vice-like clutch around my stomach that I'd had when Julie wore that lifeless expression, and when Melissa slammed her head into the gravestone ... I didn't know any of these kids personally, but that didn't matter. They all had families they'd been torn from; loved ones they'd give anything to be with again.

It made me mad because Cillian's actions were so ... *unnecessary*. He was just an evil bastard who'd given himself the right to determine when their time was up; a psychopath who decided they had no worth. If only the victims left their houses a minute later, or didn't wander away from their parents, or stayed at the hotel instead of going to the beach – if only, if only, if only – maybe they'd still be alive. Knowing my brother's death could've been avoided, *that* was what gnawed away at me every night. Because it was my fault Danny was in the forest where Cillian was lurking that day.

"Don't worry," I told them. "I'm going to find that scumbag and make him suffer. I'll avenge all of you. And with your help we can really do some damage. We'll completely mess him up! Mark my words, he's going to regret what he's done."

I had to clench my fists to stop them shaking so

noticeably. I wanted to hit something, but I knew it wouldn't get rid of the hatred burning inside me.

The three ghost children stared back at me. They looked shocked, maybe even worried ...

Aaron glanced at his feet. "None of us want revenge," he said.

I screwed up my face. "What d'you mean? The man *killed* you. Surely you don't think he should get away with it. That's *insane!*"

"We're tired," Emily said. "We just want closure. The same goes for Danny."

Well, I knew that last part was a blatant lie. And what the hell did she know about my brother anyway? "Look, maybe you lot don't want to get back at Cillian, but Danny does, all right? He told me so five years ago."

"But Danny doesn't speak to you like we can. He takes on a different form that uses less energy so he can stay with you longer."

Was that really how it worked?

"I know he doesn't *talk* to me!" I cut in. "But he gives me signs, and he didn't object in any way when I promised I'd make Cillian pay. In fact, he's seemed pretty eager about it these past few days."

Emily shook her head. "He wants you and your mum and dad to know the truth. More than anything, though ... he just wants you to be safe. That's all. He doesn't want –"

"That scum murdered my brother! I'm not letting him walk out of this house alive!"

"You're the one who wants revenge."

"We *both* do. So what? We're twins, we think the same about everything!" Of course that wasn't true – we disagreed loads – but right now I was so pissed off and just wanted them to shut up.

Emily got the hint and backed away. Aaron, on the other hand, wasn't giving in so easily. "You don't know why Danny came back, do you?" he said.

For some reason those words stung me. How *dare* he make out I didn't know my own brother.

I gritted my teeth. "Course I do. I know him better than anyone. We're really close and –"

Aaron crossed his arms, like he felt important or something. "What you and Danny have isn't special. Everyone's close to someone. Danny came back because he knew you blamed yourself. He was afraid you were going to get yourself killed trying to find the person who did it."

I wasn't buying it. "If he didn't want revenge, why didn't he spell it out like he did with everything else?" Let's face it, I gave him more than enough chances with the Scrabble pieces and my laptop before I left the house.

"Maybe because he knew you'd react like this," Aaron said; and I didn't care how old they were. I swore.

Danny yanked the hood of my jacket up over my head. He wanted me to shut up and listen; to follow his orders, as always.

"*You* can pack it in for a start!" I hissed at

Danny, wherever he was in the room. I pulled down my hood and went to start a whole new rant when I noticed the silent boy in the middle was crying.

And that was it for me. How could I go on when he was already so upset?

I took a deep breath and let it out slowly through my nose. I wasn't the only victim here, I reminded myself, and I certainly wasn't the only one who had suffered a loss.

"My mummy and daddy don't know where I am," he sobbed.

I moved closer and knelt in front of Brett. When I reached out my hand, it passed through him and my fingers tingled, like he was a cold projection.

"The police never found our bodies," Aaron said. "Cillian kidnapped us and then he strangled us in this room."

Emily stepped forward, finding the courage to speak to me again now that my mood had changed. "Aaron was the first one."

I swallowed. "You, um … you saw him do it?"

She shook her head and the relief I felt was insane. That would've been such a barbaric, messed-up thing to witness. "None of us met when we were alive. He killed me in May 2019, Brett in August 2016, and Aaron in June 2014."

I thought back to those agonising three days when Danny was missing, before we knew he was dead. I couldn't eat, couldn't sleep … I could barely function at all. It affected me mentally and physically, but it was the "not knowing" part that really screwed with my head. Not knowing if he was hurt or lost or being tortured, if he was begging us to find him … Not knowing if it was too late to save him. During that time, I couldn't help picturing all kinds of evil things – for years, the families of these three children had lived with those tormenting thoughts.

"Where did he hide your bodies?" I asked, finally understanding why closure meant so much more to them than revenge. Aside from Cillian, I was about to become the only living person to know the truth.

"I'm buried next to the big tree in the back garden," Emily said.

"I'm under the rose bed," Aaron said. "And Brett is under the patio."

Now I knew why Cillian put so much effort into his garden. Even if he enjoyed pulling up weeds and planting seeds, nobody would suspect three dead bodies to be buried beneath such a well-kept garden.

I felt the beginning of another migraine. There was just one thing I didn't understand, something Danny refused to tell me but maybe these ghost kids would:

"Why now?" I asked. "Danny was killed five years ago. Why's he waited so long to tell me?" I could have reported Cillian years ago and stopped him from killing anyone else. It made my skin crawl to think what this room had been used for only one year ago.

"He hasn't told you?" Aaron asked.

"Told me what?" The twinge at the back of my head was quickly turning into a dull ache.

The three of them exchanged looks, as though silently nominating one of them to speak. In the end it was Emily who told me the truth, and in two simple words: "Cillian's dead."

Everything stopped: my headache, the breath I was inhaling; even the ticking of the hidden clock seemed to have been silenced. "Cillian is … *dead?*"

She nodded. "He died three days ago."

I looked at them all in turn, but their expressions never faltered. Just like that, Cillian was …

"What the hell am I doing here then?" I got to my feet, staring around the room in search of Danny. "I wanted him to suffer – you *knew* that! You sent me on this quest the moment he was dead!"

"You don't understand –" Emily tried to intervene.

"Don't I?" The three of them backed away, as though I'd just set fire to a stack of Cillian's old books. "The man … *monster* … I hate most in the *entire* world … I don't get a confession, I don't get to see him hate me in return, I don't even get to break a single bone in his worthless body … There's been no *point* in this trip! No point at all! So thanks a lot, Danny. Thanks a frickin' bunch. You had no intention of giving me what I wanted. And all the sneaking around this house, the build-up, the whole friggin' *trip* … You just let me worry and fear a man who's already dead!" The three ghost children had disappeared and the dogs outside were barking madly at the yelling they couldn't get to. "You've outdone yourself this time, Danny," I continued. "You really bloody have –"

Ping!

I jumped at the sound. It was short and shrill, kind of like an egg timer.

Behind me, I spotted the old typewriter, now with a single sentence printed on its yellowed paper. I was surprised the ink hadn't dried up over the years.

I knew the writing had come from Danny. I considered ignoring him but that feeling didn't last long. I sat on the dusty carpet in front of the typewriter and read his message:

```
Cillian is dead but he isn't gone
```

"What does that even mean?"

I figured it out as soon as I asked. If Danny was dead but could still communicate with me – if *any* of Cillian's victims, and others, could get through to me – why couldn't he do the same? "Cillian must be a spirit, like you."

Keys were jabbed down and then the typewriter *ping*-ed again as the paper carriage was set back to the start of the next line, completing a second sentence:

```
Not like me
```

"You know what I mean." But how could I make him pay if he was already dead? "All right, Danny, no more cross-country. I'm in Brookston, Mr Butch isn't with us ... Where do I go from here and what do I do?"

Go to Brookston Juniore Orfunage ruins. Talk to April.

I rubbed my face with my hands. More talking. "Is April another victim?"

I never did find out who she was.

No. She's the one who started it all.

Vague much. "So ... I'm guessing I need to be April's voice too? Pass on her messages and all that."

Yes. You need to bring them together but Cillian can't see her.

I sighed. That seemed to be all I was doing; bringing everyone together. Why did they have to latch onto *me* in order to leave the places they were murdered? No wonder Danny didn't tell me where I was going from the start. I was collecting spirits on my hike across Devon. The whole thing was frickin' insane.

Before I asked anything else, I needed to make

sense of what I already knew. I took the sheet of paper Danny had been typing on and told him to write out a list of Cillian's victims, in order, on the fresh piece of paper behind it.

He immediately started typing. Within minutes, I had the basics in front of me:

```
2013 April O'Hagan: Brookston Juniore
Orfunage Ruins

2013 Grant Luther: Brookston Juniore
Orfunage Ruins

2014 Aaron Boid: Cillian's house

2015 Me: Brookston Forest

2016 Brett Miller: Cillian's house

2017 Melissa Cundille: Brookston Cemitree

2018 Julie Davis: Saint Edwards Castle ruins

2019 Emily Porter: Cillian's house

2020 ...
```

I picked up the sheet of paper. Since 2013, Cillian had murdered at least one child a year. He didn't target a specific gender, but they all seemed to be around the same age. There was only one other victim I hadn't yet come across – Grant Luther. I had a feeling I'd be seeing him when I met April.

There was no name written beside this year, but since Danny had left it open it could only mean one thing: he suspected he might kill again. After all, if Cillian really was a spirit, what was stopping him? Was *I* supposed to stop him? I didn't know any mediums and I wasn't a priest – is that why I needed help from the other ghost children? They needed closure and I needed protection. A *lot* of protection. I didn't know what Cillian was capable of now. A couple of days ago, I'd never sensed a spirit that wasn't Danny – now I was going up against some evil entity …

One thing that baffled me, though, was the surname, "O'Hagan", on the top of the sheet. "Are Cillian and April related –?"

I jumped at the sound of those damn dogs again. Danny didn't get a chance to reply. They were barking and scratching frantically at the kitchen door, trying to get inside. I didn't know why they were so desperate to get back in. Then I heard a noise that made my heart skip a beat.

The latch downstairs clicked as the front door closed.

Someone was in the house.

CHAPTER TWENTY ONE

I held my breath, listening out for movement. This was far more terrifying than meeting any ghost. Spirits could disappear; people couldn't – and I wasn't supposed to be here. Would the person who'd just walked in batter me for trespassing?

I heard slow footsteps traipse through to the living room, and then … "Cillian?"

It was a man. He had a deep, somewhat strained voice with a slight Irish accent. He called out again. "Hello? You home?" Whoever this man was, he didn't know Cillian was dead.

I was tempted to stay hidden in the spare room. If he was looking for Cillian, though, I knew he'd end up searching every room. I couldn't let myself get cornered.

The man made a noise from the kitchen – he'd found the mess – and then he opened the back door to let the dogs in. I heard the scampering of their heavy feet as the three Wolfhounds rushed inside to greet him, their claws tapping against the tiled floor, their long, wagging tails whipping against the cupboards. They seemed happy to see him, whoever he was.

This was probably going to be my best chance to escape. Hopefully the racket downstairs would distract him long enough for me to leave the house. The sealed window behind me was not an option – the only way I was getting out that way was by smashing the glass. That left the front door; all the way along the landing, down the stairs, across the hall … It was risky, but as long as the man stayed in the kitchen, it should be easy enough to slip away.

"Watch my back," I muttered to Danny – and any of the ghost children, if they were still listening.

* * *

I folded the sheet of paper Danny had written the list of victims' names on and shoved it in my pocket. Then I slowly pulled open the door. It was now or never. I inched across the landing, listening out for any sign of movement downstairs. The dogs were still excited and now the kettle was boiling; he was making himself a drink.

So far, so good, I thought, as I reached the top of the stairs.

I couldn't remember if any of the steps creaked, so I moved carefully, testing my weight on each one before moving to the next. It was a slow but necessary process. I didn't want to mess up. If whoever was here heard me, that was it. I was only halfway down, though, when I heard one of the dogs panting.

I froze, one foot hovering over the next step. *Please, please, please, go away,* I silently begged. But the sound was growing louder as the Wolfhound got closer. Then, as though fate itself was against me, the living room door was nudged open by a big, wet, coal-black nose.

God-frickin'-sodding-dammit! The dog stopped in his tracks as soon as he spotted me, and then his whip-like tail began to wag, hitting the door and the furniture close to him. *Thump! Thump! Thump!*

"Ssshhh!" I hissed, but all that seemed to do was lure the thing over to me. He placed his front paws on the third step in an effort to reach me, his hind legs still on the hallway floor. I backed up and luckily, for whatever reason, he didn't try to follow.

"Arnie! Whut're you up to?" the man's voice called out. He was in the living room.

Shit.

I turned and bounded up the stairs, no longer caring how much noise I made. That's when Arnie started barking again. The door opened fully before I could reach the top.

"Oi!" the man shouted. "Stop right there!"

Checkmate. With nowhere to hide, I did as he said.

Arnie was still barking at the foot of the stairs

and I could feel the man's piercing gaze, as hot as used fire-irons. I turned to face him, only a step away from the top. I wondered why he hadn't given chase until I got my first real look at him, standing there under the living room doorframe. He was old, maybe early seventies, leaning on a wooden walking stick with a gold-tipped handle. He really didn't look in top shape. He was either recovering from or diagnosed with something serious. His face was red and his chin was twitching; but he was also dead focused. He stared at me and as I stared back, I realised I'd seen this man before: the balding crown, angular nose and suede waistcoat.

I glanced at the photograph on the wall next to me, the winter one of Cillian and his grinning family. He was the man standing at the edge of the picture, his coat half open to reveal what could have been the same waistcoat he had on now. He looked much older than he did in the photo, but that was probably because of whatever health condition he has. With a slight shudder, I couldn't help noticing how similar he and Cillian looked. They were definitely related.

"Miscreant!" he spat. "Whut are you doing in this house?"

No sooner had the words left his mouth than his ruddy cheeks paled and his sharp eyes widened.

I looked behind me, thinking he must have caught sight of one of the ghost children. He hadn't, though. I was still alone.

"It's *you*," he said. The anger and the accusing

tone had vanished completely. "That boy from the papers."

I felt the colour drain from my own face then. *I was in the papers?* Mum and Dad must've reported me missing. I'd only been gone three days! I was going to be in so much trouble if this man turned me in.

"Whut are you doing *here?*" he asked, now sounding more concerned than anything.

"I ... don't know." I was unsure how to respond.

"Did Cillian bring you here?" he said.

The penny dropped. He didn't think I'd broken in; he thought Cillian had kidnapped me. I decided to use the excuse he'd just handed me. "Yeah ... he did. Who are you?"

The man shuffled closer to the stairs. "I'm Iollan O'Hagan. Cillian's father. Listen –" he pointed to his chest with a spindly finger "– I had no part in this. *Honest!* A-and I know Cillian didn't mean anything by it. It's just a misunderstanding, that's all."

"You think Cillian's *innocent?*" Judging by his leap to kidnapping, I figured he knew Cillian had some sort of history.

"Please!" Iollan's grip on his walking stick tightened so much that both his hand and cane were trembling. "You can't ... You don't understand. Can I at least talk to you, see if we can work something out? I won't let Cillian near you, I promise!"

"What don't I understand? Your son's a maniac!"

Iollan flinched at my words. "Please," he

persisted. "Come and have a chat."

I didn't trust him, but I could tell he had information that might help me piece together his son's motives.

"I just want answers," I told him. With Cillian dead, there was no chance of an ambush, so I made my way back downstairs, pushing past Arnie. Danny stayed close as I let myself be ushered into the living room by a psychopath's father, playing the victim of a crime that was never committed.

* * *

The three dogs joined us in the living room, lying on the floor in different places. I sat on the settee in front of the coffee table that was covered in the letters addressed to Cillian, an open TV guide, two scrunched-up crisp packets and half a cup of tea that smelt as bad as it looked. Iollan took the armchair, positioning it so that we were facing each other across the table. He hoisted up the legs of his pressed trousers before lowering himself into the chair. When he placed his walking stick on the floor by his feet, he too spotted the tea and grimaced.

"Listen," he said, moving the cup under the table and out of sight. His eyes were darting now, like he was worried his son might come back at any moment. "I'll pay you compensation if you don't go to the police. No real harm's been done, has it? It's just a big misunderstan –"

"Stop saying that word." It baffled me how he thought his son's actions could just be swept under a rug. "Why shouldn't I go to the police?"

"How does two grand sound?"

"Like bribery," I said, before repeating the exact same question.

Iollan fell silent.

He licked his chapped lips, clearly trying to think up a response that might justify what his son had done — not that there was one. "Look, he doesn't ... I mean, I've *tried* to help him, but he struggles to grasp what I tell him. It's not his fault. What he's been through ... it's difficult to deal with."

"I'm sure the court will take that into account." I had to refrain from hitting him. How was any of that an answer? Iollan was about to say something else but I beat him to it. "By the way you reacted earlier, this has clearly happened before. If I take the money, who's to say he won't kidnap somebody else?"

"I don't know! I can't pretend to know what's going on inside his head."

"Hasn't he ever told you why he does it?"

"No! Well, in a sense ... His sister died, all right?" He broke off to sigh. "Like I said, it's not his fault. Since her death he's been hung up on some twisted form of revenge that makes less and less sense each year."

His sister. She must have been the girl he was hugging in the photo. "You mean April?"

"*April?* No, my daughter's name is Clodagh."

Goddammit, there were too many names to keep track of. Just when I thought I was starting to get it, another twist formed. I made a mental note to add her to the list Danny had written for me. "What happened to her?"

Iollan swallowed. I was making him re-live the event, but I didn't care. I needed to know. "She was with a group of kids from her class." He paused, and for a second I thought that's all I was going to get from him. Then he continued, and when he did his voice was much harder. "The ringleader said they were playing 'Dares' – *Pft!* Idiots. The lot've them. Clodagh should've known better, but she was just a kid. Twelve years old, what a waste ..." He shook his head and I could see the sadness in his eyes. It was all too familiar.

I didn't bother doing the maths. Cillian's mum must have been young when she had him, and the age difference between her and Iollan must have been at least a decade. Whatever, though. That was their business.

Iollan swallowed. "It's horrible, losing a child. Especially one so young. She was going to change the world, my Clodagh. I knew it. But instead she got herself killed – climbing down a well, of all things, at some ruins near Brookston forest. No charges were brought. I still hated the brats who egged her on, but I accepted the facts. It's all you can do if you're going to move on."

"But Cillian didn't accept it?"

Iollan shook his head again. "They were close. Their ma died not long before, but losing Clodagh was easily the toughest thing he'd ever been through. He wanted someone to be punished, needed someone to *blame* ..."

"That's why he killed Grant Luther." I was only guessing, using the names I remembered Danny writing to piece the story together. "He was the ringleader, wasn't he? A boy in her class. Killing him was all about revenge, like you said. But what about the others?"

Iollan drew in a quick breath. He knew. Of *course* he knew. Did he witness his son's crimes? Maybe Cillian confessed to him? "How ...? Why would ...? What on *Earth* are you talking about?"

It was too late for him to hide it now. I leant forward in my seat. "Cillian blamed Grant for Clodagh's death so he dragged him back to the orphanage ruins."

"Who told you that?" His voice was a strained whisper.

I was right again. "But that doesn't explain the others," I said.

"There are no 'others'!" He was shaking now, and because of his age (and whatever health problems he already had), I wondered if he might have a heart attack or something. That didn't stop me listing the remaining victims. I even jerked a thumb in the direction of the garden when it came to explaining about Emily, Brett and Aaron, indicating where they were buried.

Iollan got to his feet, no longer needing his walking stick. Instead of collapsing with a failed heart, he glanced out of the window like he expected their dead corpses to be sticking out the ground. "How much do you know?" he demanded. That cold voice I'd first heard on the stairs was back again, but now with a touch of desperation.

I stood up too. We were almost the same height. "More than the police, that's for sure." I went to walk around the coffee table but Iollan blocked my path.

"You're not going anywhere," he said, and the memory of Mr Butch at the Yonder Square flashed to mind. If I could escape from Mr Butch I could definitely get away from this old kook. "Where's Cillian?"

"I don't know," I said, not wanting to complicate matters by telling him that his son was dead. "But believe me I'll find him. I need to know why he killed those kids."

Iollan raised his hands to his head. When he brought them down again, I saw he'd pulled out two thin clumps of wispy grey hair. "I told you – it's for Clodagh! He needs someone to blame!"

So each year, after the anniversary of his sister's death, he killed another child – that was *it?* Sick, twisted, on-going revenge?

I thought about all the brutal ways Cillian had

taken those children's lives and how Iollan knew so much about the murders. This wasn't a one-man job. I bet my entire savings (which now technically belonged to Mr Butch) that Iollan was involved in some way.

"That's why you're here," I said. "You hadn't heard from him in a few days so you thought he might be out finding a new victim – who you assumed was me. You help him, don't you? You knew it wasn't Grant's fault but you killed him anyway. And you did the same with all the others."

Iollan rushed forward, making me fall back into the chair. He bent down, his face so close that his nose touched mine. His skin felt oily and his breath stank of cigarettes and rotting teeth. "I'm not a murderer. Don't you *dare* try to pin his messed-up deeds on *me*. Yes, I thought he might be out looking for another one, but I came here to try and discourage him – like I've been doing for the past seven years! He doesn't listen, though. If Clodagh can't be here, then Cillian can't see why they should be."

"Course he doesn't listen – he's a psychopath! He should be locked up and you know it!" I leant back until his greasy nose was no longer touching me, although his putrid breath still lingered.

Iollan smirked. I think it was supposed to be a show of confidence but all it did was make him look like he had gas. "He's my son, the only child I have left. If I can't dissuade him, I'll cover for him.

Nobody's taking my boy. *No one.* That's why you're not going anywhere. I don't know how you found out about my Cillian, but it's going no further."

"What? He's going to kill me too, is he?"

Iollan's lip curled. I knew he wanted me out of the picture, and I knew he'd do whatever it took to get it done, but I wasn't afraid anymore. He was outnumbered – me and his victims versus him alone – so I couldn't see how it was possible for me to lose.

Iollan straightened and made his way over to the window. He drew the curtains – there'd be no witnesses. I wasn't sure if he was going to wait for Cillian or attempt to finish me off himself.

All three dogs suddenly got to their feet. Did they sense a change in Iollan's mood? The barking and whining started again, only this time their long tails were between their legs. The one closest to the kitchen nudged open the door, letting in another waft of shit before scarpering from the room with his brothers in tow. I heard one of them barge something out the way in their hurry to escape and then they were out in the garden, taking their spooked cries with them.

"What the –" Iollan turned from me to the dogs, his eyebrows low. He was confused but I'd already figured out what they were running from. Standing by the mantelpiece stood three of Cillian's victims: Emily, Brett and Aaron – three of the dead children Iollan had helped bury. They were watching him with a haunting, unforgiving look.

When the old man followed my gaze, he gasped so loudly he almost choked – and then he lurched backwards, stumbling over the coffee table. I moved aside and watched him crash to the floor, spilling the cold cup of tea. I'd never seen anyone that old jump so far.

When he looked towards the mantelpiece again, the three children had vanished.

"Wh-what … What the h-heck was *that?*" he stuttered, glancing round the rest of the room. He had the same stiffness in his neck as a meerkat checking for danger.

"Recognise them, do you?" I said.

He shot me a glare. "How much more do you know?" he hissed. He was staring up at me, his nostrils flaring.

"Enough."

"Then you know I wasn't involved."

I scoffed. "Yeah, *clearly!*"

"What do you expect me to do? Let him get locked up? I've already lost one child, I'm not going to lose another."

I wanted to deck him. Cillian belonged in whatever form of Hell there was, and so did he.

I knelt down in front of him, watching his face for any kind of reaction. "My brother was killed because of your cover-ups. You and your son will always be hated by me and my family – *and* all the other families, when I tell them the truth. He deserves to suffer, and I won't let you or your deranged reasoning get in the way."

Iollan didn't react the way I thought he would. His eyes widened, not with grief, but realisation. "Cillian was never here, was he?"

I stood up and turned to leave. As I did, though, Iollan grabbed my ankle. I wasn't expecting it, so I lost my balance and landed with a thud next to him.

Iollan reached round and grabbed the front of my shirt. "I told you," he said, spittle flying in every direction. "You're not going anywhere!"

I didn't even try to resist. My neck tingled; the room was ice cold ... My brother wasn't happy.

Within seconds, Iollan let go of me and began clutching his throat, as though trying to pull at something blocking his airway. He coughed, wheezed, squirmed on the floor ... The invisible force choking him was Danny.

I let him struggle. He had this coming. I got up and made my way over to the front door. When I turned back, Iollan's face had turned a nasty shade of purple. I unlocked the door. "You can let go of him now, Danny."

He did, but it took a while for the colour to return to Iollan's usual pasty face. He stared up at me, quivering and gasping for breath. I didn't need to worry about him calling the police. The last thing he'd do was get them involved. His son was a murderer, and he an accomplice.

"I'm going," I said, daring him to stop me. But the fight in him was gone. He shuffled back, unable to look away. *The coward.*

I opened the door without another word. Iollan had closed the picket gate but I left it wide open again as I walked out of Cillian's front garden.

It was a good job for Cillian that he was already dead, because I wanted to kill him. I guess I'd have to settle with tormenting his restless spirit for a while until April kicked him out of this realm for good. But who the heck *was* April? And what happened to Clodagh? Where was Cillian's body and how did he die? All my original questions had been answered but a ton of new ones had formed in their place. But the main one I kept asking myself was, even though Cillian was already dead, was there still a way for me to make him suffer? Danny might not have been bothered about revenge, but I was.

CHAPTER TWENTY TWO

Now that I knew why Danny was killed – in a cycle of revenge that had nothing to do with him – I wanted to curse, scream and break stuff. I wanted the world to *burn*. It just wasn't fair ... It wasn't *right* ...

I thought finding answers would make me feel ... I don't know. *Better,* I suppose. At least in some way or another. Instead, everything I'd learnt in that house was a burden on my shoulders. Not just the stuff about Danny, Cillian or the other victims – it was also the bit about me. Iollan wasn't the only one who could report me. If I was in the papers, anyone could tip off the police, including Natasha or Mr Butch.

I had to get back to the B&B. Mr Butch had wanted to drag me back to Woodlock since driving up that death-trap of a cliff, so I knew he'd rat me out as soon as he saw the article. And if the police were informed, I'd never make it to Cillian.

I prayed that the Brookston Junior Orphanage ruins weren't too far away. I needed to get to April before the police found out where I was. I still wasn't sure how she tied in with all this (maybe she was a relative, or perhaps a friend of Clodagh's?) but whoever she was, she was going to lead me straight to Cillian – his body and spirit – and then I needed to pass on her messages, force him to see her, so she could finally stop him.

Danny tugged my arm, urging me down a wide alley next to a fish and chip shop. It looked like a dead-end, so I continued walking.

I wondered how long Iollan would wait at the house before going to find his son. Maybe a couple of hours. Possibly three.

Danny tugged even harder on my jacket sleeve.

"Stop it," I said. He didn't, though, and as I rounded the corner, passing a convenience store, I realised why. A police car was parked on the curb ahead of me.

Great, just what I needed.

I should've kept going but I panicked, turning back the way I'd come and bumping into a man in dark uniform: hat, radio, badge … *Crap.*

"Easy there," he said. He didn't sound gruff like Mr Butch but there was a definite air of authority about him.

"Sorry," I mumbled, avoiding his eyes.

Before I could make a move, he asked, "Shouldn't

you be in school?"

I blinked. "Um … Well, I …" It was difficult to think. Did he recognise me from whichever newspaper Iollan had spotted me in? His face was blank, so it was impossible to tell. I cleared my throat and said the first thing that came to mind: "Me and my family have just moved here. I don't start my new school 'til Monday."

"Is that so?" The policeman arched an eyebrow. "Where did you move from?"

"Woodlock," I said automatically. (Why was I such an idiot?)

"Woodlock, huh?" The officer mulled this over for a few seconds. (*Stupid, stupid, stupid …*) He was gonna twig it. I felt hot and sweaty waiting for his response. "Where's that? Doesn't sound local –" He was interrupted by crackling static from the hand-held radio clipped to his belt. I had to hide my relief when I overheard he was needed at "The Green by Stanton Bridge" or wherever.

He replied promptly before turning back to me. He looked really serious. "Right, well make sure you're in school on Monday. If I catch you again, you'll be in big trouble."

He headed to his car and I walked towards the convenience store again. It wasn't too late for him to realise who I was, so I bolted as soon as I rounded the corner. I flew down the street and shot down the alley Danny had pointed out next to the fish and chip shop.

The brick wall at the end was too high to climb, so I hid instead. I tried not to gag as I crouched behind an industrial bin that smelt of seaweed and rotting fish. *Perfect place to hide a body,* I couldn't help thinking. The stench made my lungs feel dirty and contaminated, but I stayed there just long enough to feel that the coast was clear. When I stood up, though, there was a man staring straight at me from the other side of the bin.

I jumped – but it wasn't the officer. It was Mr Butch.

I almost didn't recognise him. He was shaven like the day we met, and his clothes – although damp in places – were even cleaner than before. But that's not what threw me off. It was the sunglasses and navy ascot tied around his thick neck. The shades were fine, I suppose, but the scarf looked ridiculous on him.

"Thought you could hide from me, did you?" He was out of breath, as though he'd had to run to catch me up. At least now I didn't have to walk back to Natasha's house.

"Course not – I left you a note for a reason." Then I got distracted and asked, "What's with the ...?"

"What, *these?*" He yanked off the scarf and glasses. That's when I noticed he also had a copy of the daily mail under his arm. My stomach churned. I knew what he was going to say next. "Didn't buy them by *choice,* if that's what you mean. In fact, I got them from the same place as this ..." He tossed the paper over to me and I caught it clumsily. "Turn to page seven."

I did, with a sense of reluctance.

The thin pages stuck to my sweaty fingers as I clocked the numbers: 2-3, 4-5, 6 ... There, my own photograph stared back at me. It wasn't the best picture – my hair flicked up at the front and my dimples were more obvious than usual – but there I was, under a caption that said: BOY MISSING SINCE WEDNESDAY.

This must've been what Iollan saw.

I couldn't look at Mr Butch. Dad, being in the Woodlock police force, must've pushed the story for it to have spread this fast in such a short time. I read through the article, shocked by how much the police and journalists knew about my whereabouts. Surprisingly, though, that wasn't the worst part. They'd made Mr Butch out to be some kind of dangerous, kidnapping criminal! No wonder he'd bought the sunglasses and scarf. If he was spotted, he'd be done.

I read the final paragraph one last time:

The police have analysed CCTV footage and interviewed potential witnesses in search for Jordan Richardson. A student at Charbonville College in Devon reported seeing Jordan and Leslie at The Yonder Square Inn – the pub she works at part time. They arrived on Thursday 26th March at around

05:00PM. The witness stated: "They seemed like any other customer at first. But when the boy (Jordan Richardson) tried to leave, the older man (Leslie Butch) stopped him. The boy shouted 'get off' so I went over to ask if everything was okay. Nothing happened after that ... He let the boy go but I did hear him (Leslie) make a threat, saying that if he (Jordan) didn't come back, then he (Leslie) would 'track [him] down'. The boy left by himself; I'm not sure if the man eventually followed or if the boy returned. I only wish I did more," the witness concludes. This was the last sighting of Jordan Richardson and suspect Leslie Butch. The Richardson parents plead for anyone with information regarding their son's whereabouts to come forward. The number for the police helpline is at the bottom of this page. We do not advise approaching Leslie Butch.

"You better start explainin', kid!" Mr Butch hissed, snatching the paper from me. He leaned in close. "I'm wanted for *kidnap*. I could get locked up for this. We're goin' straight to the police to sort this mess out." That's why he'd come to look for me. It wasn't about the money anymore. If he turned up at the police station alone, he'd look far guiltier than if I was there with him, safe and willing to explain the whole misunderstanding.

And I *was* willing to explain – just not yet. The police would take me home straightaway and I couldn't go back until I'd found Cillian. If Mr Butch wanted to go, I'd just have to reach the orphanage before they could catch me.

I stepped away from him. "I need more time."

"You're a runaway, aren't you?"

"No."

"Then why are we wanted?" Mr Butch's voice was quiet but his tone was colder than a room filled with poltergeists. "I'm turnin' us in. I don't care if I have to drag you the entire way."

"I'm not sure that'll help your case."

He shot me a dirty look. Nostrils flaring, fists clenched, he'd made up his mind, and if I couldn't convince him otherwise in the next thirty seconds, I was going to be dragged to the nearest police station.

"Listen, I promise I'll tell them the truth, but I really can't go with you yet."

"Why not?"

"Because ..." There was no way to finish my sentence without sounding insane.

Danny was still close by. Surely he could see I had no choice but to tell the truth. If I opened up, though, would Danny show himself or would he disappear like he usually did?

"Well?" Mr Butch said.

Because I'm avenging my brother ... Because I'm tracking down a dead man ... Because I need to cast away the spirit of a serial killer ... I couldn't go with any of these.

I sighed. "It's something you need to see." Words would never be enough to persuade him.

"What d'you mean?"

I hadn't tried this in years, not since I was put on my first dosage of meds a few years ago. I closed my eyes, concentrating. "Danny? Please show yourself."

When nothing happened, I opened my eyes and saw Mr Butch looking at me gone out. I ignored him, talking directly to my brother again. "Show yourself or this trip is over. You know I'm not playing games. I've done everything you've asked. This is out of my control now!"

Still, there was no sound, no movement ... This was so *typical* of him. This was *exactly* what happened with Mum and Dad, with Dr Ashton, with everyone at school – I wasn't letting him make a fool out of me this time. We were literally out of options. He had to show himself. If he didn't, I was going to be taken home.

"Just give him a sign!" I begged. "Rattle the bin lids, kick some rubbish around ... anything!"

But still nothing happened.

"All right, that's enough," Mr Butch said. "I don't care what you do after we've sorted this, but I'm clearin' my name. Come on."

When I didn't move, Mr Butch dropped his ascot, shades and newspaper and grabbed my upper arm. I tried pulling against him as he dragged me towards the main road but it made no difference. He was too strong. And since there was nothing I could say to make him let go, I knew the mission was over.

Danny started to panic. He was pinching me

and tugging my hair, but what the hell could I do? He must've realised I was telling the truth, that it was all up to him, because he stopped assaulting me without me having to tell him. I thought he'd gone – whether it was to get help or create an obstacle, I wasn't sure – until Mr Butch and I were near the opening. Then something clattered loudly behind us.

Danny had actually done it.

Mr Butch stopped. It had come from the other end of the alley. I didn't bother hiding my smile. There was more clattering as Danny shook whatever was inside the industrial bin, and then – *Bang!*

Mr Butch's head snapped round in the direction of the noise. "Right, pack it in," he told me. "You're not funny."

"I'm not doing anything. I'm standing right here."

"You know what I mean. What you said earlier 'bout rattlin' bins and chuckin' rubbish … This is obviously some kind've prank. And who's Danny?"

A small pile of cardboard lifted into the air. It spun several times before dropping to the floor again.

"Danny's my twin brother," I said. "He died five years ago."

Mr Butch kept glancing between me and the dustbin. "Seriously, kid. Stop bein' stupid. What are you up to?"

"I'm not being stupid. Danny is a ghost, a spirit,

and there's something I need to do for him. He's been leading me this whole time. My parents don't believe me so I didn't tell them I was ditching school, but I wasn't expecting to be gone this long." Danny started opening and closing the metal bin lid. "I'm so close to finishing what I set out to do," I went on. "And after I'm done, I promise I'll go with you to the police and clear all this up."

Mr Butch said nothing. He was staring into the alley where the bin lid continued to clatter, and then he shook his head. "No, I ain't buyin' it. Ghosts don't exist, you're just tryin' to get out've comin' to the station with me!"

He was still gripping my upper arm but instead of pulling me towards the main street, he led me down the alley again. It was much colder now, and I could tell by the look on Mr Butch's face that he felt it too.

He made his way over to the rattling bin. It was louder now as Danny used more energy. I could tell he was getting impatient. They both were.

Mr Butch let go of my arm and thrust the lid open, releasing a wall of stench. I wrinkled my nose but Mr Butch didn't seem fazed by the smell. He peered inside, his blank expression revealing he hadn't spotted anything out the ordinary. Then – *Woosh!* – what seemed like all the rubbish in the rusty container flew into the air: plastic, rotting food, crushed packaging ... Mr Butch jumped back and watched the mess land around us, littering the entire alley.

He looked at me, quickly closing his mouth after realising that it was hanging open.

I shrugged, remembering the number of times Danny had wrecked my room. "He likes to trash things."

That wasn't enough of an explanation for Mr Butch, though. "How –?"

"*Hey!*" a familiar voice shouted out.

We turned around and saw Natasha standing at the top of the alley. She was looking straight at us. My stomach dropped and I knew Mr Butch felt just as anxious because I heard him groan under his breath. He was wondering the same thing as me: had she seen us in the papers yet?

"What a mess," she said, glancing at the rubbish around us. Danny was still here but he was being quiet, now, observing.

Natasha looked different with make-up. Her skin seemed smoother and her eyes bigger. She smiled at us and I figured that if she knew a missing boy and potential criminal had stayed in her house, she wouldn't have batted an eye at the litter. "Fancy bumping into you pair again," she said. "I thought you'd be out of town by now. Where are you off to?"

"Uhhh ..." Mr Butch was at a loss. I knew he didn't want to raise suspicion by mentioning the police.

"The Junior Orphanage ruins," I put in.

"Oh!" Natasha sounded impressed. "Me and

Ethan used to go up there a lot before we moved in with my mum. It's quite a trek from here. Would you like a lift?"

Mr Butch declined the offer before I could open my mouth.

"Don't be daft," she said. "I'm heading into the city to do some shopping anyway. It's pretty much on the way."

"Actually, Natasha," I said, "a ride would be great." I'd deal with Mr Butch's response later but right now, with Natasha as witness, he couldn't drag me anywhere. Besides, if she dropped us off exactly where I needed to go, it would speed up the journey by several hours. And the sooner I was done, the sooner Mr Butch got what he wanted. It was a no-brainer, really – not that he cared if I got where I needed to go.

"No, it's okay, Jordan. We'll walk." Mr Butch looked calm, but I knew he was anything but.

"You can walk if you like, but I might as well give Jordan a lift," Natasha said. She winked at me, as though this was a silly disagreement between an uncle and his nephew.

Mr Butch hated that idea even more. There was no way he was letting me out of his sight now. Stalemated, he agreed to the lift.

We kept our heads down until we reached Natasha's blue Toyota, parked at the edge of an Argos car park. I got in the back with Mr Butch, clipped on my seatbelt, and then I saw it – today's paper, neatly folded on the passenger seat.

Cool it, Jordan, I told myself. She was hardly going to read it while she was driving; and after she'd dropped us off, she'd be going shopping. By the time she got round to seeing the article we probably would've turned ourselves in anyway.

I settled into my seat as Natasha started the engine. The only thing that mattered now was Danny.

Watch out, Cillian. I'm coming for you.

FiVE YEARS EARLiER

It was a lot darker beneath the trees. Leaves and branches stretched across the sky, so very little sunlight could break through. I'd been in plenty of woods before, going for walks with Mum and Dad, but this one was very dense. Once my eyes had adjusted to the dim light, I asked Lewis who would be on first.

I watched him snap off a long stick from an ugly-looking tree. "Dunno yet. Wait 'til we get to the clearing," he said, and began hitting other trees and plants with it as he walked.

I checked behind me. Danny had fallen to the back of the group. I wanted to join him, but he had a look on his face that meant he'd rather be left alone. I let him be, following Lewis deeper into the forest.

The clearing wasn't far. There were fewer trees here, so sunlight flooded down like holy light. In the middle was a huge rock big enough to climb, and a brook running through a bed of flat stones. Leanne said that if you followed it upstream for about half a mile, it led to a lake. "I saw a deer there once," she said. "It even let me stroke it." I didn't know if I believed her or not, but it was a nice thought to have.

"Right, I know a fair way to settle this," Lewis said. He stopped and began snapping the stick he'd been carrying into several smaller pieces. "Whoever draws the shortest is on."

After choosing our twigs, leaving Lewis with the remaining one, the nine of us revealed what we had. It didn't take long for me to realise Danny had drawn the shortest.

"Unlucky!" one of the boys called out.

I turned to Lewis. "Can we do it again?" I didn't want to leave Danny by himself.

"Sorry," he said in a voice that didn't sound very sorry at all. "Rules are rules."

I opened my mouth to try and persuade him, but Danny cut me off.

"It's fine, I don't care," he said. And it was easy to believe that. He just wanted the game over with so we could go back.

"But —"

"But what?" Lewis interrupted. He was looking between me and Danny, as though we had some kind of hidden agenda. "Dan said he's fine being seeker. Where's the problem? Would *you* rather be on or something?"

If I became seeker, though, Danny would be alone with Lewis. He'd probably hate that more than seeking. I closed my mouth, realising I had nothing to add.

Lewis, now talking to Danny, pointed to a dead tree on the other side of the brook. "Go over there and face that tree – you see it? Then close your eyes and count to a hundred. Give a shout when you're ready."

Danny said nothing. Everyone watched him head towards the tree, but it was only when he'd reached it and started counting that they all made a move, silently disappearing into the forest. I was about to head upstream and follow the water close to the lake Leanne had mentioned, when Lewis grabbed my arm.

He held his index finger up to his lips and whispered, "Follow me."

We headed downstream instead. At first, we were careful where we stood, trying hard to avoid snapping twigs, rustling leaves or crunching fallen pinecones. The further we got, though, the clumsier Lewis became as he started picking up the pace. I could still hear Danny's muffled counting as Lewis took off: "Forty-four … forty-five … forty-six …"

I sprinted after him, following left, then right, then right again. He seemed to be heading in a specific direction. A couple turns later and we eventually reached some old barn. "Come on," he said, leading me inside. He was no longer whispering.

The wooden door creaked ominously when he opened it – a horrible nails-on-chalkboard sound. It was obvious the place hadn't been used in years. The yellow paint was chipped and faded, the walls weather-beaten and rotting, and the mould had become part of its design. Inside was no better. The place stank of old hay and dampness. There were three empty window-frames set at the top, letting in minimal sunlight, and the beams were draped in spiderwebs. And then in the corner was –

"Hey guys," Lewis called over. He shut the barn door and sauntered up to his friends. Shane, Mike and Sophie were sitting round a crooked, plastic garden table on the other side of the barn. We sat down with them. I thought them being here was just a coincidence until Dave, Ben, and Leanne turned up too. They'd planned this.

"Shouldn't we be hiding separately?" I asked.

Lewis shrugged. "What difference does it make? He's never gonna find us."

That's when I realised just how far away we were. I'd been running with Lewis for ages and I couldn't remember when I'd stopped being able to hear Danny counting. He must have reached a hundred by now, but I never heard him shout to say he was coming to find us.

Lewis would've laughed if I admitted that I wanted to be found quickly. There was no way to keep track of time, though. The longer we stayed, the more fidgety I became. I couldn't keep up with what everyone was saying; all their loud voices told me was that the chances of Danny finding us were very low.

Eventually, I decided Lewis could laugh all he wanted; I wasn't enjoying the game. My chest felt heavy and my throat was tight. I stood up from the table and the conversation ended.

"Listen," I said. "We've won, all right? Danny doesn't know the woods like you guys. He could be lost!"

Predictably, Lewis laughed. "He's not lost. He just can't find us."

"I don't care. I've got to look for him. It's been ages …"

"It's been fifteen minutes!"

But I was already halfway to the door.

It took a few seconds for the others to decide to join me. I guess they had nothing better to do. I opened the creaking door and stepped out into the cool fresh air.

"This is pathetic, you know that?" Lewis said.

I couldn't look at him. But my desperation to find Danny outweighed my embarrassment.

As always, Lewis took the lead, and the rest of us followed him back to the clearing, calling Danny's name the whole time.

"No offence, Jordan," Sophie said, when Danny didn't reply, "but your brother is a terrible seeker."

That's just it, though, I thought, *he actually isn't.* Usually nobody could hide for long from Danny.

The eight of us split into three uneven groups to cover more ground. We searched for ages, but by the time we all met at the clearing again there was still no sign of Danny.

"He must be on the beach!" I said, trying hard not to panic. I ran the entire way back, and even though the others had longer legs, they still had a hard time keeping up. When we got there, we split up again and agreed to meet at the bottom of the hotel car park steps. I really thought we were going to find him this time, but just like in the forest we met up empty-handed.

"Just chill," Lewis said to me. "He probably gave up and went back to the hotel."

This sounded as unlikely as a tsunami hitting Brookston Beach – Danny would never leave me. But maybe he did go back, I reasoned. Maybe, when he couldn't find me, he got worried and assumed I'd gone to the hotel myself.

I climbed the concrete steps two at a time. The others followed only as far as the entrance, so I raced through the lobby alone and hit the button on the lift for my floor.

The door to our room was unlocked again. I burst in and hurried over to the living room area, where Mum was busy painting her toenails.

"You're back early," she said, dipping the tiny brush into the sparkly red polish.

"Is Danny here?" I blurted out.

She stopped what she was doing to look at me. "I

thought he was with you."

I wanted to cry. I wished more than anything for him to be in our room playing on his tablet and being pissed off with me again. My face felt hot and my legs heavy. I didn't want to worry Mum, though.

"We're playing hide-and-seek ..." I said. Her face seemed to relax a little then. I didn't tell her that *I* was supposed to be hiding and *him* seeking. "If you see him, tell him to wait for me here," I added, before running out of the hotel room again. I didn't have time to explain. He must still have been in the forest.

I raced down to the lobby and over to where Lewis and his gang stood waiting for me. I shook my head. "He's not there." It was easy to detect the sound of panic in my voice.

"Relax," Lewis said. "He can't be too far. I've been out by myself way longer than this—"

"Danny's not you!" I was sick of him telling me to relax, to chill, to calm down. "He's in trouble. I just know it."

"No you don't. *How* can you know? You're just scared because he's not here to hold your sissy hand."

I tried to ignore the laughter that followed. "We have to find him," I said.

"*We* don't have to do anything," Lewis interjected. He stared at me, long enough for me to look away on any normal occasion; but this was for Danny, so I stood my ground. "Find him yourself."

"Come on, mate," Ben piped up from behind

him. "It kinda *is* our fault."

Sophie nodded next to him.

"Are you guys thick?" Lewis looked between the pair of them. Nobody said anything, so Lewis shrugged. "Whatever. *I'm* not staying. You guys do what you want." He barged past them and the rest of his posse followed him. Ben and Sophie gave me a sheepish glance, but they weren't going to hang back just for me.

I watched them go. Were they being serious? "But I don't know my way around the forest!" I called after them.

"Shame!" Lewis spat over his shoulder.

None of them turned back.

"Please!" I held my breath but they carried on walking. For the first time ever, I was on my own.

There was no time to beg; I sprinted back to the forest. I jumped the ditch and squeezed past the fence, cutting my arm on one of the jagged ends. My chest was tight and a stitch was stabbing my sides, but I couldn't waste seconds recovering. After a few deep breaths I began calling my brother's name. I pushed myself into a half-walk, half-jog and shouted louder and louder. All I heard was my own lonely echo bouncing back.

I circled around the clearing, past the clearing and up by the barn too many times to count. I searched in every direction, no longer caring if I got lost as well.

"Danny!" I shouted into the forest.

Danny ... my echo mocked.

When the sun started to set, I decided I had to go back. It would soon be too dark to see. I wiped my tear-streaked face with shaking hands and headed for the beach, with the setting sun behind me and my gaunt shadow looming in front.

When I got back to the hotel room, Mum and Dad were furious and Danny was still missing.

CHAPTER TWENTY THREE
FRIDAY - PRESENT DAY

It didn't take long to drive there. Then again, I wasn't paying much attention. All I know was that we eventually turned onto a dirt road that ran through the middle of a field. Then, a bit further ahead, I saw it: the orphanage ruins.

It was impossible to tell where the fire had broken out. The roof was completely gone and so were a lot of the walls, but the basic shape remained. It would've been a massive Victorian building, with high ceilings and lots of windows.

There was a forest at the other end of the field, maybe only a hundred metres from the orphanage. I was sure the kids who used to live here told some scary stories about that forest. It probably tempted a few kids with its tease of freedom, the same way it terrified others.

As we drew closer, I saw that the ruins were sectioned off by a wooden barrier – an attempt to keep people away, I guessed – and parts of it were being held up by scaffolding and recently inserted brickwork. It'd been preserved in a way that Saint Edward's castle never had.

Not too far past the ruins I also noticed a water well. The pitched roof was missing, leaving the two posts that used to hold it up sticking out of the circular stone wall. Something seemed to have been placed over the top of it, though, covering the hole. Wooden boards, perhaps? I felt a pang in my gut. Was that the well Clodagh fell down?

"Here we are," Natasha said, pulling up at the side of the road. I unfastened my seatbelt. "Do you know much about the history of this place?"

"A little," I said, just to shut her up. The only history I needed to know was that a boy was murdered here for revenge.

I got out of the car and crossed the road, trying not to slip on the squelching mud and wet grass as I made my way towards the ruins. Weeds and moss clung to the walls that remained, tangling around chipped bricks and crumbling cement.

I stopped at the wooden barrier that marked the ruins' boundaries, reading the signs attached to it. One of them said, in bold, underlined letters, "*__No Trespassing__*"; the other was a metal plaque engraved with information about the fire that had destroyed the orphanage.

I could sense Danny instantly beneath the gale, but I also sensed something else. Just like at the church, a feeling of pain and suffering washed over me. Was it the orphans being burned to death or was it Grant and April?

"Bloody wreck, ain't it?" Mr Butch said, coming up alongside me.

I was about to step over the barrier and head towards the ruins when I heard Natasha approaching. *I thought she said she was going into the city ...*

"It burnt down in 1899," she said, zipping up the coat she'd just slipped on. "Some managed to escape but fifty-one people were killed, including thirty-seven orphans and fourteen members of staff. The children were between the ages of six and twelve."

Mr Butch was impressed. "You know your stuff."

I didn't bother telling him that she'd recited the information from the plaque next to him.

A cluster of leaves began to swirl next to one of the closest walls. It wasn't the wind – the tingling feeling in my forehead assured me of that.

"How long are you planning on staying here?" Natasha asked. "Only, I can drive you somewhere less remote if it's a quick visit. The buses aren't very regular around here."

"No kiddin'!" Mr Butch said, remembering the palaver of reaching Charbonville. He thanked her for the offer and then nudged me, hard. "You ready to go back?"

He knew I wasn't.

The leaves were spinning faster now, as Danny's patience wore thin. "Wait here," I said to Natasha and Mr Butch. Without giving it a second thought, I stepped over the barrier and began making my way towards the swirling pile of leaves.

"Hey! What are you doing?" I could hear the panic in Natasha's voice. "You can't go over there. The sign says 'No –'"

"Relax," Mr Butch said. "There's nobody around. It's not like he's going to break anyth –"

A piece of slate cracked clean in half under my feet. I thought it was going to be solid, being wedged in the ground. I could almost sense Mr Butch cringe as I contradicted him.

"Oops," I muttered. I was careful not to tread on anything else.

Once I reached Danny's checkpoint another small pile of leaves began to swirl up ahead. He was leading me further into the ruins, out of Mr Butch and Natasha's line of sight. I looked behind me; neither of them was paying me any attention, so I carried on.

Just as I'd expected, I could feel others here as well as Danny. It still caught me off guard, though, when I rounded the first corner and saw one of the orphans. My heart beat fast. Why did it always freak me out?

A boy no older than eight was sitting against a wall hugging his skinny legs close to his chest, his colour desaturated like every ghost I'd come across. He was wearing a creased shirt with his sleeves rolled up, plain trousers that looked a size too small for him, and a pair of worn-out boots – all of which were singed and blackened by soot.

He stared at me for a few seconds with vacant eyes. Then he got to his feet and sprinted, soundlessly, along the uneven ground. My mouth fell open as I watched him pass through another wall.

The leaves were still rustling up ahead – I needed to follow Danny. Feeling as composed as I was going to be, I headed on, venturing deeper into the ruins. It wasn't too difficult, as long as I didn't think about the other spirits lurking there. I stopped again, though, when I heard an ominous, echoing whisper –

"Go back ..." it said, over and over. I couldn't decide if it was male or female, young or old. It simply existed. I didn't hear Mr Butch or Natasha react so I knew it was in my head, being projected only at me, exactly like on the bus.

Whoever it was sent shivers down my spine. But I wasn't going anywhere unless Danny told me to. I headed on, taking a turn that put me completely out of Mr Butch and Natasha's sight, but the voice didn't stop: "He's here ... He's here ... Go, now ..."

Then a high-pitched scream broke out. I jumped. It was frickin' loud. How could nobody else hear it? I covered my ears but it made no difference. The sound was coming from *inside* my head. When it stopped, the voice had gone and a horrible ringing noise was left in my ears.

Everything was suddenly way too quiet. My

joints stiffened and my jaw was beginning to chatter. I needed to get back to Mr Butch. I didn't care about the leaves spinning up ahead and I didn't care about finding April. This was by far the creepiest place I'd ever been to.

I turned and spotted the same boy from earlier, leaning against that same wall. He looked at me, but I didn't have the courage to pass him again. I went to run in yet another direction and that's when I saw two other boys. They were sitting on a low wall detached from the main structure. One of them was slightly older – maybe twelve – and the other was about seven. Pale, translucent: they were also ghosts.

I sprinted the other way, taking my chances with the lone boy from before.

I'd almost reached the final corner when I felt something wrap around my ankle. I tripped, immediately looking back to see what had snared me: a vine as thick as my wrist had managed to coil itself around me. I tried pulling myself free but it was as though someone was controlling the vine. It tightened around my ankle, dragging me away from the corner.

I was about to call out when a cluster of leaves began circling me – Danny was reassuring me. I let out a shaky breath. The vine didn't loosen, though, until I'd stopped struggling. I unwrapped the weed from my ankles and could feel the heat where Danny's energy had passed through it.

"Shit ..." I said, but that's all I could manage.

What the hell was he playing at?

When I looked up, the three ghost boys were still staring at me. It was frickin' unnerving, but that wasn't what had tipped me over the edge. It was the voice and that piercing scream.

Taking a deep breath, I got to my feet and brushed down my school trousers. They'd seen better days. Mum would go ape when she saw the state of them. I was about to say something to Danny when I noticed that a fourth boy had appeared. He was sitting next to the two orphans, bouncing his heels against the wall. This kid looked different, though: jeans, Nike trainers, a Spiderman T-shirt ... He smiled as though he was pleased to see me. I knew exactly who this was.

I swallowed the wall of saliva that had been building in my mouth. "You must be Grant Luther."

The boy nodded. "And you're Jordan."

I know I'd only just met him, but there was something about Grant that I really liked. He seemed like the type of kid I knew Danny and I would've got on with in the playground. I smiled back at him, and then I saw movement from the corner of my eye: a man – I mean, ghost – was walking through the ruins, head down, carrying a pile of thick rope over his left shoulder. He passed through a wall that was in his way, continuing towards the forest.

"Who's he?" I asked, watching the man stop at one of the farthest walls. He was in plain view of Mr Butch and Natasha but of course they couldn't see him. They remained oblivious as he dumped the rope in a pile and started tying one of the ends.

"I don't know," Grant said. "He can't hear us, though."

"What did Cillian do to him?"

The man hefted the rope onto his shoulder again and then started climbing the wall. Once he reached the top, he threaded the rope through a gap that used to be a high window and secured it in a knot by his feet. Then he gathered up the other end and I saw the hoop he'd tied earlier hanging limply in his hand.

"Nothing," Grant said.

I'd already figured as much. He slipped his head through the noose and tightened it just enough. I turned away before he could step off and plunge to his death. "He committed suicide two weeks ago," Grant explained. "I saw him throw his wedding ring, so I figured it had something to do with his wife."

I checked behind me, as though I would see the ring and somehow be able to make sense of the man's situation. Of course that didn't happen. Instead, I saw the man reappear at the other end of the ruins and begin his slow and silent walk towards the same wall, ready to jump again …

"Don't mind him." It was a girl's voice. I turned back and there she was, standing in front of the wall next to Grant's dangling legs. I recognised her instantly from one of the photographs in Cillian's house, the one at the top of the stairs: she'd stood next to a younger Cillian, held the arm he'd wrapped around her shoulders … "He's in a loop."

"Um, are you —" I began, but she cut me off.

"I'm April. I can't believe you actually showed up. Danny said you would, but I've been waiting for such a long time and … well, here you are!"

This was April? I assumed the girl in the photograph was Cillian's sister. They seemed really close; they even had the same-shaped nose! Unless she was his half-sister or something? If that was the case, though, why would Iollan be in a photograph with April and not his actual daughter, Clodagh? Even if they weren't related, surely the two girls knew each other. "Did you happen to know a girl called Clodagh?" I asked.

April smiled. Course she did.

"You do, don't you?"

She was close to laughing now. She glanced up at Grant, who was also grinning, before explaining to me what was so funny. "My birth name is Clodagh," she said. "Ma liked the name 'April', but Daddy wanted me to have an Irish name. He's *very* patriotic. He didn't live with us, though. He only came back on birthdays and near Christmas, so my ma and brother went around calling me April. It's what everyone knows me by and I'm glad. If I hadn't died, I would've changed my name for real as soon as I turned eighteen."

I didn't know what to say. The mystery about

April and Clodagh was solved. April *was* Clodagh; she died playing dares with her friends; Cillian was her older brother and he murdered kids to avenge her. It was that simple. Unlike the others, though, April and Grant had known each other when they were alive – they were even in the same class, if Iollan's words were anything to go by. Grant was there when April fell down the well, and she must have seen her grieving brother drag him back to the scene of the crime and murder him in cold blood.

I was still dwelling on this when the lone boy behind me suddenly took off, sprinting silently through a brick wall. He did not appear on the other side. A few seconds later, the boy materialised in the same place I first saw him, hugging his knees.

I thought back to Natasha's mother; to the man who stumbled out of the Yonder pub; the man who kept hanging himself on the other side of these ruins; the piercing scream and the voices I kept hearing – first on the bus and now here … This was probably the only chance I had to get answers, so I told April everything. I didn't understand how I could go from sensing only Danny to seeing all *this*.

"It's the link between you and Danny," she said.

I must've looked pretty clueless because I didn't need to ask her to explain. She just did. "Basically, until a few days ago, Danny had always put up a sort of barrier to stop anyone else from getting through. He was protecting you. But now he's lowered that barrier so that me and everyone involved can talk to you. Sometimes others slip past the barrier, too." She shrugged. "It can't be helped."

"So they have nothing to do with Cillian?"

April shook her head. "And as for the scream – that was probably me. When I slipped down the well. I'll always be connected to this place because of it. It happened so fast, I didn't even think it was that dangerous at the time … I'd never been so scared and then," she opened her arms, gesturing to the ruins and ghost boys around her, "this became my new home."

I didn't know what to say. I'm guessing the same went for April too because in the end Grant had to step in.

"It takes a lot of energy to keep so many spirits out," he said, referring to Danny again. "Once the gate, or *barrier*, has been opened – even a bit – it's difficult to monitor. Besides, like April just said, we see them all the time. It's easy to forget what a big deal it is for people who're not dead. But when –"

"Wait a second." I had to stop him there. "You mean … you see this all the time? Like people's final moments, dying wishes, lingering grief, restless spirits – that kind've … *stuff?*"

Grant hopped down from the wall and glided towards me. "It's what happens when you die and can't move on."

"Or don't want to move on," April added. "What you've been seeing, that's nothing! You'd be surprised how much room it takes up on the surface."

Shit. Danny had been surrounded by this for five years, because of *me*. "Why didn't you *tell* me?" I said, searching for my brother's presence. I knew he was here somewhere.

"He didn't want you to worry," Grant said. "That's the whole reason he came back – to watch out for you. Not to give you *more* stress. Anyway, it was his choice to stay."

"Yeah, only 'cause I was selfish and wouldn't move on." I pressed the heel of my hands against my eyes. He had never wanted to be avenged. That's what *I* wanted. And because of that, Danny had stayed around to keep me safe. I'd trapped him in a place that seemed hellish in every way: watching the living go on without him while constantly being faced with grief and death.

"He's out there now, you know," April said.

"I know. He led me to you." I removed my hands from my eyes. I was starting to see stars in my vision.

"Not Danny," she said. "Cillian."

His name alone brought back all the ugly, bitter feelings of vengeance that had driven me here in the first place. I breathed in slowly through my nose, trying to block out the man committing suicide behind me for the tenth time or more – now aware that my brother had been seeing this kind of stuff for far too long.

"He knows you're coming," April continued. "He's known for a while and he's not happy. He wants to kill you."

"I thought he only went after children," I spat, hoping the coward could somehow hear me. I didn't care if he was her brother.

A stone hit the back of my head. I cursed, turning to face the empty space behind me.

"Danny won't rest until he knows you're safe," Grant said. "He told us so."

I picked up the stone by my feet and lobbed it. "Well, he should quit throwing stuff at me and get on with protecting me then."

The same pile of leaves that had swirled around me earlier started to rise until they were above my head. Before I could react, Danny dropped them on top of me.

"Knock it off!" I said, brushing bits of twigs, leaves and dirt from my hair and the back of my hood.

"Jordan, this is serious," April said. "Even if you show my brother's body to the police, it won't make any difference to you now. Cillian refuses to move on. He still wants to avenge me, and he wants to keep our dad from going to prison." April's eyes were glistening (*could ghosts cry?*), and then I felt a pressure on my chest: heavy, painful, like that feeling at the hotel all those years ago when I first found out that Danny wasn't coming home. It was heartache – but this wasn't *my* sadness. It was April's. She pushed an image of the Wolfhounds into my head: they used to walk the dogs together. I don't know how I knew; I just did.

Tears pricked my eyes – again, though, I knew it was coming from April. It wasn't just her life that was taken that day: a friendship had ended, too, and now she could only watch over her brother and witness him deal with it in the worst possible way.

Then, just like that, the pressure on my chest lifted and the tears went away. It was so *strange*. I knew I hadn't been possessed; April had just put her emotions onto me, physically sharing her feelings so I would understand, I suppose.

"Cillian doesn't spend a lot of time in one place," April said. She was doing her best to keep it together. "You know how Danny's connected to you? Well, we're all connected to our families and the places where we were killed. And because you came to us, we're now connected to you as well. Cillian's no different."

"So …" I tried working this out for myself. "His house, your dad, and wherever the hell he died?"

Grant nodded. "He's also linked to you."

"*Me?* How come?"

Like before, April did the explaining. "He kept hearing you curse his name. The closer you got, the more he homed in on your negative energy. It's pretty hard to miss, actually. You carry a lot of hate towards my brother – which I understand – but that's what's led him to you. Remember back on the bus? That voice you heard was Cillian, and it's a good job you left when you did because he was going to kill you there and then."

Shit … *For real?*

I remembered the menacing voice, the sing-song threats, and how uneasy I'd felt when the bus engine cut out. It wasn't paranoia; my gut instinct had been right all along.

"How do you know all this?" I asked. "Were you there too?"

"No, Danny told me what happened. Cillian put a thought into the driver's head that made him pull over and leave. He wasn't possessed but because he was so tired, his mind was susceptible enough for my brother to plant ideas in his head. Danny doesn't know what Cillian said but it was enough to make the driver abandon his bus and run away." April glided closer to me, standing beside Grant. "Cillian knows you know what he did. He might be dead, but our dad can still get in trouble – and Cillian doesn't want that. Since you know everything, the only way he can be sure you won't say anything is if he gets rid of you for good." She looked at me, making sure I understood the implication. I already knew he wanted me dead, though. What more could I say?

She continued, "And, let's say you *did* tell the police before Cillian got to you: he would haunt you for the rest of your life *and* carry on killing kids. It doesn't matter if his body is buried or cremated, Cillian will still be here. Like we are …" April folded her arms. "… Unless you help me guide him into the spirit realm where he can't kill anymore."

She made it sound so easy. Before, it was just

about killing him; then finding his body so the police could gather enough evidence to give everyone closure. I thought that was why Danny was leading me to all the other victims: I was the only one who could hear their stories and pass on the truth. Turns out there was an even bigger reason. One I wasn't so keen on.

I ran my fingers through my hair. I had to stop thinking about revenge and closure. Neither would do me much good now. Instead, I needed to focus on getting rid of Cillian — because if he killed me, Danny would never be able to rest. His spirit would never be at peace and he would continue to see death. And what if he was forced to watch *my* death, repeatedly, over and over again?

"How do we get rid of him?" I said. "I've been told you're the key, April. You're his sister, you're the reason he …" I couldn't bring myself to finish the sentence. It wasn't her fault Cillian was a maniac.

"He'll listen to me," she said. "Go into Brookston Forest at the back of these ruins. You'll find his body there and his spirit won't be far. I'll get him to come with me, away from this realm — but first, I'll need you to convince him that I'm here. He can't see me or hear me or even sense when I'm close by. He never has."

I sighed. "And how the hell do I get him to see you?" He needed to be on the same frequency to communicate with her but that would be impossible if he was angry, bitter and narrow-minded.

"Whatever way you can. He doesn't have a physical form anymore but he's still the same Cillian. Talk to him, *persuade* him ..."

"And if he attacks me?" I doubt he'd listen for long, especially if he considered me a threat to his father. Besides, why would he believe a word I said? I couldn't even get Mum or Dad to believe me.

"We'll protect you," Grant said.

"But what if you can't –" I heard a branch snap somewhere behind me. It was immediately followed by heavy footsteps.

Crap ... Shit ...

I spun around. Only the living made a noise when they walked, and I wasn't on good terms with a lot of them. Surely Iollan hadn't followed me ... Surely it wasn't the police –

"Jordan!"

Mr Butch. Thank God.

I turned back to April and Grant, but they'd already disappeared.

"Jordan? Jord –" Mr Butch rounded the corner and then stopped in his tracks. He frowned, noticing the bits of leaves I must have still had in my hair and hood. "What happened to you?"

"Nothing." I quickly brushed myself down again and then felt Danny drift towards Mr Butch.

Play nice, I warned.

Mr Butch shivered the instant Danny passed through him. He turned around, but of course he didn't see anything. The man, the three boys and

Danny were all on a different frequency to him. "Come on, let's go," he said to me. "Natasha's waitin' for us."

I followed his long strides, checking over my shoulder one last time. Other than Danny, the three boys and the man tying the noose on a distant wall, we were completely alone.

CHAPTER TWENTY FOUR

I stole a glance at Mr Butch. I still needed to tell him my next plan. I knew he'd be livid – *again* – but what could I do? I had to keep going, and whether he came with me or not, I had to tell Natasha that I wouldn't be hitching another lift. If I left without telling her, she'd get suspicious, and neither of us wanted that.

We were now nearing the wooden barrier. Here goes: "I need to go into Brookston Forest. It's literally across from these ruins," I blurted out.

He swore. *(Livid. Called it.)* "This is just a never-endin' piss-take with you."

"It's the last place I need to go – *honest*. Danny wants me to find something in there." I could tell him that much because I knew he was still curious about what he'd seen in the chippy alleyway; but I wasn't sure if I wanted to give him the whole "casting Cillian's spirit away" details. "After that,

I'll go straight to the police with you. I promise."

"Your promises don't mean shit to me," he said. "And you're very bloody vague, you know that?"

I didn't know how to respond, so I said nothing.

"Look," Mr Butch stopped and turned to face me. I did the same, although I couldn't quite meet his eyes. "I don't know why but for some stupid reason I believe you, okay — not about all that ghost rubbish," he added when my face lit up, "but about you comin' with me to the police when you've finished whatever it is you're doin'. A delinquent or runaway would've fled by now. Besides, I've already come this far. Might as well follow you for another couple've hours."

Did I just hear that right? I half wondered whether Danny had planted the idea in his head.

Mr Butch sighed, but not his usual fed-up sigh; this was more reserved. "Here's what's gonna happen," he said. I forced myself to look at him. "You're either gonna surprise me and do a runner after all, makin' me look like an even bigger bleedin' mug, or … I'm right and I can trust you to pay up and clear my name. I'm warnin' you, though —" Mr Butch's voice reverted back to its usual threatening tone "— if this turns out to be some huge bloody wind-up, I can promise you'll end up regrettin' it. You saw how fast that story of us spread. The truth'll come out eventually. I'll make sure everybody knows what a troublemakin' time-waster you really are."

I couldn't help grinning. Mr Butch actually

trusted me – well, sort of. That made everything so much easier. "I won't let you down," I said.

Mr Butch didn't return the smile, but I felt like some of the tension between us had finally lifted.

"We'll get Natasha to drop us off closer," Mr Butch said, as we continued towards the car.

That was fine by me. I was just glad there was no more extra hassle.

We stepped over the wooden barrier and crossed the road. When we reached the car, I saw Natasha talking on her phone. Mr Butch went around the other side, and when I opened my door she quickly hung up.

"Are you ready to go back?" she asked. She was smiling but it looked false in every way.

I shut the door behind me and told her what Mr Butch and I had arranged.

"Oh! Okay then. Yes, I can drive you closer. Would you like me to wait around until you're finished there too? Like I said, buses are a nightmare out here and it's really no bother for me. I'm not going shopping now anyway."

Mr Butch had just got in the back with me. "Why not?" he asked, picking up on her change in plans. He probably felt the same way I did, like she was hiding something.

"No reason. I've just changed my mind." She spoke way too quickly, like someone who was guilty. I glanced over at the passenger seat and my heart skipped a beat. The newspaper was missing.

Crap – did that mean she'd read the article?

When I looked back at Natasha, she was staring right at me. I didn't want to be in her car anymore.

"Um, you know actually, since it's not raining, I think we'll just walk to the forest instead …" I said, trying to play it cool. "Thanks for the offer though. Come on, Uncle Leslie –"

"Wait!" she said.

I ignored her. If Mr Butch hadn't figured out something was wrong by now, he really wasn't as sharp as I thought he was.

I pulled the handle, but the door wouldn't budge. I tried again, and again, and Mr Butch did the same on his side – but it was no good: both doors were locked.

Mr Butch sighed. "Natasha, please let us out."

She shook her head.

"Come on, this is ridiculous!" he said, and I suddenly felt cold all over. "You shouldn't believe everythin' you read –"

"Of course *you'd* say that," she remarked.

"You're makin' a pretty dumb decision then, keepin' me locked in 'ere with you if you fell for all that rubbish. Don't you remember the part that said not to approach me?"

Natasha's face hardened, making me shiver. "You wouldn't dare touch me. I've already called the police so if you lay even a *finger* on me, they'll know exactly who it was."

Oh God. The police were on their way. They

were coming *right here*. That meant we only had minutes to get away and put some distance between us and her.

I turned to Mr Butch.

"Open the doors," he said to Natasha, looking completely nonchalant. "Or I'll unlock them myself."

"Not a chance. You're staying where you are!" Natasha's voice quivered at the end of her sentence. She turned in her seat, eyes fixed on Mr Butch. "People like you … You're *sick!* How can you live with yourself!"

"Natasha," I said. I was about to explain that the papers had got it all wrong, that I wasn't being kidnapped, when Mr Butch moved forward in his seat.

"STAY AWAY FROM ME!" she screeched.

I flinched at the noise but Mr Butch kept going, trying to climb between the front seats to unlock our doors. The gap was slim, and he was hardly supple – that didn't stop him, though.

Natasha scrambled for the handle to let herself out. She was still screaming when my own door suddenly swung open, and then I was being pulled from the car. The police had got me. I was going to be taken home.

I'm so sorry, Danny …

They were rough, whoever was dragging me. Soon they'd be cuffing Mr Butch, and Natasha would spin whatever story her panicked brain thought it had seen.

The police officer dropped me to the ground, rolled me onto my back and –

And it wasn't the police.

The first thing I saw was the glinting blade he held above his head. I tried pulling away, but the man had a tight hold on my arm. His eyes were rolled to the back of his head and a long line of drool hung between his mouth and the collar of his lopsided fluorescent jacket. The way he moved ... the way he looked ... I'd never seen anyone possessed before.

I thrashed, I kicked, I squirmed – he wouldn't let go. Shit, he *wouldn't let go!*

My fight-or-flight instinct abandoned me. Instead, my mind went blank and my body froze. I could hardly breathe. All I could do was lie there shaking. Panicking.

This was the end.

I could feel his fingers digging into my upper arm, could see the string of drool now dripping onto my chest, and could smell the metallic of blood mixed with days-old sweat. I saw the rust on the blade above his pale, muddy fist. And then the knife came down.

"URGH!"

That wasn't the sound of me being stabbed. It was me being thrown to the side by Mr Butch as he lunged at the man on top of me.

Natasha started the engine. The tyres spun for a second, covering me in dirt before tearing off down the road.

289

I sat up, coughing and rubbing dust from my eyes. Across the road, the possessed man and Mr Butch were wrestling on the ground. Mr Butch was holding the guy's wrist with one hand, that same blade that almost finished me only millimetres away from his face. The man was doing the same to Mr Butch's other arm, as if restraining him in turn. It took me a moment to realise that Mr Butch was holding a knife of his own. It was much smaller, but it glinted brighter than the rusty one he was trying to prise out of the man's hand. Had he found it in the guy's jacket?

Mr Butch grunted with every calculated block and hit, whereas the fluorescent-jacket man was silent and manic. Somehow the guy managed to get his arm free and began swinging his knife around, missing Mr Butch by mere inches every time.

I held my breath.

Oh God. Just run, Mr Butch ... I thought. But he didn't. He stayed close to the man, dodging mostly, and throwing in hits of his own when he could.

I glanced behind me. Natasha's car was nowhere in sight. She'd completely abandoned us. I'm not sure what she could've done to help but the fact that she'd left without a moment's hesitation made me hate her ...

Thwack!

I turned in time to see fluorescent-jacket man fall to the floor. Mr Butch's fist was clenched – he'd just decked the guy.

Sprawled on his stomach, I saw a bus company logo printed on the back of his hi-vis.

No way …

The man sat up. Blood was now mingled with his drool and as I kept staring, I realised who it was: bald head, smooth face … it was the driver who went missing before we reached Brookston. Last time I saw him, he was cheery, sane and wearing glasses. No wonder I didn't recognise him.

The possessed bus driver got to his feet, and once he'd spotted me, he started heading my way.

"Oi!" Mr Butch called out at him. "Where d'you think you're goin'?"

Mr Butch was already on him. He punched the guy again and I watched him fall back down. Mr Butch didn't stop there, though. Every time fluorescent-jacket man tried to stand, Mr Butch would flatten him, refusing to give the driver even the slightest chance of getting up.

The heavy blows looked hard enough to knock out a professional boxer. Being possessed, though, it didn't affect him the way it should've. It was terrifying, like watching an actual Terminator or something.

Mr Butch eventually started to tire. His swings were wide, and the speed of each delivery had slowed. The bus driver was in a league of his own. Eventually, whoever had possessed him managed to evade one of Mr Butch's hits.

Mr Butch fell through his punch. Before he had

a chance to recover, the possessed driver gave him an almighty shove in the chest.

The power behind it was something else. Mr Butch skidded past me, across the road and onto the muddy grass.

Christ, that must've hurt. I thought that was it, game over, when Mr Butch staggered to his feet. He was made of tough stuff. I knew it was a good idea to keep him around.

"COME ON, THEN!" he bellowed.

But the possessed bus driver had lost interest in Mr Butch. With his eyes still upturned, his attention was all on me.

I wasn't sure if it was a good idea to try and connect with this spirit, but I did. Now that I wasn't so focused on the knife, I was able to raise my frequency enough to open up.

My chest tightened and I was suddenly fuelled with rage – not my rage, though. It belonged to whoever had just tried to kill me.

The spirit was definitely male. He was cold, unforgiving, and he had a *lot* of energy. He pushed an image of a shovel into my mind – digging holes, planting flowers, covering the roots with wet dirt … Gardening? No, not gardening. It was something else.

I don't know how I got all this – I just did. Like the way I had been able to read April.

I thought back to the voice inside the orphanage ruins, telling me to go back because *"he's here"*

... And then I remembered what April had told me about her brother's whereabouts. Cillian was here, and it had taken me until now to realise I was looking right at him.

I wish the hatred I felt for this monster gave me the strength to at least insult him. But I was a goddam coward, no denying it, and I swear I saw Cillian smirk in agreement.

He raised the bus driver's hand, bringing the knife up to his neck. I knew what was coming next ...

I tried not to gag as I watched him press the blade into the driver's skin.

Mr Butch swore, stepping forward until he was between the two of us. He was trying to shield me. "Look away," he said, but I couldn't. I watched Cillian force the driver to slice open his own throat, hacking away with that dull knife as if sawing through a joint of beef. Blood ran down his neck and squirted out as he severed an artery. The flow seemed to thicken the more he hacked.

When he was finished, he dropped the knife in the wet grass. The driver was still standing upright, still staring straight at me with upturned eyes ...

I could hear Mr Butch breathing heavily in front of me. God knows what he was thinking, but because I was on the same frequency as Cillian, I knew exactly what this meant. It was the same gesture as a finger across the throat, just in a more graphic, more horrific way – a threat that said: *'You're dead'.*

Satisfied that I understood his message, Cillian fled, abandoning his host.

The driver collapsed, with gouts of blood still gushing from his neck. He flailed, he twitched, he gargled and spluttered. And then nothing. Nothing but more red.

CHAPTER TWENTY FIVE

I couldn't take my eyes off the body. A pool of blood seeped out from beneath him, soaking into his clothes, dyeing the ground a shade of crimson I never wanted to see again. And it just kept spreading. I had to fight the urge not to throw up. How could there be that much blood?

"You all right?" Mr Butch asked.

The answer was no, and I wasn't going to pretend otherwise.

"Kid?"

He was dead. No doubt about it.

"Come on, Jordan." Mr Butch pulled me to my feet and helped steer me away from the mess that used to be a living person. After a few steps, though, my shaky legs gave way and I collapsed to the ground again.

Cillian had killed him – and he'd almost killed me. I could've been lying in my own pool of blood …

"She's ratted us out. I know you're in shock but if we don't leave soon the police are gonna catch us red-handed."

Red.

I didn't move.

Danny pressed a leaf against a small cut on the back of my hand. Instead of helping me back up, Mr Butch knelt beside me and started wiping the dagger in the grass. There wasn't much blood on it but there was enough to make me gag.

When it was as clean as it was going to get, he took off one of his boots and slid the knife under the insole where there was a hollowed-out place especially for it. The knife didn't belong to the bus driver – it was his, and it'd been with him this entire time. Maybe I should've felt wary, but the shock seemed to have dulled all my senses.

With the knife now secure, Mr Butch slipped on his boot, tied the lace and turned to me.

"Are you hurt?" he asked.

"I don't think so."

"So you can stand?"

There was only one way to find out. My body was still trembling but maybe I'd be able to stay on my feet.

Mr Butch pulled me up again and this time he didn't let go. He supported my weight as he walked us away from the bus driver's body. And I knew it was pointless to dwell on anything other than getting out of here, but I couldn't help wondering

… What was the driver's name? Did he have a wife? Any kids? Had he made plans for the weekend …?

No. Block it out, Jordan.

"You carry a knife." I said to Mr Butch, distracting myself.

Mr Butch continued walking. "A small one, yeah."

"Why?"

He shrugged. "Never know when you're gonna need one."

Without thinking, I turned back to look at the dead driver.

"Hey." Mr Butch jerked me forward. "Just put it out your mind. The shock'll wear off."

"Easy for you to say."

"I was in the Reserves for nine years, kid. I know what I'm talkin' about."

That explained the knife. And a lot of things, really. Even so … "The army can't help me with what I've got to do."

I hadn't meant to say that out loud.

Mr Butch stared down at me, looking kinda insulted. It was true, though! What good was being trained to fire hundreds of bullets if they wouldn't even graze the enemy? I couldn't kill a man who was already dead – as much as I wanted to – but the dead man could still kill me.

"I just saved your life, didn't I?" Mr Butch said.

"Yeah, but I'm not sure how much time you've bought me."

"And what the hell's *that* supposed to mean?"

I yanked my arm away and met his steely gaze. Suddenly I had no problem standing. "I saw him!" I said. "In his eyes."

"What are you talkin' about?"

"I'm talking about that bus driver. He was the one who stopped the bus before we reached Brookston. He was possessed by Cillian O'Hagan."

"Cillian *who?*" Before I could answer, Mr Butch said: "Look, I know you meetin' your brother was a lie, but all this talk about your brother's ghost and people bein' possessed ... Are you –?"

"What? *Crazy?*" I was sick of everyone thinking I was mental. I had thought that maybe he was starting to get it, that he would take my word even if he didn't fully believe. I guess I'd thought wrong. "Yep, that's me. Go back to Woodlock and everyone'll tell you the same. In fact, tell the police while you're at it. My therapist can back you up on how *delusional* I am –"

"Jordan." He reached out to grab me but I stormed off. We couldn't waste any more time standing around. The police were on their way and now there was a dead body lying only metres away from us.

Mr Butch cursed, catching me up in several long strides. "I just want to know what's goin' on!"

"You know enough to know I have a fucking screw loose –"

"All right!" Mr Butch clenched his fists. Ex-army

or not, I wasn't backing down.

He was probably waiting for me to collapse again. I didn't, though, and it only took a few minutes to reach the edge of the forest. "All right," Mr Butch said again. Calmer this time. He must have realised he'd hit a nerve. "I'm sorry I implied you might not be all there," he added, pointing briefly to his head. "You've gotta admit, though, it does sound a bit crackers."

I said nothing.

"Kid, all I know is that there's *somethin'* you need to do for your brother. But what is it? What the hell are you doin' out here?"

"You really want to know?" I swallowed. All the lies and secrecy were getting too much; I was up to my neck in it all. I needed to come clean, even if it changed everything. With that thought, I took a deep breath and finally confessed. "I'm going after a monster. A *murderer.* That Cillian O'Hagan guy I mentioned – he's the one who killed ..." I choked on my words, even though I'd said it a hundred times before. I guess some things never get easier to say.

"Your brother." Mr Butch finished my sentence for me, having pieced the story together. He nodded as if he understood – and maybe he did, who's to say – but it wasn't the reaction I was expecting. "I'm sorry, kid. Criminals like him should be used as target practice." He sounded proper sincere.

"He deserves worse than that."

I could feel him looking at me. And then came

the lecture. "I get that you're angry," he said – story of my life. "But do you even have a plan? You can't act on your emotions, Jordan. That's never a good idea. This man is *dangerous*. What, you think that just because you want to hurt him bad enough, you'll develop super-strength to pin his arse down? Unfortunately, mate, that's not gonna happen. And let's say you *do* pin him down – then what? You gonna kill him? I'm sure that's exactly what your parents would want: one son buried six feet under and another behind bars. No, you've gotta think things through in life. Especially in these circumstances." He shook his head. "Maybe we ought to wait for the police to –"

"No!" I looked at him, making sure he didn't stop. I thought we were past the whole 'waiting for the police' idea. "Listen, it's … it's not like that."

"What d'you mean?"

What *did* I mean? Did I really want to tell him the *whole* truth? I suppose I had nothing to lose. He already knew about Danny and that I talked to dead people – whether he believed it or not. "Cillian died a few days ago. He's … well, he's still here. As a spirit. And you're right – he *is* dangerous. He refuses to move on, and that's why I'm here: to connect him with his sister so she can cast him into another realm."

There. I'd said it. There was no going back now

Mr Butch was silent for quite some time. I didn't know what to say – or even if I should – so I focused on walking, heading further into the forest like April told me to. Eventually, Mr Butch said, "Ghosts are a tricky topic. I've seen a lot've killin' in my time — that's a ton've ghosts wanderin' around, don't you think? And how come hardly anyone's ever seen them? Nah … I believe that when you're dead, you're dead. That bus driver *could've* been possessed, but most likely he was a ravin' lunatic."

"He seemed pretty sane last time we saw him," I muttered.

"Who's to say it was definitely him, though? We only saw the driver for a few seconds while he printed off our tickets. I know *I* can't remember much about him." Mr Butch looked up at the branches above us and sighed. "I don't think you're crazy, all right? I just think if you can give me some hard evidence, it'd be easier for me to understand."

It wasn't an unreasonable request …

"I *want* to believe you," he added. "Maybe if you get your brother — Daniel, is it? — to 'appear' again … it might help change my mind."

I knew he didn't expect to be convinced, but he was being more open-minded about it than Mum or Dad ever was; more than *anyone* ever was. I decided it'd be worth the effort to try and convince him. "Just remember," I said, "he doesn't always show. Sometimes he's busy, other times he's just plain stubborn."

Mr Butch nodded, as if he expected the excuses.

Danny wasn't here yet, so I stopped walking. I

really needed to concentrate in reaching out to him because I was still feeling ill from seeing all that blood.

I tried to feel for any change in temperature as I began to call his name in my head. I knew he'd hear me eventually but whether he listened or not was a whole different matter:

Danny, I need you to show Mr Butch another sign. It's important. He'll believe everything if you do this one thing.

Nothing happened. I ignored the expectant look on Mr Butch's face and carried on:

Please, Danny. Just do what you did in the alleyway back in the village.

Still nothing.

Why is it always such a challenge to get you to cooperate with me!

"Forget it, kid," Mr Butch said. "Let's keep movin' before – *urgh!*" Mr Butch gripped his chest and for a second I thought he was having a heart attack. Then a familiar chill cut through me.

"He's here," I said, unable to contain my smile. Danny had just passed through Mr Butch, just like in the orphanage ruins. It wasn't a very nice sensation, I'll give him that – Danny had done it to me plenty of times – but it wasn't painful. Having said that, Danny had seemed more aggressive this time. He was probably annoyed at being told what to do.

Mr Butch looked around, trying to find him.

"You won't be able to see him," I explained.

"He's basically a ball of energy – like a poltergeist."

"Right ... And he's here now?"

"Yep. He just passed through you."

Mr Butch grimaced. "I'll need a bit more proof than that."

Danny tugged the sleeve of my jacket. I wasn't sure if that was the extra bit of proof Mr Butch had asked for or whether it was just him being impatient. Either way, it went unnoticed by Mr Butch.

"Danny," I said, out loud this time. I was about to beg him one last time when I heard sirens blaring in the distance. Mr Butch and I jumped at the noise. Danny hadn't listened to me after all: he'd been trying to warn us.

CHAPTER TWENTY SIX

We set off, sprinting deeper into the forest. "That Natasha's really gone and done it for us," Mr Butch said.

"Tell me about it," I muttered, before directing my thoughts to Danny: *Is there any way you can keep them off our trail?*

The police would spot the body in no time. They could hardly miss it. And it wouldn't be long until they searched the forest. Natasha's brief, panicked statement claiming she'd found "the missing boy" was probably enough to bring out half of Devon's police force. And if we were still here by the time dogs and helicopters got involved, it would take a miracle to escape.

Up ahead our path branched out in four directions. The far left and right pathways led away from the forest; the two middle paths headed downhill, one route short and steep, the other longer with a gradual decline.

"We should stick to the outskirts," Mr Butch said. "If we head too deep into this place, we'll lose our way and might backtrack straight into them."

It made sense, but Danny was telling me to take one of the two middle lanes. He was directing me just like he had in the taxi.

"Let's go left." Mr Butch grabbed my arm, pulling me towards the path he wanted us to follow.

"Hold up a second," I said, and even though I tried to resist, Mr Butch didn't slow down. "Danny wants us to go further into the forest."

"Trust me, it's a bad idea."

"I know but …" I shut up, suddenly on high alert. I could hear something: a rustle from one of the trees and a continuous splintering of wood …

Mr Butch heard it too. He stopped, trying to work out where the sound was coming from. We both clocked it at the same time: up ahead, a thin tree over three times my height was bending into the pathway he'd planned to take – like some heavy invisible force was weighing it down. I didn't know Danny had that kind of strength. He kept pulling the tree, causing it to creak under the strain until it finally gave way.

Birds all around us took to the sky as the tree landed with a crash. The police must've heard it, but all I could do was stare in awe. Its branches were caught in the hedge, suspending the trunk at an angle over the path. This made trashing my room look like nothing.

Mr Butch swore, and then the same thing happened to the fourth pathway: creaking … straining … *Crash!* The trunk of a similar-sized tree snapped, blocking the way. We could've climbed over either tree but the message was clear, even to Mr Butch: we were not to pass.

"*That* …" He pointed to the tree blocking the left lane, and then did the same to the one on the right. It might not have been enough to fully convince him of ghosts or spirits or whatever you want to call them, but at least it made him question the truth.

"You get used to it," I said, although I had never seen Danny knock down a tree before.

Mr Butch stared back at me and shook his head. "No … No, that's not normal."

"He wants us to keep going," I explained, and then Danny lifted the hood of my jacket over my head – in plain view of Mr Butch. My brother was getting impatient again.

"What the …?" Mr Butch actually took a step back.

"You're not afraid, are you?" I smirked. "He won't hurt you – as long as you don't hurt me."

"I'm not *afraid*. I just weren't expectin' a bleedin' magic trick halfway through our getaway."

I remembered the first time I'd seen Danny knock something over. It was a couple of days after the funeral. I was choosing my cereal when Danny pushed a half-full box of Coco Pops out of the cupboard. I ran off screaming even though I knew it was him. I guess by comparison Mr Butch was handling it better than I had.

"Let's go," I said to him. We had to make a move. The middle lanes were left untouched, so now there was only one way to go – Danny's way.

Mr Butch breathed in through his nose, and then we set into a jog down the steeper of the two paths.

I had to concentrate on keeping the same steady pace. Any faster and the momentum would trip me over. I kept hearing Mr Butch curse as the stones skidded from under his feet, too. Maybe we should've taken the other path.

Now that I was moving again, Danny left – no doubt to distract the police. Without a guide, though, I didn't know where to go when we reached the bottom of the slope.

Then Julie appeared, a few metres away.

"Holy shit!" Mr Butch had spotted her too. He slipped but somehow managed to keep his balance, stumbling to a halt instead of falling flat on his face. I did the same, stopping just ahead of him. "That's who I saw up on that cliff …" he said.

How was he able to see her? And wasn't it too dark for him to make out any details at the time? Unless he just knew … like a supernatural sense he wasn't even aware of.

"She's going to show us where to go," I said.

Mr Butch looked at me. "You *know* her?"

"She's one of Cillian's victims."

"*What?*"

A dog barked somewhere far away. It was followed by the shouts of several men. They were in the forest.

Please, Danny, hold them back.

"I take it you're going to lead us to Cillian?" I said to her.

Her face was solemn; she was nervous. I wanted to reassure her but what could I say? Even I was panicking. Without a word, Julie ran on ahead, her footsteps silent as snowfall.

"Come on!" I said to Mr Butch. He was staring at Julie, his mouth agape. He soon came to his senses, when we heard the barking start up again. There was definitely more than one tracker dog with them.

"This is insane," Mr Butch said, setting into another run with me. He made sure I stayed ahead of him, using me as a barrier between himself and Julie.

She led us through a thorny thicket where all the bushes and trees looked identical. We would've got lost without her, for sure. She was zipping left, zipping right, passing straight through branches that Mr Butch and I had to bulldoze our way through. I almost twisted my ankle at one point.

When we were back out on another stony pathway, Julie came to a sudden stop.

Mr Butch and I slowed to a halt behind her. I bent double with my hands on my knees. "Which way?" I asked, gasping. My chest was on fire.

Julie pointed right. We were to go on by ourselves. Like Danny, Julie must have been staying to distract the police. Even if they didn't see her, she'd still be able to throw off the dogs and spook any superstitious cops.

Mr Butch and I headed on, our feet dragging and our minds racing. I knew he must have a million and one questions, but either he was too out of breath to ask or he didn't want to risk the police hearing him. Not that I would've been able to answer. It hurt to breathe, let alone speak. My mouth was watering and my stomach was threatening to heave.

"What the ...!" Mr Butch stopped again. Melissa had just materialised next to a patch of purple flowers ahead of us. I wasn't used to seeing Mr Butch so shaken.

I kept going, clutching my side and trying not to throw up.

"Hey," I breathed. "Which ... way?"

"Cut through there," Melissa said, pointing to the bushes next to us. Heading off trail again was probably a good idea. "Just keep going as straight as you can until you come across a brick wall. It says 'private property' but the owner has been dead for years. Nobody's bothered to tear it down."

"Okay ... Thanks ..." I was so desperate for another drink.

"April is already there and the rest of us will join you when we can. We're just holding off the police until you're inside. Did you know they have specialist search teams in here looking for you?"

"Fan-bloody-tastic!" Mr Butch spat, not too spooked by Melissa to comprehend the amount of trouble we were in.

"You should go," she said.

I wasn't sure how close the police were, but the look on her face convinced me that they couldn't be far.

So I ran, pushing past more branches, thorns and stinging nettles, with Mr Butch right on my tail. We headed straight as best we could, exactly like Melissa had told us. The trees here were much closer together than the ones we'd sprinted through with Julie. Twice my trousers snagged on something, but I just let them tear.

I was starting to think we might never make it out of the damn thicket, when we came across an uneven field with an electricity pylon in the middle of it.

"There's that wall," Mr Butch said. The brick wall Melissa had mentioned was just on the other side of this field.

Mr Butch scanned the wall for a way in. Before he could reply, though, one of the police officers called out: "Put your hands in the air!"

My stomach dropped. I looked behind me and saw two cops at the other end of the thicket, pushing their way through the thick-branched thorn bush we'd already battled our way through.

Shit. They'd found us.

How the hell did they get here so fast? –

"C'mon," Mr Butch pulled me forwards, into the clearing. When had he decided to help me all the way? Was it when Danny knocked the tree down, or when Julie and Melissa showed themselves? Did this mean he *believed* me?

We set into one final sprint, crossing the open field that stood between us and the wall Cillian lurked somewhere behind. It would only take us a minute, two at tops, but I could already hear the bushes rustling behind us, could hear our pursuers' voices clearer than ever, and the faint beeping and static of their radios.

"Shit," Mr Butch hissed. "We're not ... gonna ... make it ..."

He was right.

"Still don't ... see a door or gate," he added.

"I think that's it!" I pointed to a silvery glint that must have been a gate, right at the end of the wall. But it was too far away for us to reach.

"Run ... straight ahead ..." Mr Butch said between breaths. "When you get to the wall ... don't stop ... I'll give you a ... boost up ... all right?"

"But ... how will you ...?"

"STOP RIGHT THERE!" The police were out of the brambles.

"STAY WHERE YOU ARE!"

"ON THE GROUND, NOW!"

I looked down, watching my feet so I didn't slip

in mud or trip on any rabbit holes or molehills. We were nearly there, very nearly there.

Mr Butch ran on ahead of me. The police were bellowing at us to stop and shouting orders into their radios – I could hear their voices, their panting, their footsteps … I could hear the hard breathing of one of the officers behind me. If we messed this up, then we'd both get caught.

Mr Butch approached the wall but didn't slow down. He slammed into it at full force, crouching and cupping his hands all in one fluid motion, ready to boost me up. It was now or never.

I ran at him and, at the last possible moment, leapt, my foot landing perfectly in his hands. I was instantly hoisted high into the air.

I grabbed the top of the wall and managed to heave myself up the rest of the way. We'd done it! We hadn't screwed up. When I looked back, though, the cop who'd been at my heels had already seized Mr Butch, forcing him to the ground and cuffing him.

"Just go!" Mr Butch called out to me. Two other officers had almost caught up and behind them were half a dozen more. I also spotted three dogs, now off lead, galloping and overtaking everyone.

I did as Mr Butch said and jumped down to the other side. My legs tingled from the impact; there was no time for me to recover, no time for me to get my bearings. I was immediately up and running again. Only an aged brick wall separated me from all the chaos, and it wouldn't take long for them to scale it.

CHAPTER
TWENTY SEVEN

Everything was darker now that I was back under the cold shelter of trees. My eyes quickly adjusted but I had no idea if I was heading in the right direction — and even if all this running did throw off the police, I knew the Alsatians would sniff me out. Luckily, I had a plan for that.

"Danny?"

He was already by my side.

"Get rid of the dogs!"

I had seen back at Cillian's house that a ghost could spook a dog into submission. Hopefully the same would work on these.

I felt a stone in my left shoe that stabbed into my heel whenever I pressed down. I couldn't stop to remove it, so I carried on with an almost-limp, losing myself deeper and deeper in the forest.

The storm had turned the place into a waterlogged obstacle course. Twice I almost skidded on soggy leaves and wet grass, but it wasn't enough to stop me. I pushed myself into another run, my feet pounding against stones and dirt. In the distance, dogs were still barking and men were still shouting. They must've been over the wall by now.

"Just find his body," I said, not letting myself get distracted. Cillian's spirit wouldn't be far from it, and neither would April.

I was covering a lot of ground and I wanted to keep it that way. Despite my best efforts, though, the stitch in my side was getting worse. I tried to stick it out as long as I could, but eventually I had to stop. Bending over to catch my breath, I was about ready to pass out.

As the wind blew through my hair, cooling my face and stabbing my throat, I wondered how fast it would carry my scent to the police dogs.

I took the stone out of my shoe then pushed myself on, trusting that Danny would correct me if I strayed too far. I rounded the trunk of an old thick tree and –

"Oh-my-God!" I jumped back, my heart thudding so hard I was sure I was going to throw up. Grant was standing in front of me, translucent and pale as ever. "A simple *"Hi, Jordan"* would've been nice," I said.

"Danny told me to show you the way," Grant said by way of explanation. He didn't say anything else. He just ran, silently, along the muddy path.

I groaned, clutching my side. *If I get out of this*

alive, I swear I'll never run again.

It was strange to think that the last time I was alone and sprinting desperately through a forest, I was searching for my brother. *(I jumped the ditch and squeezed past the fence … calling my brother's name …)* And now, five years later, the only thing that had changed was the person I was looking for. *(… All I heard was my own lonely echo bouncing back …)* It was still about Danny, though. It always had been.

"How much further is it?" My sides and throat were burning.

Grant didn't reply. He stopped by the opening of another clearing and waited for me to catch up.

"Look," he said, pointing to the other side. "Over there, by the tree with the broken tree-house."

To call it a tree-house was an overstatement. It had a jagged wooden floor and three torn bed sheets that hung as makeshift walls. Maybe it was possible for it to hold the weight of a child, but I wouldn't have bet on it.

There was a small pile of branches on the ground beneath it, and …

And poking out behind the tree trunk was a pair of legs, splayed at a very weird angle. Stained baggy jeans, old walking boots …Definitely male; definitely dead.

Even though the torso and head were completely hidden from view, I knew exactly who it was. I ignored the pain in my sides and throat, forcing myself into the clearing for a better look. And when I rounded the tree, there he was. Cillian O'Hagan.

I remembered his face – the photographs of him along the stairs were ingrained in my mind – only now his skin was grey, and his stupid smile had been replaced by a pained expression, frozen into place.

And there was blood. Not as much as I saw gushing out the bus driver, but it was enough to make my stomach turn. It had soaked into his clothes, matted his thin hair and absorbed into the ground, contaminating where he lay.

There were cuts on his face from where he'd hit other branches on his way down, and a dark patch of dried blood stained one of the roots sticking out the ground – that must have been where Cillian cracked his head when he landed. Did he slip or did his branch snap? Whatever the case, I hoped he hadn't died instantly. Please let him have suffered.

I looked down at his calloused hands: the murder weapons that finished off my brother and so many others. The only reason I didn't spit in this monster's face was because I didn't want to interfere with any potential forensic investigation.

Then the temperature dropped, colder than I'd ever felt it before. It wasn't the weather – and it wasn't Danny, Melissa or Julie … It wasn't *any* of the ghost children.

No. I knew exactly who this was.

"Crap," I hissed, backing away from Cillian's body. He was here.

There was no way to tell which direction the icy chill was coming from. It was everywhere all at once, making it impossible for me to find him. "Show yourself!" I said. I didn't have the nerve or desire to prolong it.

Grant had already disappeared. Did the others need him, or was he just afraid? Either way, I didn't blame him for leaving me.

At first the only sound I could hear was my chattering jaw — whether it was from the cold or the rush of adrenaline, I wasn't sure. Then I heard something else: a faint creak, right above me. I looked up into the tree Cillian's body lay beneath, and …

There he was, sitting on a thick branch beneath the flimsy tree-house. Maybe that was as high as he'd climbed before the fall.

I couldn't move. He was pale, desaturated, translucent — just like all the others — but the look he gave me was something else. It was a look that seemed to say he'd got what he'd wanted; like he'd planned this all along. All I could do was watch his mouth stretch into a smile that made him look even more sinister. "You're here," he said.

I gritted my teeth. Even though my jaw was still chattering, my voice never faltered. "Yeah," I replied lowly, staring back at him. "I'm here."

CHAPTER
TWENTY EIGHT

Killer. *Killer.* It was all I could think as he stared down at me from his stupid tree. My body froze, and even though I wanted to insult him, even though I wanted to kick his corpse and make him suffer, I was still afraid.

"I hear you've been looking for me," he said, his voice as smooth as running cement.

I couldn't reply. I was too riled up to form a coherent sentence, let alone follow a conversation. How the hell was I supposed to convince the scumbag, if I couldn't even talk to him?

"Well," Cillian continued, "you've got your wish. Any last words?"

Screw you, I thought. Danny would kick his ghost arse way before he got close enough.

"What were you doing up in that tree?" I asked. I needed to know. The failed climb that gave him an undeservedly swift death ... what was the point of it?

The temperature dipped as April materialised in the bushes next to his body. No Danny yet, though. She'd left the others, ready to convince her brother into leaving this realm ... just as soon as I got him to see her – a task that now seemed virtually impossible.

She was right there! How could he not see her? Especially if they were as close as she and Iollan claimed they were?

Cillian laughed, as oblivious as a corpse. "I found a new target. She didn't know I was watching. Then again, none of them ever do."

I balled up my fists. "You *sick* demented bast–"

He soared out the tree, stopping inches away from me. He was about half a foot taller but some of that was due to him levitating.

"I'd think carefully before insulting me – your next words could be your last. You come here trying to get my father arrested the *second* I die ... I *won't* let that happen. He understood why I did what I did. The police wouldn't help us, and those brats ... *worthless* ... they deserve what they got!"

"My brother isn't worthless," I said.

" *'My brother isn't worthless'* – oh, piss off. You're just a stupid, scared kid. Ever since I first heard you curse my name, you've relied on your dead brother and that taxi driver the entire time. I'll tell you something, though ... Danny's no match for me."

April shook her head. "Don't," she pleaded

with me.

Don't what, though? Retaliate? Torment him like he was tormenting me? He thought he and April were above everyone. How wrong he was ... I was reminded of what Aaron said back at Cillian's house: "What you and your sister have," I repeated. "It's nothing special. Everybody has someone they love, people they'd do anything for. Those children you killed — they all had families. And Danny ... he wasn't just my twin. He was my best friend. No doubt like April was to you."

"Don't make me laugh," Cillian snarled. "If you cared about your brother half as much as I cared about April, you would have found a way to kill me years ago. That's what *I* did." There was a gleam in his eyes as he began listing off his victims, declaring them like they were trophies. "I got the ringleader in April's class. And then I got the fat boy I took back to my house. Then there was your brother, then the scrawny boy, then a girl with long hair in a graveyard ..."

I shivered, the hairs on my arms now standing on end. It wasn't a supernatural chill; it was more of an *I-want-to-wrap-my-hands-around-his-throat* kind of chill.

Since Cillian admitted he could sense Danny, I knew he'd be able to let in others. Did he know about his other victims? The ones in his house; the ones who had followed me since the castle ruins and the cemetery ...?

God knows. For now, though, sensing Danny was enough. It meant he knew how to get onto their frequency. Even if it was a mistake.

But if I was going to get him to connect with April, I needed him to direct all his thoughts to her – like I did with Danny. He'd never do that, though, if he didn't think she was there.

The only other way I could think to make this happen was by talking about April. If he thought about her enough, maybe, *maybe* she could reach him: "I get it, you lost your sister."

"No," he spat. "She was *taken* from me."

"Right. Just like Danny was taken from me. *You* took my brother …" *and I want you to burn in Hell for an eternity for it.* "You drowned him in June five years ago …" *you vile, vicious, inhumane monster...* "and like April, he was innocent. You killed him for *no reason!* It didn't change anything, though, did it? Your sister's still dead. Killing doesn't bring anyone back!"

"Nothing brings them back. What I did wasn't to turn back time. It was to punish others with the same irreversible sentence April got. I don't care who they are. If I could take them, I would. Their laughter, their games … it all reminded me of her. I had to *do* something other than clinging to the past."

So it wasn't just revenge. He was killing *because* of her, not *for* her.

I breathed in through my nose. April. I had to

get him to think about April. "How do you think your sister would feel if she could see what you've done?"

Cillian gave a single dry laugh. "She'd understand. She knows me better than anyone. Doesn't Danny know you? Speaking of which …" He clicked his fingers. "How do you think your brother felt when you ditched him by that tree?"

He didn't even give me a chance to reply. "I'll tell you," he said, and I could tell he was starting to enjoy himself. "When you ran off with your friends and left him all alone – before he spotted me – he turned around to watch you leave and I saw the look of betrayal on his face. Is that what you did? Betray him? I never did that to April."

Wait … Danny *saw* me? He watched me take off with Lewis, leaving him alone by the dead tree … "We had a disagreement," I said. "That's all. It didn't mean anything." Breathe in … Stay calm … He was just trying to wind me up. "We were kids. It was just a game. We would've ditched those guys eventually and I had the rest of the day to make it up to him! If *you* hadn't …" Breathe in … Stay calm … "It was a stupid game. Not a *betrayal*." April … I needed to get him to focus on April …

I was about to ask him if he had ever argued with his sister, when Cillian said, "Say what you want, I don't particularly care. It just made him an easier target."

My blood ran cold. Forget April.

"You're a *fucking psycho!*" I pulled out the piece of paper Danny had written the list of victims' names on, my hand trembling with rage. "You see this? I'll make sure the whole world knows what you and your dad did. You think you're the only one who wanted to get their own back on whoever tore you're world apart? The moment I found out what'd happened to Danny ... I wanted you *dead* for what you did to my brother. Not like this –" I pointed to his body, sprawled beneath the tree house "– I wanted to do it myself."

"HA! You wouldn't have got far. I'd have smashed your skull in before you even knew what'd hit you."

Suddenly, the piece of paper I was holding was torn free from my hand, as if the wind had carried it off. I reached for it, but I knew it was gone. Without touching the paper, using some sort of supernatural power, Cillian had snatched it from me. Then, still without touching it, he shredded the paper into a thousand tiny pieces.

Whatever, I thought, trying not to give him a reaction. It was hardly proof anyway. The police would pin him and his dad down in other ways.

"Besides," he continued. "I got your brother – what, five years ago? And you've done nothing until now. Building up the courage to face me, were you?"

"I didn't know where you were."

"Is that so? Well, I bet it angers you knowing I was in Brookston the entire time. Literally only a few miles from where I killed him." Cillian shrugged.

"It's not like *I* was playing hide-and-seek."

April tried to say something to me then, but I wasn't listening. I had the same exact feeling as when I went for Matt in Mr Anderson's classroom. My muscles tightened and my heart raced. I knew my punch would pass straight through Cillian, yet I clenched my fist anyway, drawing back my arm ready to strike his dumb leering face. He disappeared, though, before I had the chance.

Bastard.

My back turned cold; he'd already materialised behind me. This put April in plain view of him, yet still he couldn't see her. Nothing I said was getting through to him.

I spun round to look at him. "You've been so obsessed with killing that you've shut April out this whole time," I said. "She's here! She's behind me right now, next to your body –"

"No she's not!"

"Why don't you believe me?" I'd spent five years failing to convince people that Danny was still around, so I understood why he hadn't been able to see April when he was alive: some people refused to believe in ghosts. But he was now a spirit himself! *And* he could sense Danny. Surely this should make him at least *consider* the possibility of his sister being here.

"You're lying," he said. "If she was here, I'd be the first to see her."

"Not necessarily. Not if she can't get through to

you."

That's when I heard April shout out to me. "Tell him I was always with him whenever he walked the dogs, that I was with him just last month when Kasper chased a squirrel up a tree and then got spooked by a twig that fell on him."

I did, being her voice just like we agreed. And then April began telling me more and more: stories, secrets, special memories ...

Cillian said nothing as I repeated everything April said. He simply stared at the ground, his face as empty as a freshly dug grave. I gave him time to process everything. Surely he didn't need any more proof. There was no way I could've guessed half of what April had just told me.

Cillian's silence was almost reassuring, until he shook his head. He looked up at me, his expression suddenly contorted – and then he vanished again.

"Cillian!" April screeched.

For God's sake! I honestly thought we were close to convincing him.

I scanned the clearing for any sign of him. The air was cold and my forehead was tingling, so he was definitely here somewhere.

"Show yourself!" I called out.

He didn't. Instead, a stone clipped the back of my ear.

"Ouch." I reached up to touch the spot where I'd just been hit, and then a leafy branch was thrown at the back of my head.

"Stop it!" I said, knowing Cillian would ignore me. I dodged a conker and then dived out of the way of a stumpy log that rolled towards me. I may have been used to Danny chucking stuff at me but he only ever meant to get my attention that way, whereas this guy wanted me dead. "Just listen to — *ow!* Your sister's still here!"

April rushed in front of me to try and stop the blows, but they passed straight through her. All I could do was wait it out — and then Danny showed up.

My brother blocked most of what Cillian threw at me, launching it across the clearing and into the trees: I watched another branch that had been thrown suddenly change course and soar away from me into some brambles; then a handful of stones stopped dead in front of my face, levitating for just a second before dropping to the ground. I still tried to dodge out the way, but since Danny had got involved, I'd not been hit by anything.

I could tell that Cillian was getting annoyed. He hurled a couple more rocks — which Danny stopped, letting them fall to the ground in front of me — before releasing this horrible, wailing scream.

I covered my ears. It was frickin' terrifying, like some half-demon, half-banshee type thing. It only lasted a few seconds, but it made the Alsatians bark like mad in the distance. They must've heard him.

I was preparing myself for the next attack when the temperature around me became warmer. Cillian was gone.

"What happened?" I asked. "Where is he?"

Danny and April didn't respond.

Surely that wasn't it. Cillian wouldn't waste a perfectly good opportunity to get rid of me, especially when the police were so close – I could rat out his dad the second they spotted me. No, he was planning something, I knew it.

I stood there, waiting, constantly checking around me. I was expecting Cillian to reappear at any second. The more time passed, the more on edge I felt. What cruel scheme did he have up his sleeve? Maybe he'd try and sneak up behind me ... Maybe he'd –

I shivered. There was something in the shadows. Was it Cillian?

I stepped back, watching as he began to approach.

It was a human figure. Definitely a man's silhouette. He was way too sluggish to be a police officer and far too gangly to be Mr Butch. And anyway, the police would surely reach the clearing from the opposite direction – like I had done ...

I held my breath, watching the man slowly stagger out of the shadows and –

"Oh, it's just you, Iollan," I said. My body relaxed. He might've been Cillian's accomplice, but I knew he'd be wary after seeing what Danny could do to him.

As Iollan made his way into the clearing – staggering, shuffling, without the aid of his walking stick — I remembered Cillian's body behind me. Cruel or not, the monster was his son. I stepped aside for him to see.

I thought he'd be hysterical, maybe even break down in front of me or ... *something*. But Iollan remained silent. He must've been in shock.

As he got closer to Cillian's body, though, I saw that wasn't the case at all.

Iollan was now slumped, his face slack and his eyes rolled to the back of his head — just like the bus driver back at the orphanage ruins. He was being possessed by Cillian.

"Found a new host, have you?" I said. *What a coward.* "You going to kill him too when you're finished with him?"

My legs were shaking. The last time Cillian possessed someone, I almost ended up dead.

April ran to my side. "Convince him," she begged, as if I hadn't been trying. It was hopeless, though. Surely she could see that.

I knew the other ghost children were holding back the police, but I needed them all here now. Cillian was strong. There wasn't a lot Danny could do by himself.

"You're pathetic!" I said to Cillian, taking a step back. I was deciding whether it was worth making a run for it. "If you'd stop being so narrow-minded, you'd be able to see your sister!"

His silence was unnerving.

"Leave your dad and face me on your own!"

He slowly shook Iollan's head – *No* – and then he lunged at me.

CHAPTER TWENTY NINE

Wham! Iollan's fist slammed into the side of my face. I should've been expecting it ... don't know why I didn't prepare myself. I stumbled and Cillian seized his moment –

Whack! to the head.

Thump! in the stomach.

I could sense Danny darting in all directions trying to protect me, but the punches kept raining down. Cillian's host may have been a seventy-year-old man with deteriorating muscles, but his movements were as agile as something inhuman. It was impossible to predict his moves. I blocked and dodged as best I could until eventually, he got close enough for me to hit. I drew up my leg, fast and sharp, kneeing Iollan in the stomach.

I knew it wouldn't hurt Cillian – ghosts didn't feel physical pain – but the impact knocked him backwards. He tripped on something and I took my chance. I ran. I had to get away. I had to regroup with the others. To hell with April's plan.

Before I even reached the edge of the clearing, Cillian caught the back of my arm, swinging me round to face him. His grip was so tight I could feel Iollan's bitten nails digging into my flesh.

Danny turned colder. He was desperate, but he just wasn't strong enough to help me on his own. April was still invisible to Cillian, and Cillian was hardly going to give up his host. In the end Danny resorted to throwing whatever he could find: stones, pinecones, twigs, branches ... He wouldn't lob anything heavy, though, in fear of hitting me by mistake.

Cillian made Iollan's thin lips curl into a malicious smile. His upturned eyes and twisted mouth looked like something out of a nightmare. Danny's efforts didn't faze him. In fact, he seemed mildly amused. He reached forward, grabbing my hair ...

"*Aahh!* Get off!"

As Iollan's face came close to mine, I could smell the rotten teeth and cigarettes on his breath. "You spend so much time with your brother." His cracked lips moved as Cillian spoke, but the voice didn't belong to Iollan: it belonged to Cillian. "You should join him."

I tried prising his bony fingers from my hair, but they were locked in place like a pit bull's jaw. I couldn't get away. He dragged me over to the tree where Cillian's body lay and: *slam!*

The pain was red hot and like nothing I'd felt before. It completely dazed me; I didn't know what to do. Still clutching my hair, he hurled my head into the tree again. And again. And again.

"No ..." I mumbled. I held out my hands to try and soften the blows. Coloured dots were already dancing across my vision and everything was out of focus. I wasn't sure how much longer I could hold out for ...

Slam!

I felt blood drip down the side of my face, warm and thick, which made me panic even more. Danny couldn't protect me this time. I was on my own.

My trembling legs gave way and I felt a tuft of my hair tear out as I fell. Cillian only let go to grab an even bigger chunk. He tried dragging me to my feet, but I was unable to support my own weight. My body was clumsy, heavy, not my own. I couldn't move. I couldn't think. It was taking too long to get me to stand, so Cillian continued the job from where I knelt. *Slam, slam, slam ...*

The world cut out for a few seconds. So, this was how it ended. This was how he would finish me, just like Melissa in the graveyard. Just like all the other ghost children. Just like my brother.

"Please ..." I begged, to no one in particular.

When I opened my eyes, everything was spinning. And I swear I saw someone standing by the tree.

I couldn't make out any details. It just looked like a short white silhouette ...

Slam!

... Although I could've been hallucinating by this point.

Cillian drew my head back again, and as he did, the silhouette lunged towards me ...

* * *

Leave.

Him.

ALONE!

I pulled my brother away before his head hit the tree again. Cillian tore out another huge chunk of Jordan's hair but it was the only way to get him out the way, to break him free of Cillian's hold. I've never possessed anyone before, but I couldn't float around watching him get beaten to death. I won't let Cillian take him as well.

Still controlling Jordan, I ran, stumbled, ran, to the other side of the clearing, and then I leapt, fell, stood behind a bush. Not to hide. I was getting used to handling his body. He was kind of flimsy and heavy to move but it didn't take me long to adjust.

I looked over at Cillian. He was staggering towards us, Iollan's jaw tightly clenched. I could tell he had sensed the change in energy. Oh yes, he knew exactly who he was staring at through Jordan's upturned, swollen eyes.

"If you come near my brother, I'll kill your host,"
I said, using Jordan's vocal cords, moving Jordan's

lips – although it was my voice that came out his mouth. "Your dad's blood will be on your hands. Not ours."

He knew I wasn't kidding. I'd almost strangled Iollan earlier. Cillian's dad wasn't just his weapon – he was also his weakness.

Frustrated, he let out that horrible scream – the one that frightens Jordan. It didn't scare me, though, and he knew it. Instead, he bared Iollan's yellow teeth and charged, sending us to the ground.

He raised his fist above Jordan's head and I knew it wouldn't go through me anymore, that it would end up hurting my brother.

I dodged out the way, letting Iollan's fist smash into the ground by Jordan's head. The momentum threw Cillian off balance, so I took my chance and pushed Iollan away.

I tried to stand but he kept pulling and grabbing and lashing out – he wouldn't let go of Jordan. I jumped on top of him and tried to pin down his thrashing arms. Cillian may have been stronger but Iollan's weakened muscles held him back.

"Stay away from Jordan," I warned, digging my nails into Iollan's wrists.

Cillian shook Iollan's head. "He knows the truth. I won't have him reveal my secret."

"So you'll frame your dad for killing my brother? Seems like he'll go to prison no matter what."

"I'm not framing him. I'll burn the brat, and everyone will forever blame that Leslie Butch."

I stared into my killer's eyes. How much time did he think he had? "The police are already here, and the smoke will only lead them straight to your dad."

He smirked. "I know how to get away with murder. I've been doing it for seven years!"

"Well, I've been protecting my brother even longer, since we were in preschool, and I WON'T LET YOU KILL HIM!" I punched Iollan's face. I wanted to see the old man bleed, but I also knew I couldn't let my anger get the better of me. That's how mistakes are made. I remembered what Mr Butch had told Jordan earlier: you've gotta think things through in life ...

Cillian thrashed and screamed some more but I managed to keep Iollan pinned to the ground. There was no way I was letting him back up. No way at all.

With nowhere to go, I felt his energy disappear from under the old man's skin, taking with him all the fight, strength and resistance I'd been battling since I'd joined Jordan in the clearing. He'd left his father's body.

Iollan immediately started gasping. He looked confused. He was shaky, scared, out of breath ... pathetic. I could block his airway again but there was no time. Cillian was still close by. I could sense him.

I needed to keep him from ambushing Jordan, so I regrouped my energy and left his body.

CHAPTER THIRTY

I took a breath, and then another. It felt like all the air had somehow been knocked out of me.

There was a slightly discoloured Iollan sprawled out beneath me, but no sign of Cillian. And wasn't I by a tree before, being beaten to death? This must've been Danny's doing. He'd saved me.

I rolled off the old man, who was groaning and gasping for air.

"Wha-what happened?" he asked, trying to sit up.

Should I tell him we'd been possessed?

My head was much clearer now. I wiped away a thin trail of blood coming from a cut somewhere on my forehead before it got in my eye.

"You!" Iollan exclaimed. He pointed at me, his raised hand shaking something fierce. "It's you again."

Yeah, yeah. It's me.

Before I had a chance to reply, Iollan spotted his son's body.

"Cillian," he muttered.

I stood up, wiping away more blood as it continued to drip down my face.

Iollan was pleading under his breath as he struggled to his feet. He kicked up leaves and twigs as he half ran, half stumbled to the body. I swallowed, watching Iollan collapse to his knees again next to his dead son. It reminded me too much of Mum and how helpless she had been when … yeah.

He was silent, checking for a pulse that clearly wasn't there.

I scanned the clearing for Danny or Cillian but there was still no sign of either of them. What was the point in me being here if Cillian wasn't going to show? I could see April standing by the bushes only a few feet away from her father. As I'd expected, Iollan couldn't see her either.

"Danny?" I said under my breath. "You there?"

My right side stiffened from a sudden draught. I assumed it was my brother but when I turned, there was the translucent white figure of Melissa. I was about to say something when the other five ghost children materialised behind her. But still no Danny.

Iollan was too preoccupied to connect with any of them, so I knew he would stay oblivious. I was as good as alone with them. If they were here, though, it meant the police couldn't be far.

"They're coming," Melissa said. "We couldn't

distract them for much longer, so we came back to warn you."

"Thanks," I said. They'd done well to hold them off this long.

"You have maybe ten minutes until they get here if you want to run," she continued. I couldn't run away, though. Like April said, if Cillian didn't leave this realm with her, a kid was definitely going to die – and there was nothing stopping him from killing again, year after year. No, running away wasn't an option. Besides, the monster would haunt me forever if he stayed.

I heard the distant shouts from a team of police officers, clearer than ever now.

Iollan looked over at me. "Who's that? Did you call for help?"

It was sad that he thought Cillian could still be saved.

I nodded, swallowing the truth. If Iollan left, maybe Cillian would appear again. "You should go and show them where he is."

"Right … Yes, I'll …" He scrambled to his feet again, his stiff joints and trembling limbs making it look like an almost impossible task. I thought he'd at least question me, but he didn't hesitate. He scarpered into the forest after the voices.

With Iollan now showing them the way, it didn't leave me with a lot of time.

I took a deep breath and let it out slowly. "I'm ready for you, Cillian. Come out and face me!"

Nothing.

"Your idiot father's gone now. Show yourself!" I waited some more but still nothing. This was getting old now. "If I was April, I'd be so ashamed. You want to protect your dad: you should've listened when he told you to stop murdering innocent children. You wanted to avenge your sister: you should've known that killing her friend was the wrong way to go about it – let alone the others you went after!"

Goosebumps formed along my arms and I could suddenly see my own breath. It worked. He was back.

I scanned the clearing, trying to find him. Before I could take another step, though, I was pushed back by my throat and pinned against another tree. His invisible hands were around my neck, his thumbs pressing into my windpipe. I tried prising his fingers off me but there was nothing there. I mean, I could *feel* the pressure on my throat, but I couldn't grab the ghost hands that were holding me in place.

My lungs were burning, my throat closing ...

I felt Danny return. He and the other ghost children were close by, I knew, but I couldn't see what they were doing.

I lashed out towards where Cillian's arms and body should've been, but my fists swiped through thin air. I kept going, though. It was all I could do. Then a horribly familiar sound cut across the clearing.

Cillian loosened his grip. It wasn't the police.

This sound was coming from the opposite direction – where possessed-Iollan had entered the clearing. We listened closely: low, deep, menacing …

Growling.

Now Cillian revealed himself. His translucent arms were outstretched, hands around my throat, exactly as I knew they were. He was smiling. "They've found me," he said. "My dad was out walking them and now they've come to protect me."

He let go of me and I bent double, choking. It was his and April's dogs. "You do realise you left them locked up in your house with no food or water?" I croaked, massaging my throat.

The bushes rustled. We both turned and watched as the three brindle Wolfhounds emerged from behind the leaves. Their teeth were bared and their hackles raised; they looked ready to tear limb from limb.

"You look nervous," Cillian said to me, like that wasn't a normal reaction around a pack of angry, lion-sized creatures. He grinned. "You should be."

My legs shook. I wanted to take a step back but I was afraid that any movement might trigger them to attack. They were behaving differently to when I saw them earlier, when they were begging for food and attention. Would they remember me as the boy who let them outside? Would they care? Probably not when their master was around.

I looked at the ghost children and remembered how spooked the dogs got at the sight of Emily, Brett and Aaron back at the house. The dogs may have been submissive before; however, I knew the ghost children would only agitate them this time if they interfered. The wolfhounds were already behaving aggressively – anything could trigger them to flip.

"Cillian," I said in a low voice, "you don't need to do this. April's still here."

"Liar."

"I'm not lying! You just need to let her in. She needs to talk to you – like Danny talks to me!"

"Shut up!" Cillian's voice was suddenly sharp. Even the dogs fell silent. Their eyes were trained on him, ready to attack on his command. "I'm not letting you reveal the truth. My dad's a good man, I won't let him get locked up. And as for April – she's dead, *gone*, and if you mention her one more time, I'll go after your entire family."

April ran in front of me, pleading her brother to stop. Of course he didn't hear her, though.

I don't know if she meant to pass her feelings on to me, but she did. My heart suddenly felt heavy with April's panic – so heavy that it was making me feel nauseous. She didn't want any more blood on her hands.

"Please," I said, to anyone who would keep the dogs from reaching me. "Don't –"

Cillian gave the word.

I flinched, bracing myself for the impact. All three dogs bent low, ready to pounce, but none of them made a move. They were still growling, looking at me through Cillian. I reckon they could see April, or maybe they sensed her, Danny and the others. Why else would they be holding back?

"What's wrong?" Cillian said to them. "Come on – go get him!"

But still his dogs didn't move.

This was probably the last chance I had to persuade Cillian. "April doesn't want revenge. You can ask her yourself. She's standing right in front of me – *look!*"

Cillian had had enough. April held out her arms, trying to shield me as her brother glided towards us. Only then did his dogs make a move. They crept forward, following his lead. I didn't know what would be worse: their teeth digging into me or Cillian choking me to death.

The growling got louder as they came for me. They'd catch me in a matter of seconds if I ran, so I shut my eyes and braced myself for the impact, praying that Danny and the others would be able to hold them off.

I heard April whimper somewhere close by, and then the dogs leapt towards me.

Oh shit …

I tensed, waiting to feel claws and teeth rip into me – but it never happened. I knew they were in front of me, though; I could hear their barking, snarling, snapping … But the attack never happened.

I let out a shuddering breath, plucking up enough courage to open my eyes. When I did, I was expecting to see the other ghost children somehow holding them off …

They didn't need to, though.

The three dogs were standing inches away from me, but they had their backs to me. Their menacing growls were aimed at Cillian. They didn't want to attack me; they were trying to *protect* me.

I looked up at Cillian. His face was scrunched up like he was about to explode. "You turned them against me!"

"No, I didn't –"

"Liar!"

Cillian took a step closer, but this only made the dogs nervous. The one on the left inched forward, ears back, ready to pounce again. He'd pass straight through Cillian if he went to attack, but that didn't stop him snarling.

"Cillian –" I tried, but April cut me off.

"Cillian, stop it! *Please!"* she screeched.

"They're *my* dogs," he hissed, still gliding towards me. They were going to flip out any second. "You've already hurt my father, I won't let you take *them* as well."

"I'm not taking anything!"

"Jordan!" The muffled shouts of the police officers could finally be distinguished. They were saying a bunch of stuff but mostly they were just calling my name. I was out of time.

"Listen to me!" I said.

He knelt down in front of his dogs. They were

still barking madly, saliva dripping from their foaming mouths. The sound was going to lead the police straight to me, if Iollan hadn't already done that. I turned to April. I'd run out of ideas.

"Cillian!" She materialised between him and the dogs. "Please look at me! I'm right here! You have to move on. You have to stop killing people!"

"He still can't hear you," I said.

I watched Cillian stretch out his arm. "Come on now, Arnie … Kasper … Luke …" His hand passed straight through April. I felt bad for her. All her efforts were wasted on a man too ignorant to even try and reach her.

"Jordan!" The police.

"Jordan!" April.

"Cillian …" I tried one more time, but it was all over.

"There's a good boy," he said to the closest dog, still holding out his hand. They were barking louder than ever now. "Come on. That's it Kasp – *OW!*"

He yanked his hand away, as if Kasper's bite had actually torn flesh. The dog's sharp teeth went through his hand like a hologram, but the pain that showed in Cillian's face was real.

He looked up and I braced myself for another attack. I expected the anger that fuelled his hatred to return any second, but it never did. Instead, his entire face lit up.

He wasn't looking at me; he was looking at April. I didn't know if it was the shock of being bitten or the feeling of betrayal – all I knew was that, without his rage, he could finally see her.

A smile as wide as Devon spread across Cillian's face. I couldn't bring myself to look at him. He didn't deserve happiness and he didn't deserve closure, yet I was letting it happen.

April laughed, rushing into his arms like he wasn't the psycho we all knew him to be. I guess even though he was a monster, he was still her big brother.

She could take over from here. Whatever she said, he would listen. April would lead him out of this realm.

I still wished Cillian could've suffered more, but there was no way I was going to get that, and I'd just drive myself mad thinking about it. I needed to remember how many families I'd given closure to; how many lives I may have saved … I'd listened to my brother and I'd done what he'd asked. *That's* what really mattered.

The dogs stopped growling. Since Cillian was calmer, their hackles went down and their ears moved forwards. Then Arnie (the one who'd stopped me on the stairs back at Cillian's house) began sniffing the air. He wasn't interested in the ghosts anymore.

Arnie passed me without a glance, his nose fixed on the ground. It didn't take long for his brothers to notice what he was doing. Curious, they followed him until they too picked up the scent.

I knew what smell they were tracking before

they'd even got there.

The three of them stood by their master's rotting corpse beneath the tree, tails low and heads bowed. This was the Cillian they knew; the Cillian they would mourn.

"Jordan!"

Instead of panicking at the sound of the police, my body felt lighter. I was ready to go home. Cillian's victims could finally rest – *Danny* could finally rest – knowing that their families would soon hear the truth. All I had to do now was show Cillian's body to the police, tell them about the other victims and where the missing bodies were buried, and let them take it from there – and then clear Mr Butch's name. And pay him all the money I owed him. And apologise to Mum and Dad like crazy. And expect an endless amount of sessions with Dr Ashton and other psycho-whatever people. Oh, and my clozapine dosage might go up, or maybe I'd be put on something stronger – and Mum would no doubt expect me to take them in front of her from now on …

"Cillian – *wait!*" April's voice cut across the clearing.

I quickly turned to see what was happening, and then saw Cillian fly towards me.

I didn't have time to react.

He passed straight through me. Danny had done the same to me before, but never with this amount of force. What was usually just an unpleasant, spine-tingling sensation knocked all the air out of me. I stumbled, tripping on something behind me and then:

CRACK!

My head ... There was a blinding pain in my head. I wanted to move, but I couldn't. I wanted to talk, but I couldn't. I was paralysed. *OW* ... my fucking *head*.

With a shaky hand I managed to reach up and feel the cold rock under my head, and also something warm and sticky that could only have been blood ...

"Jordan!"

... My blood.

Three police officers and an Alsatian came rushing into the clearing. And then the world turned black.

CHAPTER
THIRTY ONE

Brightness. I could see it before I opened my eyes.

Now that I was awake, I was expecting the worst kind of pain to come rushing back. Nothing happened, though. I felt normal. *Better* than normal, in fact. I wasn't aching or tired or numb ...

A gust of wind made the forest rustle and I could hear the faint sound of running water from a nearby stream.

I blinked, squinting up at green and bronze. It took a moment for everything to come into focus. I saw leaves towering above me from the treetops, beams of sunlight piercing the gaps.

I must have been lying down.

I moved my fingers and felt the softness of grass, the coolness of dirt. It was reassuring. I could still feel stuff – so I couldn't have been bleeding to death, because surely I'd feel that.

I reached up anyway and tried to find the blood or clot or matted hair. But I appeared to be unharmed. Did I really hit my head? Maybe I just thought I had, after the shock of Cillian passing through me. In fact, where *was* Cillian?

I sat up slowly and glanced around. I was in the middle of a clearing. I knew I was in a forest before I blacked out, but everything looked different: the trees were greener, flowers were flourishing, and there was nobody else around. Nobody, except ...

I froze.

I couldn't speak ... couldn't even open my mouth.

He made his way towards me from the tree he'd been leaning against.

He had the same dimpled smile and messy brown hair that I remembered so clearly. "Is it really you?" I asked as he knelt in front of me.

Danny nodded.

Impossible.

I was laughing before I knew what to say next. I reached out to hug him and he fell into my arms, his small hands gripping the back of my jacket. His body was firm, his weight solid. I could feel the creases in his clothes, the warmth of his skin. He wasn't pale and he wasn't a projection – he was exactly how I remembered.

"How come I can see you?" I spoke into his hair. It smelt of that cheap strawberry shampoo Mum bought on holiday in Brookston. "You've never shown yourself before."

Danny moved away. "It takes up too much energy – like Aaron said. I wouldn't've been able to follow you as much if I'd put my energy into a physical form. Right now, though ... its only temporary. I needed you to see me."

Why?

There was still so much I wanted to ask him but all I could do was stare in awe. He was here. He was actually here. "I've missed you so much," I said, wiping away my tears.

Danny dived into my chest and hugged me again. "I've missed you, too."

It felt good to be this close to him. Like I was being given a second chance. I ignored the cold seeping into my knees from the ground and held him tight, afraid that if I let go he would disappear.

Speaking of disappearing ...

I couldn't help noticing that all the stones and branches that had been thrown around earlier were gone. The forest floor was clear save for grass and patches of wildflowers; and I could still hear the running water behind us.

"Where are we?" I asked. This wasn't where I'd faced Cillian. And what had happened to the police?

"Don't you recognise it?"

I looked again but it was his voice that was the giveaway: this was the clearing where Danny had ended up drawing the shorter stick, where he'd become a seeker – and just over there was the dead tree Lewis had told him to start counting from.

I let go of Danny as a shudder raced down my spine. "I hate this place."

"I think it's peaceful," Danny said. "It's the brook I don't like. Just up there." He pointed past the dead tree, further into the forest. I knew the stream was somewhere over there but all I could see were bushes, brambles and more trees. I wasn't about to go looking for the spot where he was murdered.

Why the *Hell* did I follow Lewis that day?

I stared back at my brother. None of this made any sense. "How did I get here?" I asked. "Am I dead too?"

My heart raced – *ironically* – at the idea of not being alive. Part of me didn't want to find out.

"Not quite," Danny said. "You hit your head and fell unconscious. You can choose to stay if you want but it's not actually your time."

"What d'you mean?"

"The doctors are trying to bring you back. I just wanted to say a final goodbye first."

A final … *What?* "I don't want to say goodbye."

"Jordan –"

"I've just found you! I won't leave you again."

"Jordan –"

"It's my fault you're here –"

"Jordan!" Danny's voice was nothing but serious. "You've got to stop blaming yourself for my death. It was Cillian's fault – you *know* that. How were you supposed to know what was going to happen?"

I swallowed. I guess I wasn't quite ready to forgive myself – even with Danny's permission.

He smiled, placing his hand on my shoulder like he'd done at his funeral, all those years ago. "You did it, Jordan. You saved me."

"If only."

If I'd truly saved him, we'd be playing videogames together right now, full from too much junk food or one of Mum's home-made dinners.

"But you *did* save me!" Danny persisted. "I can finally rest. Mum and Dad know who killed me – they were told yesterday. *Everyone's* families were told: Julie's, Melissa's, Grant's, Aaron's, Emily's, Brett's …"

"And where are they now – Melissa and the others, I mean? They were right in front of me before I tripped."

"They've already gone. April couldn't come back without Cillian following her, and the others were just too desperate to leave. They wanted me to thank you, though. Honestly, what you did … we couldn't've done it without you." Danny grinned so wide it was almost contagious.

"Well, how was I supposed to ignore you with all the pinching and breaking stuff?" I gave his shoulder a friendly punch and he laughed. God, I'd missed him.

"I kept telling them that you'd help," he continued. "I told them, 'Jordan will save us – just you wait!' And you did. I'm so proud to have you as my brother."

I could feel myself welling up again. Why'd he have to go and trigger me? I cleared my throat before I turned into a blubbering mess. There were still a few things I needed to know. "That scumbag Cillian," I said. "He's definitely gone, is he?"

"Yeah. There's no way he'll be coming back."

"And Iollan? What's happened to him?"

"In custody. You'll need to tell the police what you know but they've got enough evidence to send him down. He pretty much broke straightaway, confessed everything. He even came clean about the bodies in Cillian's garden. The police then went ahead and cross-checked Cillian's DNA with the samples in my case file, and then did the same with Grant, Julie and Melissa's files too. They were all a perfect match."

Good. "There's no rush to go back then; I can stay with you. The doctors can keep me on life support."

"And what if they don't?"

I pulled a face. "Come on – Mum and Dad wouldn't let that happen."

"So you'll just let them go on worrying?"

I said nothing. Of course I didn't *want* to worry them: I'd hurt them enough already. But Danny was right here and –

"Mr Butch is in custody too, by the way," Danny added.

He just *had* to find another reason for me to

leave.

"He'll be fine without me," I said, hoping I was right. I didn't like the thought of being responsible for ruining his life.

Danny didn't look convinced. "Nobody believes him. They still think he kidnapped you. On top of that, he's actually stayed loyal to you – he's not mentioned anything about you going after Cillian or any of the spirit-talk that would've freaked Mum and Dad out …"

I was taken aback by this. Nobody, besides Danny, has ever had my back like this. I know he needed me, but I was still hanging onto the idea of staying with Danny. "The police have no evidence! They'll have to let him go eventually. *Surely*. Won't they?"

"If you tell them, they will –"

"I'm not leaving you!" How could he be this selfish? How could he be this … I didn't want to go. "You said I have a choice! I'm staying with you. School's absolute hell and nobody believes a word I say. Every day's a frickin' battle to convince anyone I'm normal and I don't wanna do it anymore, not on my own … If you're not with me, I'll have no one."

I didn't realise I was crying until I saw the tears rolling down Danny's face, too.

"You're never alone, Jordan," Danny said.

I covered my ears. I didn't want to hear it.

"Besides," he went on, "school doesn't last forever. You'll leave one day and then you can go wherever you want."

"I don't want to leave *you*." I sobbed like I had five years ago.

"I know – I don't want to leave you either. But I have to rest, and Mr Butch needs you. Mum and Dad need you. And who's going to look after the baby the way only an older brother can? You have to be there for them because I can't. You understand, don't you?"

I nodded. There was nothing else left to say. It wasn't my time. I had too many people counting on me, too many people I cared about, too much to live for. If I stayed with Danny, all that would be on my conscience and I'd never find the peace that Danny and the other ghost children now had.

"Will I be with you when it *is* my time to move on?" I asked.

"I'll find you, I promise." Danny leaned forward and hugged me again. "You'd better be grey and wrinkly the next time you're here, though!"

I laughed and sobbed at the same time. My tears were wetting the back of his T-shirt and I was trying my best not to shake as I promised to live for the both of us.

And then, just like that, everything became colder.

White clouds began to swirl in the sky as if a tornado was about to form. The trees swayed violently as bits of bark, dirt and dead leaves were blown around us, like plastic flakes in a shaken snow globe. This was it: the storm that would take me home.

'Wait!' I wanted to scream. I still wasn't ready ... It was all happening too fast ... Would I ever truly be ready though?

I felt some invisible force trying to pull me back, but it only made me hold onto Danny tighter.

"It's okay, you don't need to fight it," he said, trying to reassure me. "You're stronger than you think."

I couldn't speak. I felt dizzy and the sunlight was suddenly way too bright. I closed my eyes, knowing that our time together was over.

"I love you, Danny," I choked.

"I love you too," he said back — the last words I heard him say.

The light around me shone even brighter and my head was now spinning so fast that I struggled to keep my balance. I couldn't breathe. Was I still holding my brother?

Too much spinning, too much light ...

And then I blacked out again.

CHAPTER
THIRTY TWO

My head is on fire. Noises everywhere: Beeping, rustling, clanking, talking …

I opened my eyes. The room was bright. Monitors and equipment along the walls; the smell of disinfectant; two women standing in a corner, one of them holding a clipboard. I was in a hospital bed, with tubes and wires sticking in my arm.

"Hello, Jordan."

A smiling man with teeth like a dentist was standing over me.

"I'm Dr Holden," he said. "You're in Meadowview Royal Hospital. Can you tell me how you're feeling?"

I blinked. *"Pain,"* I wanted to say. *"I'm in pain."*

"You've been in a coma for five days," the doctor continued. "Do you remember what happened? Blink once for yes and twice for no."

I swallowed, and then said, "Why do I need

to blink?"

Dr Holden's smile widened. "I wasn't sure if you could communicate verbally yet. Your parents will be glad to hear you're awake. They've just gone to get a bite to eat, but they'll be back soon. In the meantime, I'm going to run some tests on you and ask a few basic questions. Is that all right?"

I nodded.

Even though I'd been out cold for days, I was frickin' exhausted. Luckily, though, Dr Holden didn't take long. I answered everything as best I could and sat still while he prodded and scanned me with all kinds of medical equipment. I fell asleep before I could hear the results.

* * *

When I woke the next day, Mum and Dad were sitting by my bed.

"Oh, thank God!" Mum cried out, instantly reaching over to hug me. I cringed with the thought of her knocking the needles in my hand. When she sat back, though, I saw that they'd already been removed.

They were both smiling but they looked beat. There were shadowy bags under their eyes and their skin was pale, just like on the day of Danny's funeral. And then I noticed how much smaller Mum's belly was. I mean, she was still pretty big, but I could tell she wasn't carrying – she didn't hold herself in that way. Had she miscarried? Was that why they looked so empty? Shit – it must've been the stress I'd put her through …

"How are you feeling?" Dad asked me.

I gave him a weak smile. "All right, I guess." That was a lie. Mentally, I was drained and now overwhelmed with guilt and self-loathing for what I'd done to Mum and my new baby brother or sister; physically, my head still ached and every now and then I felt sick, but Dr Holden had already warned me about the side-effects.

"You scared the hell out of us, son," Dad admitted, and then he told me the results from the tests I'd taken yesterday. Apparently, my CT scan showed that I should make a full recovery. Fatigue, muscle weakness and difficulty concentrating was a given for the next few days, but as long as I had no problems during the night, I would be discharged tomorrow.

What a relief. I couldn't stand hospitals.

I stayed quiet as Dad went on to explain about the past few days I'd been unconscious. I found it hard listening to their version of the story. There were too many thoughts in my head: Mum's bump, Danny, Mr Butch …

I felt my body jolt. "Where's Mr Butch?"

Mum stiffened, just like back in Mrs Patel's office when she'd found out what Matt had said to me.

Dad cleared his throat. "Leslie Butch is in custody," he said, with all the seriousness of a constable. "They have no evidence that he kidnapped you, so they'll need a statement as soon as you feel up to it, preferably this afternoon."

Jeez, I had a lot of explaining to do. "Mr Butch didn't kidnap me. *I* got in the taxi. I left *by myself.* When we lost the cab, he stayed with me because he felt responsible – not because he was kidnapping me. *I* dragged *him* along, if anything."

Mum and Dad looked confused. It was a lot to take in, especially if they'd all but convinced themselves that the man was guilty.

"I don't understand. If he didn't take you, why did you leave?" Mum watched me closely and when I didn't reply she asked, "Did you know about Cillian?"

I tried my best not to give a reaction. "What d'you mean?" I said.

"They found you in the same forest as him, literally across the clearing from you. Did you see a body, before you tripped? Because if you did, *that's* who killed Danny. Forensics found traces …" Mum looked away. Talking about Danny would always pain her. She took a breath and turned back to me. "Forensics found traces of that man's DNA in Daniel's records."

Dad's expression hardened. "Turns out that sick bastard is a serial killer. His identity wasn't on record at the time, but they found evidence that linked him to at least six other murders. His father confessed what his monster-of-a-son did to them all. He even gave them the location of the three missing bodies."

"How did you end up in the same place as Cillian?" Mum asked. She was determined to get an answer out of me. "That's why you were there, wasn't it? Did you know who he was? What he did?"

Danny was right: Mr Butch hadn't told them a thing ...

"Debbie." Dad sighed. He knew the facts (or lack of) better than anyone. "We've been over this. The entire police force was clueless – how could Jordan have known?"

"That's what I'm asking! Everyone's going to want to know how Jordan knew where to find him–"

"I didn't know!" I said, because I couldn't tell them about Danny and the other ghost children. No one would believe me. I stared down at the plain white sheets that covered me and told them what Dad thought was the truth, that it was all a huge coincidence. "I just wanted to visit the forest me and Danny were in that day. His grave is just a hole we put him in; the woods were the last place I saw him alive."

I knew one of them would answer with a follow-up question, so I told them straight out. "Please, I don't want to talk about this right now."

Dad nodded, giving my shoulder a reassuring squeeze. "I understand, Jordan. The detective chief inspector *will* want to speak to you about it though."

I'd deal with it later then.

Mum took my hand, gently rubbing her thumb

over my knuckles, and suddenly there was only one thing I wanted to know, even if the answer choked me.

I looked up at her. "The baby?"

Mum's lips stretched into a smile, and her free hand instinctively reached towards her stomach.

"Your Uncle Ryan's got her at the moment," Dad said.

Her. It was a girl. I had a *sister.*

"They're in the nursery," Mum added. "Do you want to see her?"

I nodded. "Course I do!"

Dad's smile was as big as Mum's. Happiness suited them and it was a look I'd missed. The reason they looked so aged wasn't because they were grieving over a stillborn; they'd been worried sick because of *me.*

They left the room holding hands. They were tough, my parents. After everything with Danny ... after all the crap I'd put them through ... they were still standing tall. I should've at least left them a note. And I couldn't believe I'd missed the birth! I thought about how I'd switched off my phone in Mr Butch's cab, refusing to read any messages in fear of being yelled at before losing it over the cliff. Mum could've gone into labour the moment I left, for all I knew.

I watched two nurses pass my room through the window in the door. So much was happening only a few feet away, yet in here everything was reassuringly still. The longer I was alone, though, the more his name pressed down on me.

I took a breath. "Danny?"

There was no reply, and the temperature never wavered. He was gone.

I'd guessed as much. I was just hoping against hope.

I pressed my palms against my eye sockets as tears threatened to overflow. There was an empty space inside me, one only Danny could fill. It would take time getting used to his absence; the silence.

I swallowed, my throat tightened as if by illness. I was so used to my brother's presence that sometimes I forgot he was actually dead. In a way, letting him go felt like he'd died a second time.

I waited for everything to properly sink in before lifting my hands from my eyes. Danny was at peace. He wouldn't be tired any more. And even though I didn't need him to protect me, I still craved his company, his friendship, his brotherly pranks. Photographs and memories were all I had left of him now – yet I knew they would never be enough.

Dad didn't bother knocking. He entered the room quietly, still grinning from ear to ear. I sat up straight as he held the door open for Mum. She was holding a small bundle close to her chest. My stomach clenched.

Mum took a seat beside me, in the same plastic chair she had occupied only minutes ago. My eyes were instantly drawn to the baby sleeping in her arms, wrapped in a pastel-pink blanket. My sister. Her features so ... *so tiny!*

"She's a week old tomorrow," Mum said.

I brushed my finger lightly over her cheek, afraid that she would break with any amount of pressure. Her skin was soft.

"Can I hold her?" I asked, unable to look away. She was beautiful.

"Of course."

As Mum placed her in my arms, I bit down hard on my lower lip. She stirred, but only slightly. I gave her my index finger and she clutched it, whimpering softly. I managed to lull her back to sleep within seconds.

"What do you think of little Nora?" Dad asked. I could tell he was grinning again.

"She's ... perfect."

Danny would've loved to have seen her. And maybe he did, before he went away. I'd like to believe that.

I stroked her hair, being careful not to wake her. Although there were dull days ahead, filled with grieving, longing and darkness ...

Nora. She would light the way.

ACKNOWLEDGEMENTS

Where do I start? I have so many wonderful, talented people to thank over the years.

Firstly, since I started writing *Killing a Dead Man* when I was finishing my GCSEs, I would like to thank all my English teachers (especially **Mrs Suman Suri**), for making the lessons so engaging and for pushing my dreams of becoming a writer. I would also like to thank the school Librarian, **Marianne Checkland**, for believing in my writing (even if I was too afraid to enter a lot of the writing competitions back then!) and for introducing me to so many amazing books. Lastly, I would like to thank my Extra Project Qualification supervisor, **Mr Taylor**, who happened to be a fantastic science teacher but admitted he knew very little about creative writing! It was in those science labs where I was encouraged to explore the literary market, determine my audience, and research YA fiction.

A huge thank you to all the Creative Writing lecturers who have taught me over the years – especially **Jonathan Taylor**, **Kerry Featherstone**, and **Rod Duncan**. Your workshops, advice and encouragement has not just influenced *Killing a Dead Man* but has helped me become a better writer.

A big thank you to **Gatling Gun Productions** for the amazing book trailer! The cast and crew did a fantastic job – thank you everyone who was involved. (If you haven't seen the trailer, check it out on YouTube or my website!)

Thank you, **Mum and Dad**, for supporting every decision I've made (even the really bad ones!), and for letting me be that quirky, imaginative child who chased her dreams like a Disney princess.

Thank you, **Ciaran**, my little brother who now towers over me! Remember when I asked you to write the messages Danny shows Jordan so I could copy some of the spellings? Probably not – you were eight at the time! I've still got them though. And without getting too soppy (because I know you won't thank me for that!) thank you for being the coolest, funniest, brother I could ask for.

Thank you, **Aisleen**, my sister, for reading every draft I threw at you and for bouncing ideas off me. Thank you, also, for all your help with the book trailer and, most importantly, thank you for sticking by my side. Through the ups and downs we've faced in life, we've always had each other's backs! Without that friendship, this book wouldn't exist.

I would also like to thank my editor, **Martin Ouvry** from Jericho, for ironing out the creases in my novel.

Thank you, **Mark Bromley**, for all your spiritual knowledge – something that has changed my life as much as this book.

Thank you **Sophie Jarvis**, **Chloe Jarvis**, **James Eeling**, **Aisleen Hodges** and **Michael Webster** for reading *Killing a Dead Man* before it was published.

Thank you **everyone** who follows me on social media – your support means so much to me!

A huge thanks to you, **the reader**, for giving this book a chance. I hope you enjoyed it. Let me know what you thought of *Killing a Dead Man*, either through my website, on Facebook, or leave a review on Amazon. I'd love to hear from you!

And finally, **Michael Webster**, my partner and best friend and reason to smile. Thank you for believing in *Killing a Dead Man* and giving it the push it needed. Thank you also for editing the book trailer, creating my website and, of course, for the incredible book cover and layout! Needless to say, you are a talented graphic designer – but it is your strength, love and humour that anchors me. I love you.